About the Author

This is my second novel published with Pegasus. Be sure and check out my first, Lurking in Shadows. I am looking forward to a long relationship of publishing future novels with Pegasus.

I live in Tucson, Arizona, with my partner, Lori. We have been together for over twenty-three years. We live with our little rescue dog Chloe, and a tank of magically reproducing fish. We have four wonderful, supportive and loving children, a great son-in-law, and an amazing five-year-old grandson, who is the joy of our lives.

This is a work of fiction. Names, characters, businesses, places, events and incidents are either the products of the author's imagination or used in a fictitious manner. Any resemblance to actual persons, living or dead, or actual events is purely coincidental.

INVISIBLE BOUNDARIES

Ina E. Shicoff

INVISIBLE BOUNDARIES

Vanguard Press

VANGUARD

PAPERBACK © Copyright

2023

Ina E. Shicoff

The right of Ina E. Shicoff to be identified as author of this work has been asserted by her in accordance with the Copyright, Designs and Patents Act 1988.

All Rights Reserved

No reproduction, copy or transmission of this publication may be made without written permission.
No paragraph of this publication may be reproduced, copied or transmitted save with the written permission of the publisher, or in accordance with the provisions of the Copyright Act 1956 (as amended).

Any person who commits any unauthorized act in relation to this publication may be liable to criminal prosecution and civil claims for damages.

A CIP catalogue record for this title is available from the British Library.

ISBN 978-1-80016-508-3

Vanguard Press is an imprint of
Pegasus Elliot Mackenzie Publishers Ltd.
www.pegasuspublishers.com

First Published in 2023

Vanguard Press
Sheraton House Castle Park
Cambridge England

Printed & Bound in Great Britain

This book is dedicated to my partner, Lori, who has given me her love, support and encouragement to pursue my dreams with her, and new directions in my life.

Acknowledgements

I would like to thank friends and family that told me to get out those old manuscripts, dust them off and try again. Thanks to Pegasus Publishers for taking a chance on me and giving me the opportunity to accomplish my dreams of doing what I love. It is hard to believe that my first book, Lurking in Shadows was published just last year. It is impossible to adequately express how grateful I am to Lorie Frazee for her second set of eyes. My thanks also goes out to my first production manager at Pegasus, for her patience and hand holding throughout the process. Special thanks to Don Weise for his encouragement, guidance and believing in my work. To my talented photographer, and son-in-law, Ray, thank you for making my picture look good- by not letting anyone see the standard shorts and T-shirt I wear daily. And of course, I would like to thank my partner Lori for her patience and support. She is the one who adds joy to my life.

Chapter 1

Sam had never been to Chicago, and she was enjoying the view of the skyline from the seventeenth-floor restaurant. It had been a long day. The rain gently pecking at the window was calming, as was the crackling fireplace adjacent to her table. It helped that she was sitting alone in an almost empty dining room, not having to smile and make small talk with strangers.

Unfortunately, that didn't last but a few minutes. The waitress approached and handed her a menu. "Hi. Hey, are you that lady on the television commercial?"

Sam's brow wrinkled in question. "What commercial?"

The waitress tapped her finger on her chin. "I can't remember the product, but the one where that attractive older woman with the short, cropped white hair says, 'They say at a certain age you stop trying. I wonder at what age that is?' Something to that effect. If you are, you look even better in person."

Sam recalled the commercial the waitress was talking about. *I guess I slightly resemble her; at least she got the age about right.* Sam's features had softened as she aged. Her face, unlike the actress, was no longer as sharply chiseled. Sam was six foot-two, and she considered her long legs her best feature. Her arms, for the most part, remained muscular, strong and trim. There was that small wabble under her arm, but then, didn't most people have that as they got older? It was probably Sam's pure-white, spiked hair that reminded the waitress of the commercial.

"No, I'm not that woman."

"Well, you are very attractive. I hope I age as well as you."

Sam wasn't sure how to respond, so she just smiled and opened the menu to end the awkward conversation.

Just this morning, after her shower, she had noticed the crepe-paper-looking skin beginning to show on her chest, a chest that was slowly moving south, taking her smaller sized breasts along for the ride. Vanity was never an issue for her. Her aging was just a fact of life. Lately, however, she was physically starting to feel every sixty-seven years of her age. Her hip and hands had begun to ache from stiffness, especially in cold weather.

The waitress's comments took her back twenty-seven years to her younger self, in particular, the night when she and Laura had just started their second date. A phone call had interrupted a make-out session on Laura's couch. Laura answered her phone in Sam's presence and proceeded to describe her to her best friend Ann, while staring boldly into Sam's eyes. That description was the one and only time Sam heard how another person saw her.

Laura began her description with, "Well... she is the sexiest and most beautiful, androgynist woman I have ever met. She has arms like a swimmer and amazing legs that go forever. She's always in total control of the world around her. She's calm and soft-spoken, but strong and confident." That had made Sam laugh as Laura continued. "She has short, spiky blonde hair and the most beautiful sky-blue, almost transparent, eyes. Her smile is warm and sexy and makes me wet with wanting her. Her breasts are made just to fit my small hands, a theory I hope to test tonight. Her flat stomach tapers down to slim hips and firm thighs. I can already feel those amazing legs wrapping around me."

Soon after that description, they were in bed together for the first time.

Sam wondered if Laura had still seen her that way twenty-five years later, as she took her last breath and died in Sam's arms. Sam would always see Laura as that beautiful woman who had stolen her heart the first time they met; the woman that finally made her settle down and stop bedding every pretty woman she saw. That was a lifetime ago.

She looked at the short stack of books on the side next to her drink, waiting to be autographed for tomorrow's pickup at the bookstore. She decided that the sooner she signed them, the faster her day would end, before having to do others again tomorrow. She loved the solitude of writing, but book tours and signings were not something she enjoyed. Her agent and publisher were not of the same mind. Every time she got on an airplane, it sadly reminded her of all the wonderful trips she and Laura had taken together. Laura had been gone almost two years now, and Sam's heart still ached when she came to mind, which was most days of her week.

She knew she should feel grateful for all those years. Retirement had allowed her to spend the time writing, which she always wanted, and her books were selling. She signed the last novel and placed it in the box.

As she picked up the menu, a pleasant voice asked, "Excuse me, would you mind if I share your table?"

Seriously! Sam thought. *There is only one other occupied table in the whole damn dining room, and she wants this one!*

Sam looked up at the woman, who was pulling her bulky sweater around her shoulders. The woman answered her thought with, "It's the closest to the fireplace."

Sam was tempted to gather up her backpack and books and move to another table. She looked up into the woman's smiling face and hesitated a moment longer before gesturing for her to sit down. Sam placed her box of books on the chair next to her.

The woman reached out with her hand. "Hello, my name is Dani."

Sam shook her chilled hand. She took the seat across from Sam, as the waitress handed the woman a menu. Dani announced to the waitress, "I'm cold and hungry. I'll start with a cup of hot coffee, please." She pointed to Sam's menu sitting at her place setting. Have you already ordered?"

"Not yet." Sam picked up her menu. They silently studied the options. Sam had already decided what she wanted for dinner. Looking at her discreetly over her menu, she took this moment to study the woman sitting across from her. She guessed Dani was around the age of her daughters, Addie and Clancy, maybe in her mid-forties. Her one shade darker than milk-chocolate skin was beautiful. Her piercing green eyes were framed by barely visible crow's feet just beginning to appear on her otherwise smooth face and slender neck. The bridge of her perfectly shaped nose wrinkled ever so slightly, as she concentrated on her menu.

The waitress returned a few minutes later with Dani's coffee. Sam watched as the woman across from her poured several packets of sugar into her coffee, with cream, and wrapped her tapered fingers around the mug to warm them. Their orders were placed. Sam glanced at Dani, thinking that her parents must have paid a lot for those perfectly straight white teeth. *She really is beautiful.*

She realized she had literally said two words to Dani since she appeared at the table. She nodded to the fireplace next to them. "Are you warmer now?"

"Yes. Thank you for letting me share your table. Are you here for the convention?"

Sam took a sip of her water. "I saw the welcome board in the lobby; are you referring to the medical convention here at the hotel?"

Dani nodded.

Sam continued. "No. Are you?"

Dani, having warmed up, removed her sweater and wrapped it around the back of her chair. "Yes, but I wish it was being held in Florida. I can't believe how cold it is here."

Sam smiled, and quietly asked, "Where are you from?"

Dani's eyes got big, and in exaggerated sarcasm, she said, "Sunny California, thank you very much."

Sam smiled. "Well, I got you 'heat beat'. I'm from Tucson and this weather is actually a nice change."

She found Dani's chuckle very sexy.

"So, what gets you out of Arizona and brings you to cold Chicago?" asked Dani.

"A book promotion."

Dani pointed to the box in the chair. "Yours?"

Sam nodded as Dani, uninvitedly, reached inside and removed one from the box. She silently read the cover and inside flap. "You're a lesbian writer." A statement, not a question.

Nonetheless, Sam answered, "Guilty as charged."

"Wow!" Dani replaced the book in the box.

Sam wasn't quite sure if that 'wow' was meant as a surprise or a judgement. She remained silent, watching as Dani stared directly at her. Their eyes locked, as Dani continued to study her for an intense moment longer. Sam was amused and wondered if this woman was now looking at her through different eyes, given this newfound knowledge. Perhaps she may have the table to herself after all.

Finally, Dani spoke. "I have never read a lesbian novel." She seemed to mull over her thoughts momentarily and decided to confide in her by continuing. "I have wondered what it would be like to have a same-sex experience." She nodded slightly in confirmation, as she thought back to another time. "A girl in med school kissed me once, while we were drunk at a party. That is as far as it went."

A little less confused at Dani's 'wow', Sam laughed and asked, "And, how was that kiss?"

The waitress appeared with their meals and placed them on the table. "Bon appetite." She left.

Dani took a bite of her roast beef and chewed for a few seconds. "Actually, it was pleasant, and I wish I could have had that whole experience, but she passed out on the couch a few minutes later. Of course, the incident was never mentioned again. Truth be told, I don't think she even remembered it." She laughed. "Obviously, one of us just did. I dated a few men during those years. Seven years ago, on an impulse, I married my best friend, David, and we have remained best friends." She chuckled, again. "Best friends that shouldn't have gotten married. We have known each other since kindergarten, and our families are close...

so, basically it was kind of expected." She waved her comment away with a swipe of her hand. "Sorry, too much information."

Sam tried to read Dani's expression. She wasn't sure what Dani might be feeling. She didn't want her to feel embarrassed that she had put her private life out there so casually. "No, that's okay. I'm sorry to hear that. Sounds like we have things in common. I married my husband on an impulse as well." She laughed. "Well, Michael and I had a slight complication that led to that decision. A one-night experiment that turned into my daughter, Addie." Sam realized her cavalier statement might have offended her. "Oh, listen I'm sorry. I didn't mean to make light of or make any comparisons to your situation with your husband."

Dani waved her hand, dismissingly. "No, it's not tragic. David is an attorney and very busy with his career, as I am with mine. That is a plus really. We don't spend much time together having to feel obligated to act like a married couple. It makes life simpler for both of us. We haven't gotten around to divorcing. You know, our families being so close for so many years and all; it's complicated. We have no children, so it should be easy enough. We both know it was a mistake. The marriage was over before it started." Dani was intrigued about a lesbian writer being married and asked, "How about you, are you still married to Michael?"

Sam wondered whether, if Michael hadn't died, if they still would be. "Michael was my best friend, as well. We were married only a few years, before he died in a motorcycle accident. As difficult as that was, Michael and I should never had gotten married. Like you, we, too, were obligated to act like a married couple, but for different reasons. Don't get me wrong, he was a great guy, but we were both gay. Those years were very different times for gays. Michael and I both wanted children, just not within straight marriages. It worked for us. Our open marriage allowed us our separate sex lives without our families knowing we were gay. Addie, my daughter, was loved by adoring parents and lacked for nothing. Michael was clever and funny, and we had a lot of fun together." Sam surprised herself at the ease of which she was able to share this information with a stranger. She continued. "I was the luckier one and got a second chance at love. I lost my partner, Laura, a little over two years ago. We were together for twenty-five years."

Dani was amazed at how much Sam had lived through. She placed her now warmed hand over Sam's and focused a concerned look at her. "I'm so, so, sorry. That had to be very difficult."

Sam could see that Dani genuinely felt badly for her, more so than for her own present situation, it seemed. She nodded. "It has been." She looked up and added, "Her death was the catalyst I needed to stop moping around, feeling sorry for myself, and start trying to publish. She always encouraged my writing." She laughed. "So, look at me. I'm traveling around doing book signings, which I hate. I'm too old for this shit; I'd much rather be home, just writing."

Dani's stare was penetrating. "She encouraged you. How amazing of her. What did you do prior to writing?"

"I was a high school literature teacher, but I can't remember ever not writing, even as a kid."

Dani nodded. I'm sure Laura would be proud of your accomplishments."

Sam stared back at her momentarily, taking in what suddenly sounded like a profound statement. *Laura would be proud of me.* "I never thought about it that way. You're right. I am grateful she was in my life for as long as we had." *Perhaps that is what Dani wanted in her relationship, to find who she was. Okay, now I'm analyzing a stranger.* "You must be proud of your accomplishments, as well."

"I am. I work hard, and I love my work. I'm a neurosurgeon. I'm good at what I do. I wish I had as much confidence at public speaking. I have to present my research paper tomorrow morning. I'm a nervous wreck. That's probably why I'm talking your ear off."

"I'm sure you have nothing to be concerned about. You are very charismatic. I can tell that you will do great."

They remained silent for a few minutes as they ate. They had desert and coffee and continued talking and sharing their lives. Conversation came easily, and they enjoyed learning about each other.

Dani grew up in an affluent section of Atlanta. It was a small, tight, black community. Both her mom and dad came from humble beginnings. Due to their hard work and success, her parents' expectations for her and her brother were high. Their lives centered around the country club, where everyone knew each other's business. For her parents, impressive status and an advanced education were priorities for their children.

Sam could relate to some of what Dani was describing. She, herself, grew up in a small, black town. However, it was a much less desirable location and economically challenged. It was a rough place, poor, but it was also a close-knit community. Her family was one of a handful of white middle-class Jewish families that shared the same hopes and dreams for their children. Sam's dad was a blue-collar worker, and her mother was a stay-at-home mom. Sam was one of the lucky ones. With good grades, she got a scholarship to UC Berkeley and a ticket out of her small town's myopic view of the world.

Their different experiences also came from growing up in different generations. Sam grew up in an environment when being gay was still kept a secret, even as she and her generation fought for civil rights and equality. Like Sam, Dani's parents also had fought injustices on behalf of blacks. Her parents clawed their way to success and were able to hand down opportunities for their children. Dani, Clancy — Sam's stepdaughter — and Addie's generation had reaped the advantages of their parents' hard-fought struggles for equality. Not really understanding that struggle firsthand, Dani's generation basically took it for granted. As much as she and Dani had in common, Sam still found herself looking at Dani in that context. It was not a judgmental observation. Sam's life experience gave her a perspective that was different from that of her children's generation. She saw it from a historical viewpoint.

There were other differences between them. Sam's humor was understated and dry, her demeanor steady and calm. Dani's humor was upfront and bold. She was bubbly, and energetic. Their unequal ages did not hinder their enjoyable chance meeting that had turned into a delightful evening.

Dani glanced at her iPhone watch, as a vibrating text came in. "Oh damn. Sorry, I have to return this call." She smiled at Sam and stood to leave. "My goodness, we have been talking for hours. Thank you for such a wonderful evening." She reached into the box of books and took one of Sam's novels. "I don't have cash on me, but I will pay you tomorrow, if that's okay?"

The cartoon character, Wimpy, popped into Sam's mind. *I'll gladly pay you on Tuesday for a hamburger today.* The statement would be lost on Dani's generation, so she kept it to herself, just saying, "Of course. Have a good night." She liked the idea of seeing her again.

Dani took her sweater and draped it over her arm. She smiled one last time and walked away from their table. As Dani exited the restaurant, Sam admired her figure. Dani was a good three inches shorter than Sam. She walked with confidence and a sexy little sway of her shapely hips. She had a full bust that filled out her blouse and left a cleavage that invited more curiosity.

They had paid for their dinner hours ago. Sam put her backpack into the box with her books and carried them out of the restaurant. Having forgotten to pack aspirin for her aching arthritic hip, she decided to buy a bottle in the gift shop on the ground floor. She stopped at the board displayed in the lobby for tomorrow's convention agenda. Dr Daniella Masters was to speak at ten a.m. in ballroom two.

Dani had finished her call to John Muir hospital, where she worked, in Walnut Creek California. A hospital nurse had asked for Dani's permission to increase her patient's pain medication, following his surgery yesterday. Dani had flown to Chicago a few hours after that surgery and was pleased to hear that his vitals were stable. She entered her room, placed Sam's book on the bed table and put on David's boxer shorts and T-shirt, that she always wore to bed. She climbed between the cold sheets and switched out the light. She lay there in the dark, thinking about her evening spent with Sam. She liked her a lot. She was so easy to talk to, and her sense of humor and wit was endearingly funny. Unlike herself, Sam was soft-spoken, and she seemed to take things in her stride. She was easygoing and interesting. She was a beautiful and stately woman, who carried herself with a mysterious mix of grace and strength.

Dani wasn't anything like her mother. Her mother was constantly striving to impress her country-club friends. Political issues of the day were no longer important in her life. Sam's comments about her generation's fight for civil rights may have once applied to her mother, as she was coming up. Not any longer. Mother had arrived, forgotten where she came from, and those issues were no longer her concern. Her Dad was indifferent about most things and was content that she and her brother, Charles, were both successful.

Charles was the CEO of his own web-designing business in Atlanta. As kids, they had been close, but now, due to their busy lives and the distance between them, they only saw each other at their parents' home, for the holidays. He was married, but Dani didn't know much about his wife, Darla. She hoped his union, unlike hers, was supportive, loving and nurturing. Dani had never had that type of relationship, and she sadly felt she probably never would.

She and David were just good friends. Living in California gave David and herself the distance needed from their parents' expectations of their marriage.

Charles, on the other hand, was a mommy's boy, still being controlled by their mother. That was not an issue Dani shared with him. She had been the rebellious child, and her drive was to study and get out of the house. She had her career which gave her great satisfaction. That was a comfort, although not quite the best she had hoped for in her personal life.

Her mind wandered to the next morning and her presentation. *If I go there, I definitely won't sleep.*

She turned the nightstand light back on and checked her email. She stared at the coffered ceiling. She reached for the television remote but changed her mind. She picked up Sam's book, *Chance Meeting* by *Samantha Stern.* Dani's busy life gave her little time for reading non-medical material. She flipped through the book, glancing at random dialogue that brought a smile to her face. She adjusted her pillow and started the book from the beginning.

The main character, Ann, had Sam written all over her. It was like peeking into Sam's prior younger years. As she read, more layers of Sam were revealed. Ann's youthful physical description in the book was easily replaced in Dani's mind with Sam, as she was now. For Dani, the character fit better that way.

The first love scene with Ann, also known as Sam, and the book's second love interest, left Dani very aroused. Her hand moved over her breasts and down between her legs. She was wet, and she stroked herself to the rhythm of Sam's erotic play-by-play. She came with Sam's image in her head. It was the first time, fantasizing about sex, that she was able to come. Sex with David was not great, and it had been a long time since they had shared intimacy. Her career-driven mind was too busy to care much at all about sex. Although she was still young, that part of her life basically didn't exist. She put the book on the night table and turned off the light. Closing her eyes, she peacefully drifted off to sleep.

Sam's book signing was from noon until two, and it was only seven-thirty in the morning.

The throbbing in her hip signaled that it wouldn't be possible trying to go back to sleep. This damp weather didn't help. Getting older was definitely not her idea of the golden years. Each morning reminded her of a new ache she had to put up with. Mornings like these were beginning to be a sobering view of old age and becoming ever-present in-your-face. *You start to lose family and friends you love, and you like being around people less and less. Jesus, how depressing. I'm turning into my mother.*

Sam got out of bed and into the shower. She let the hot water pulsate against her hip, as she thought about last night's dinner with Dani. She had really enjoyed her company. She was an accomplished, confident woman who didn't take herself too seriously. She had a great sense of humor and, of course, needless to mention, she was strikingly attractive. Sam chuckled to herself. *Ah yes, if I were younger and Dani were gay.*

Sam dressed, and she pulled out her laptop to do some work on her newest book. Writing for Sam was more than an escape, it was more like taking a ride to an undisclosed location. She would begin a story, and the characters would lead her through her past, or into places she wished her past had taken her. Growing up in the sixties gave Sam plenty of material to write about. She had been in many gay relationships, and in and out of many women's beds.

Dani was a strong, confident woman who reminded her of her daughter, Addie. She was proud of the strong women Addie and Clancy had become. Addie had accepted Laura with open arms, after her father's death. Laura's daughter, Clancy, and Addie were best friends since fifth grade. That was how Laura and Sam had met. They were both single mothers. Laura had divorced Clancy's father a little less than two years after their daughter was born. He wasn't ready to be a dad and felt trapped into giving up his carefree life.

Their girls were thrilled that they had two moms and that they could live together in one house. Clancy was the rebellious and challenging one during their teen years. Sam related more to Clancy, having had a similar childhood. Sam and Clancy were close, and Clancy had usually come to her before confiding in Laura. Addie was always the more serious child. She worried about grades and was nerdy and funny like her father Michael, and she, ironically, gravitated more to Laura for advice.

After high school, the girls shared an apartment until Addie married Josh. Clancy never married but gave them their three-year-old grandson, Garrett. Addie and Josh gave them their granddaughter Macy, who was seven months older than Garrett. Sam smiled, thinking about her grandchildren, who were close and loving and protective of each other.

I'm a very lucky woman. I'm lucky to have such a great family; I'm lucky I had a remarkable second chance to live my true self with the woman I loved. I'm lucky to be living in a time, where coming out can no longer hurt her deceased, conservative parents. I have a lot to be thankful for.

Sam had lost friends when she came out with Laura. They were either angry she hadn't shared her secret with them or held the negative opinion of their generation about homosexuality. The few friends she has allowed in her life were mostly curious, rather than supportive, of her sexuality.

All except for Connie, Sam's only true friend. The friendship between Sam, Connie and Connie's husband, Martin, began when Addie and Connie's twin boys were toddlers. They had been through a lot together. She was there for her when Michael was killed. Sam valued Connie's unbiased and straightforward answers and sometimes unsolicited advice. She and Martin had been through it all with her. Their kids had grown up together, and Martin and Connie saw her through the death of Laura, as well. Sam had never sought out the gay community, or a lot of friends. She preferred her privacy. Laura had been the social butterfly in the family and introduced friends into their lives. All Sam had needed, besides Laura and the kids, was Connie's friendship.

All these thoughts and memories had let her computer screen time-out. She hit save and closed the cover of her laptop and decided a walk would stretch out her hip. The lesbian bookstore for the book signing was only two blocks away, so she made it her first stop, to drop off the box of books she had signed last night. Her second stop was grabbing a coffee and bagel, which she ate as she checked out the neighborhood. She stopped at a toy store to buy her grandson, Garrett, a book about a dinosaur, his current passion. In an attempt to save her granddaughter from a tearful meltdown, she bought Macy a princess outfit to change into, so that Addie could wash the one she lived in.

As she entered her hotel lobby, she saw a crowd of people making their way into a ball room. She glanced at her watch. It was just before ten. She returned to her room with the grandchildren's gifts. A smile came across her face, as she thought about Dani. She shrugged her shoulders. *Why not?*

She took the elevator back down and joined the crowd. She found an empty chair a few rows from the back of the room.

The crowd settled down, and the white noise of talking people and shuffling of chairs stopped, as Dani adjusted the mic on her blouse, waiting for her introduction to end. She was wearing matching red heels and a bold, red blouse tucked into the slacks of her well-fitted, pin-striped, grey pantsuit. Her corn-rolled-hair laid neatly in a circle atop her head. She smiled broadly, her beautiful white teeth gleaming, and she began. As she spoke, she gracefully moved away from the podium in a casual way, only returning to operate her accompanying PowerPoint presentation.

Sam understood little of what Dani was talking about. However, she was enjoying the view, and it wasn't the screen to which Dani was referring. Halfway through her speech, their eyes connected, and Sam gave her an unobtrusive thumbs up. She was rewarded with one of Dani's dazzling smiles.

Sam was lost in Dani's gestures and the graceful movements that her curvy, beautiful body made. It was about an hour later that the audience's respectful applause and the sound of chairs moving across the floor, indicated that it was the end of her presentation.

Sam started to follow the crowd to the exit when she heard, "Sam, wait!" She turned and watched, as Dani came toward her. "Thank you for coming. That was very sweet of you. I appreciated your moral support."

Sam smiled back at her. "It certainly was just that, because I had no idea what the hell you were talking about. For all I knew, you could have been speaking Klingon."

Dani threw her head back and let out a hardy laugh. "And yet, you didn't leave twenty minutes into my presentation." Her face suddenly took on a more serious look. Her thoughts had returned to Sam's novel. "Remarkable. You are really remarkable."

Sam stared at her, trying to understand the sudden shift in her voice.

Dani recovered from thinking about last night in bed. "Hey, can I return the favor? Need a little moral support, yourself? I would love to go with you to the book signing, if it hasn't already taken place."

"It's from twelve to two." Picking up on Dani's time frame reference, she jokingly added, "I can understand if you leave after twenty minutes."

Mockingly, Dani shook her head. "I'm sure I won't want to." She glanced at her watch. "I have to take down my PowerPoint equipment before we go."

"I'll help you."

The bookstore manager had set up a table for Sam and the stack of her newest book, to sign. Dani walked around the bookstore and came back with two other novels Sam had written. "Can you sign these for me too?"

"Girl, you haven't paid for the first one yet."

Dani laughed and picked up Sam's present novel from the table, and with the other two in hand, she headed for the cash register. She returned and mockingly shook the purchase bag in Sam's face. She sat down next to Sam, who had requested a chair be placed at the table for her. They remained quietly sitting next to each other, as Sam asked the next customer her name and put it above her signature with a brief comment.

During a lull from interacting with customers, Dani asked, "Are you *Ann* in all your books?"

A smirk appeared on Sam's face as she turned to her. She was impressed that Dani recognized her in the novel, and even more so that she had read her book last night.

Before Sam could respond, Dani read her mind. "I haven't finished it yet, but so far, it's pretty clear to me."

Sam said softly. "As the saying goes, authors usually write about what they know. *Ann* is usually in other books, just with different names."

"Now that I have met *Ann*, I really like her. She is very sexy."

Sam chuckled and winked. "I guess you could say she was something in her prime."

Dani put her hand on Sam's arm. "I believe that prime has yet to peak."

Sam was sure Dani must have felt the goosebumps that appeared on her arm, where Dani's hand had been placed. They held each other's stare for a moment. There were tiny golden flecks in Dani's iris's that softened her green eyes. Sam wanted to lean forward and kiss her. Instead, she said, matter-of-factly, "Why, Doctor Masters, are you coming on to me?"

Dani smiled. "That is one of the things I like about you. You are direct and come to the point."

"It appears we both are. I have never slept with a straight woman before."

"It doesn't mean we can't." Then she added, "Maybe that can be the research and subject of your next book."

The moment was interrupted, as a book appeared in front of Sam's face and a voice said, "Could you please sign your book for me?" Sam was grateful for the interruption, so that she could recover from Dani's comment. The young customer took the book and stared at the blush spreading across Sam's face. She asked bluntly, as only youth can, "Are you two lovers?"

Dani was quick to answer. "Not yet. I'm working on it."

It was the first time since meeting Dani that Sam felt uncomfortable. *Dani is my girls' ages, for god's sake! The woman is straight!* The silence that followed was awkward. Dani decided to give Sam the time to think over her brazen comment. She left the chair to browse the bookstore once more.

Two o'clock came without further discussion on the topic of sleeping together. Sam left the manager a few remaining signed books to sell. She placed some change on the counter and took a rainbow pride pin off the shelf. She turned to Dani, and without speaking, pinned it to her blouse. Dani's eyebrows raised, and a smile crossed her face. They left the bookstore. Dani stopped on the sidewalk outside the bookstore and pointed to the pin on her blouse. "Does this mean I'm officially gay, and your answer is, yes, we can proceed?"

Sam quietly said, "This means let's get something to eat and talk about it."

Dani took a breadstick from the cup on the restaurant table and munched on it, as she looked over the menu. She suddenly dropped the menu on the table. "I know I want to sleep with you, and I can tell we have chemistry, and you find me attractive too. So, there really is nothing to discuss. I'm leaving tomorrow, so is this going to happen?"

Since Dani's suggested agenda in the bookstore, Sam had considered all the things she *should* say to Dani. There were their obvious age differences, of course, and what if Dani would regret… and then there was… Sam locked eyes with her. All the things she had planned to say, dropped by the wayside. *Oh hell, this is not a life-time commitment! It would only be a one-time—*Without even finishing her thought, she admitted to herself that she had already known her answer, in the bookstore. "Yes, I think I very much would like for this to happen. I'm really not hungry. Are you?"

Dani rolled her eyes toward the ceiling and declared, "Oh, thank god, already!" She reached across the table, took Sam's hand and pulled her out of the chair.

They returned to the hotel. Dani took the 'please do not disturb' sign and hung it on the outside doorknob of her room. The door closed, and Sam gently pushed Dani against the door, taking that kiss she had wanted since this morning. It began softly and hesitantly and quickly turned into a deep exploration that left Dani feeling weak and wanting more. Sam reached under Dani's blouse and expertly unhooked her lacy, black bra. Her fingers began opening the buttons on her blouse and pulled it and her bra from Dani's body. Sam hesitated for a moment, reading Dani's face, and giving her the time to change her mind. Dani's answer was to pull Sam back for another kiss that made her moan. She fumbled with Sam's blouse, until Sam impatiently removed it herself. She took Dani's hand and lead her to the bed, where they both finished undressing and climbed between the sheets.

Sam explored the firmness of Dani's full breasts with her eager hands. She gently pulled on one of her nipples, that puckered and raised instantly, and took the second one in her mouth and sucked gently. Dani's pulse began to quicken, as she took Sam's free hand, moved it down her body and placed it between her legs. Sam hadn't planned on moving quiet that fast, but she didn't hesitate. She slipped two fingers into her wetness, then quickly locating the spot that she knew Dani wanted her to stroke. Sam asked in a whisper, "Harder?"

Dani couldn't speak and just clamped her teeth over her lower lip and nodded. Sam continued to rub a little harder and replaced Dani's biting teeth with her own mouth, pushing her tongue against Dani's tongue to the rhythm of her moving fingers. Dani arched her hips, riding Sam's fingers until she cried out Sam's name as she came, flooding Sam's hand with her silky wetness.

Now, too excited to wait for Dani to recover fully, Sam slid down, spreading Dani's legs. She savored that taste that women magically make. Dani spread her legs wider for deeper penetration, as Sam inserted her fingers. Dani pushed against Sam's demanding thrusts, as she came again. Sam rubbed herself against Dani's leg, coming herself.

It had been so long since Sam had felt this alive. She had not been with anyone since Laura had died. She lay there, almost wanting to weep from the emotion. She reminded herself that this would all be gone tomorrow. What a miraculous gift, and it would be taken away all too soon.

Dani reached down and stroked her hair. "Come up here."

Sam obeyed and was rewarded all over again, as Dani's fingers slipped deep inside her. Dr Masters was a quick study indeed. Dani's fingers were now deep inside her. Months of sexual tension was released, as she came in waves. Their sweaty heads lay on their pillows, as they smiled contently at each other.

They ordered room service, and after their dinner, they crawled back into bed. Dani ran her hand over Sam's white hair and gazed into her eyes. "I cannot believe how amazing this day has been; how amazing you have been. I have a confession to make."

Sam raised an eyebrow and waited for her to continue.

"Last night, reading your book, was the second orgasm I ever had."

Sam was not surprised by her comment, and her expression didn't change, as she stated, "Unfortunately, many women don't have them." She then jokingly inquired, "I hope today was better than last night's reading?"

Dani didn't respond to Sam's joke and in a serious voice said, "Much better. I never knew what I was missing. You showed me what I wanted." Dani's kiss lingered and after, she said, "Please show me more."

Once again, Sam and Dani explored each other's long-awaited needs.

Morning came all too fast, with little sleep. Sam awoke in Dani's bed. She heard the shower. Sam opened the shower door and joined her. She knew this would be the last time she could touch her before they both returned to their separate lives and awakened from this incredible encounter. There was no smile on Dani's face, as the water cascaded over their bodies. Sam knew Dani was thinking those very thoughts as well. She wrapped her arms around Sam and reached up to kiss her neck. Sam's hands slid down Dani's soapy, slick back, and she pulled her closer. This time, they made love softly and gently, unlike last night's passionate neediness that left them both spent. They knew this would be their final goodbye.

Chapter 2

Dani finished Sam's novel on the flight home. *Ann's* character gave her moments of such clarity into Sam, the real woman with whom she had just spent the most incredible two days of her life. She knew Sam on the written page as if she knew her all her life. The experience had been surreal, and Dani found it difficult separating Ann from Sam, as she clutched the book to her chest.

She climbed into her parked car waiting for her at the San Jose airport. *Back to reality*, she thought, as she turned on the engine. There was no need to call David to let him know she was home. He, too, had been out of town on business. Actually, she wasn't even sure when he was due back. She would know when he walked through the door. She stopped at the hospital to check on her patients before going home.

It took only a few days before she was back into her busy routine. Coming home one day, she threw her keys into the dish on the entry table and looked up to see David on the couch, talking on his phone. She hadn't seen him since returning home from the convention a week ago. He continued talking and acknowledged her with a wave. Dani waved back and went into the kitchen to get a cold drink from the refrigerator.

Their mode of communication, if they needed to say anything to each other, was to text or leave a note on the kitchen counter, since they lived their lives basically as roommates. If their professional obligations required a spouse to attend a function, out of courtesy they would, if their schedules allowed. Family get-togethers were only at the holidays. Their marriage was not even a marriage of convenience any longer. There was no hostility, never had been. There simply wasn't anything left that they had in common. Actually, when Dani thought about it, there never really was, other than their parents' close friendships.

Dani's mind wandered to Sam, as it had, daily, since returning home. She and Sam couldn't be more different, yet, in that short amount of time they spent together, they had had so much to talk about. Dani smiled. Most of that time was spent in bed. Nonetheless, there was a deep connection made on some level that Dani couldn't put to words. *I have education from books; Sam has education from life.*

David finished his call and joined her in the kitchen. "Hi."

He was still in his suit, and his unpacked suitcase sat in the hallway. He had just gotten home.

Dani handed him a cold bottle of water. "How was Arlington?"

"Good. I'm glad you're here. I have something I want to talk to you about." He sat down on the bar seat at the counter. He twisted the cap off the water bottle and took a large gulp. "I got an offer for a great paying government position in DC. I think I'm going to take it. I told them I'd let them know by Friday."

Dani was happy for him. She patted his shoulder. "Great, congratulations. When do you have to be there?"

"Thanks. I plan on telling them I'm giving two weeks' notice, and then I'll see when they want me to start. I'm hoping for a break before starting, so I can find a place and get settled." His face turned to concern. "Hey, the only thing that concerns me is what are we going to tell the folks?"

Since they were kids, both their families had lived less than a block from each other in Atlanta. Their parents were unaware that their marriage was nonexistent, practically since the wedding. She and David had basically stayed together for them. The parents loved the idea that their beautiful, black children were successful, married and made them proud. Neither Dani nor David wanted to hurt them.

This was the only part of the situation that made her sad, and her face showed it. "Right. I guess it's time we tell them. Hell, what do we even tell them?"

David nodded sadly in agreement. "I know. I think it's best that we just say we have drifted apart, busy with our own careers. Basically, that's the truth. No one's fault, no blaming."

Dani laughed. "Maybe we can stop hearing about the grandchildren we have put off giving them. I really believe that they still think we are in our twenties. Christ, I'll be forty-four!"

David smiled. "I don't know if I ever told you, but I never wanted children."

Dani suddenly felt very sad. "We never even got that far along in our relationship to talk about it. I can't believe it's been seven years."

David stood up, hugged her and placed a kiss on her cheek. "I'll get the divorce papers taken care of. Then we can tell them."

David texted her the following week at the hospital and asked her if they could meet for a very quick dinner after work to go over the divorce papers. They met at a halfway point between his office and the hospital. They didn't own property, there were no children involved and they didn't ask each other for any financial compensation. It was all very straightforward, and Dani and David signed the papers. Dani returned to the hospital, and David went to their apartment to organize his things to send ahead to the east coast. He was to leave a week later. Done. For Dani, the only sadness was losing a good friend. She wondered if David felt the same way.

Dani and David coordinated their calls to their parents. Dani told her parents a week after David left for his new job. They were devastated, and her mother insisted it was not too late for them to try again. Her father was on the call as well, and she could hear the disappointment in his voice. It was a difficult call and the news traveled fast. Twenty minutes later, her in-laws called. Again, the pleas of reconsideration were repeated.

After the calls, she was exhausted. Her feelings of sadness for her parents, were replaced by a feeling of release from the sham of a marriage that never was.

She wished Sam was here to talk to about her feelings. She and Sam never exchanged contact information. Of course, that was not an issue. She had found Sam's professional information online through her lesbian website. She had followed Sam's successful reviews with her newest novel she had read in Chicago. She even knew where Sam was heading for her next book signing. She understood that they had only shared a fleeting experience together, but Sam was constantly on her mind. It wasn't just her divorce she wanted to tell her about, it was everything about her daily life: her accomplishments made at work, every funny thing that she heard or saw. Only when she read a Samantha Stern book, did she ache for and connect to Ann, Charlotte, or whoever Sam was in the story.

One evening, a few months after David had relocated to the east coast, Dani was on her way home from the hospital. She had been thinking about Sam most of her day, and she found herself analyzing what happened between them during their time together in Chicago. Was it the thrill of having sex with a stranger? Sam, from the beginning, had never felt like a stranger to her. Maybe it was the forbidden sex for the first time with a woman. Maybe that's what kept her obsessed about their encounter. Dani had always needed to understand the logic of situations. There was no logic that weekend in Chicago. It was pure emotion, something Dani had never allowed herself to rule her decisions. It was time to finalize an answer for herself. *Of course, the sex was amazing. That's what it was, wasn't it?* True to her research mind, that could easily be tested. Dani got home, showered and dressed. She located a lesbian bar on her phone and left the apartment.

It didn't take long before she was approached by an attractive woman named Frankie, who wanted to buy her a drink. That was a refreshing surprise, after being instantly hit on by two manly-looking dykes that circled her like their next meal, as soon as she had walked into the bar.

Frankie was much more civil in her approach, but there wasn't going to be a lot of small talk, either. The place was not a community-friendly bar for gay women. It was a meat market, much like the straight bars Dani had been to while in college. But that's why she and Frankie were there, wasn't it? Frankie was pleasant, and after talking for about twenty minutes, they left the bar together.

The hotel was clean, and Frankie took the lead, as she slowly undressed Dani. It was somewhat arousing when Frankie kissed her. They made their way to the bed. Dani was touched and kissed in all the right places where Sam had been. Dani felt nothing. She even tried to pretend she was with Sam and not Frankie. Frankie tried the best she could, and finally she took Dani's hand and placed it where she wanted it. Dani's attempt at pleasing Frankie was not much better. They cordially called it a night.

A few months later, Dani tried again to prove, whatever she was trying to prove to herself, with a nurse she had gotten to know at the hospital. They had one night together, and they both agreed there was no chemistry. They stayed acquaintances, but nothing more.

This time, Sam only had to travel to San Francisco. The whole time she was there it had rained, and she mostly stayed in the hotel.

Addie picked her up from the Tucson airport. "Mom, you look tired. I hope this traveling isn't too much for you."

Since Laura's death, both Addie and Clancy were overly protective of her, and as much as they cared, Sam was constantly reminded by them of her age. They had always been there for her, and she was grateful, but since Laura's death, they tended to treat her as if she was fragile, Addie more so than Clancy.

"Addie, I'm fine." Wanting to quickly change the subject, she asked, "Tell me what's been going on the last few days."

Addie pulled out of the airport parking lot. "Aunt Julia called to say that Uncle Ed's retirement party is coming up in a few months. She expects you to clear your schedule to be there. She called me because she didn't know you were out of town and wanted to check up on you. I didn't tell her you were close by them this weekend, because I wasn't sure you wanted to visit. It's been raining in California for days now, and she was thinking about maybe coming here to get away for some sunny weather, but she doesn't want to leave Uncle Ed until he adjusts to his new meds." Addie continued to report the family activities.

Sam half listened, as she thought how close she had been to Walnut Creek, just across the bay from San Francisco, where she knew Dani worked. She had checked Dani out online and read her bio as well. Dani was never far from her mind since Chicago. It was now more than six months since they had been together. Dani had been an amazing escape from her reality. Escape wasn't really a good word; she didn't have a need to escape her life. Her life was full and busy with family and work. So, what was their experience together? Was it a moment of pure sexual impulse? To dismiss it as a one-night stand, was to belittle what had happened. There was a connection made that could not be ignored.

Yet, it couldn't be explained. They were two right people, born at the wrong times.

"Mom, did you hear me?"

"Sorry, what did you say?"

A little annoyed, Addie repeated, "I said, Garrett is starting T-ball tomorrow and wanted to know if Softa would be there? I think Clancy would like us to all be there."

Softa was Hebrew for grandmother, and that's what Garrett and Macy called her. Laura was referred to as grandma, even though the grandkids had been too young to remember her. Laura had been Christian, and their blended family always celebrated both Chanukah and Christmas and other mixed religious traditions.

"Of course, I'll be there. I'll call him when I get home."

Sam loved her house and enjoyed her garden and cooking, but for the most part, her haven was her solitude when writing. She had started a new novel and found her story line leading her into a new direction. It was beginning to change into a May-December romance. It didn't take a shrink to tell her that the subject matter was obviously an attempt to help her understand what had happened between herself and Dani. The book was about two women of different ages falling in love. It was the first time that Sam was finding her writing difficult and frustrating. She didn't know what had happened that had changed her, and she was having trouble developing her characters in the story.

Maybe she should drop it and move on with a new story line, along with her constant thoughts of Dani. That was easier said than done. The more she tried to understand her conflicting feelings, the more her plot found dead ends.

Her publisher was becoming impatient for a new submission. She put that writing aside and began another boiler plate romance.

Her new story line finally began to flow, and in a few months, she would be traveling again to promote it. She told her publisher that she definitely needed a break after this one was done. She was going to take some time off.

She submitted the completed manuscript and took two weeks off, relaxing at home. She tried some new recipes and did some gardening. She enjoyed spending more time with Garrett and Macy. They were growing up way too fast. She read four books on her 'to read list'.

Sam checked her web page, and momentarily, her breathing stopped. There was a posting from Dani. It read, 'Hope you don't mind me contacting you. I follow your website and look forward to your next book.' As generic as her comment was, Sam's heart raced. Dani had left her email address. Sam leaned back into her chair, as she pictured Dani's face, and a smile spread from ear to ear. She massaged her hands together. She typed in Dani's email address and stared at the blinking arrow a few seconds, while thinking what to say. She wanted to say how much she wished to see her again.

She wanted to tell her that she was on her mind constantly and how much she thought about her. She wanted to tell her how amazing their time was together. Sam reached out to the keyboard. Texting can be such a fertile field for miscommunication. She typed, 'Wow!' She deleted and typed, 'Of course I don't mind.' Once again, she deleted. Not knowing what Dani might be feeling, she decided on, 'What a pleasant surprise it is hearing from you. Hope you are doing well.'

Later that evening, Dani responded with, 'I'm fine, and I think about you often.'

It didn't take long before they ended each day with a shared text report of the details of their days. They both avoided discussing their Chicago weekend. Any and every other topic flowed smoothly. Sam avoided asking about David, in case Dani was feeling guilty about the time they spent in Chicago. Dani didn't ask Sam if she had started dating again; it would be too painful to know if she had. Instead, they kept their feelings about each other non-committal and light, but couldn't wait to text at days end, curled up in their separate worlds.

One night, about a month after corresponding by email and texting, Sam actually dialed her number.

Dani answered her phone. "Hello."

A shiver ran down Sam's back at the sound of her voice. "Hi, it's me. I hope you don't mind that I'm calling you? Are you free to talk?"

Dani felt an exciting, prickling sensation like she sometimes got just before a challenging surgery. She cleared her throat and said, "Of course I don't mind you calling." She felt her face getting warm from the blush that spread across her face. "I'm in bed." She gave a stifled, nervous giggle.

Sam pictured her lying there in the nude. The thought of David being next to her was very disturbing. "Oh, sorry. I will call you another time, if that's okay?"

Dani had not shared with her that she and David were no longer together. She didn't want Sam to think that's why she had contacted her. "It's fine. I'm just doing some research online about a case coming up. I could use a break. It's lovely to hear your voice."

Sam asked about her case, and Dani wanted to hear how Connie and Martin were doing, since last they emailed about Sam's long friendship with them.

Martin's health had been declining for over a year now. He was suffering from dementia, and the last few months had been the toughest. Connie had had to move him into a supervised facility. Sam was grateful she was on this short hiatus and was able to be available for Connie. They both knew it was a hospice situation. Connie had waited as long as she could to keep him home. As much as it was inevitable, it was not easy to let go. Martin and Connie had just celebrated their fiftieth anniversary, although Martin was totally unaware of who she was any more. Sam felt the weight and weariness of life's challenges and losses which came with growing older.

Her voice cracked as she held in a sob. "Dani, Martin died last night. I'm a mess. I just needed to talk."

Dani's heart sank. She knew how close Sam was to them both.

"Oh, Sam I'm so sorry. I wish I was there to hold you right now."

They talked for another hour. Dani comforted her and listened to her share the details of the last twenty-four torturous hours for Connie and herself. Finally, Sam was spent from the recap. Dani insisted she would stay on the phone until Sam fell asleep. It didn't take long. The release of emotions had come in a rush.

Two nights later, after a particularly vivid sexual dream about Dani, she climbed out of bed at three in the morning and opened her computer to revisit her abandoned May-December romance plot. Why was this so difficult to write? Unlike all her other novels, it was not an experience she had ever had before. It was hard to write because she didn't recognize herself. She had crossed over into unknown territory. She had crossed some invisible boundary. She realized her mixed feelings, all along, were really judgments that crept into her mind like a dark fog. She hadn't thought about Laura when she and Dani were together. She had slept with a straight woman. Was it their age difference? Their sexual relationship suddenly made negative adjectives jump to mind... predator, cougar, puma, all came rushing into her head. There were rules about everything in life. There were rules in her childhood about being gay, too. Finally, she understood she could no longer play by the rules of others and remain who she was. *But this discomfort is different, isn't it?*

She had shared with Connie that she had had a one-night stand while in Chicago and how she felt guilty, like she had somehow cheated on Laura. Sam could not bring herself to share with Connie their age difference. Was that shame? Why couldn't she cross that boundary even with her best friend?

Since the night that Sam had made the first phone call, they spoke often, wanting the closeness of each other's voice.

The next day Sam's phone rang. It was Dani. "Hi. I needed a break. I'm sitting on a bench in the hospital garden. The flowers smell so nice What are you up to?"

"Garrett, Macy and I are on a hike. We are almost done. It's hot and we are going for ice cream next, before heading home. How did Mr Carson fare with his surgery?"

"He did well. I'm very hopeful that he can regain some of his eyesight. The tumor was large and invasive, but I'm sure I got it all."

"Well, he was lucky that he had the very best surgeon." Sam glanced up at the trail ahead. "Hey, you guys, not so fast, wait for me." She returned to her discussion with Dani. "These guys are going to kill me. Their energy is exhausting."

Dani's hiccup of a laugh was followed with, "I know better; I have firsthand knowledge about how much energy you have."

Sam's face reddened. It was the first reference made between them about the sexually charged weekend they had shared. Dani must have realized what she had said, and there was silence between them for a moment. The subject was instantly dropped, but no amount of diversion could erase that erotic memory for either of them. Sex between them could not slip away while their backs were turned, like a forgotten text or misplaced house keys.

Chapter 3

Before getting back to work, Sam decided to go to California, to attend her brother-in-law's retirement celebration. Her sister, Julia, was three years younger than Sam. They had always enjoyed spending time together. With their busy lives, it had been too long since they had last seen each other. Sam knew that Dani was maybe twenty minutes from her sister's house, and she was debating with herself about the possibility of calling her to meet for a casual lunch. The idea excited her, but why would she possibly open a pandora's box?

Julia and Sam had shared some rough times. Sam had been the restless child and didn't always play by the rules as a teenager. Julia was the good girl. Their parents always made the comparisons that usually ended in, "Samantha, why can't you be more like your sister?" That had put a wedge between them during those years, until Sam married Michael. Instantly, everyone was glad that she had finally grown up and settled down. Then there was the illnesses and deaths of their parents and the sudden, massive heart attack that took the life of their younger brother, three days before his fifty-second birthday.

Sam's husband died, and Julia was there to help her pick up the pieces of her life.

Then there was Laura. She had been a shock to Julia. Sam knew it wasn't Laura; it was getting adjusted to the idea of Sam being a lesbian. Sam had not come out to the family until then. There was a lot of history shared between sisters. Her lesbianism was not one of them. They shared the challenges of raising their children. Through it all, they were there for each other for almost seven decades. With Martin's recent death and years of events with her sister, suddenly Sam felt very old.

Julia placed a cup of coffee on the table in front of her sister. "Sam, I'm so glad you're here. We haven't really had time together for so long. I know you have been really busy writing and traveling. I'm glad you are taking some time for yourself."

"Me too. I'm glad I'm here."

"I thought maybe we could take a couple of days and go to Monterey. I know how much you love wandering through the shops there." She leaned across the table and in a conspiratorial whisper, she said, "I could use some time away from Ed. He is driving me crazy, and now that he is retiring, we will probably kill each other if he doesn't find a hobby."

Sam laughed. "Well, doesn't he still play golf? Now he will have the time to play as much as he wants."

"He does. In fact, he was hoping you would play some golf with him while you're here."

Sam stared at the table. A silent moment passed. Sadness had crept into her voice. "I haven't played since Laura died." She quickly turned her pain into a joke. "Besides, I doubt this old woman could do nine holes any more."

Julia didn't want to bring her back to thoughts of Laura. "Well... then, how about a quick trip to Monterey with me? We have to be back here on Friday. Ed's retirement party is on Saturday. I'm having it catered, but I could use your help to get ready."

"That sounds fine. Maybe we can take in the aquarium while we're there."

She and Julia stayed at an adorable bed and breakfast cottage. They walked on the beach, catching up with each other's lives and sharing stories about their kids and grandchildren. They shopped for things that caught their fancy and didn't need. The aquarium and ocean were always calming and beautiful, and it had been years since Sam had been there.

She was glad Julia hadn't once brought up Laura. Sam didn't want to be reminded about her guilt over Dani, who was now daily on her mind and on the phone.

Only after her brief encounter with Dani in Chicago, did Sam start to feel guilty about Laura. Those feelings had been creeping back, as she tried to sort out her feeling about Dani being partially back in her life.

It hadn't taken long for Julia to adore Laura, once she accepted that her sister was gay. In her heart, Sam knew Laura wouldn't want her to be celibate and not move on with her life, but Sam was still struggling with sorting out those feelings as well. The more she communicated with Dani, she knew that her doubts would eventually have to be explored. She wasn't ready to share them with Julia.

They returned early Friday afternoon and got busy setting up the tables that had been delivered while they were away, placing them around the pool and backyard. Julia and Ed had a beautiful home in the Lafayette hills. They loved to entertain, so Ed's retirement party wasn't a stressful occasion for her sister. Julia was always very organized. The party was scheduled for two p.m. the next day.

Sam was looking forward to seeing her niece, Susan, and her husband, Scott, who were coming in from out of state. They rented a car at the airport and arrived later in the afternoon. The evening was full of laughter and catching up. Susan was her bubbly self and always had stories to share and comments to make about everything and everyone, much to her mother's annoyance. Susan had always managed to ruffle Julia's feathers. Her niece reminded her of Addie and herself growing up. Sam loved to sit back and watch the family interactions and playful teasing.

The next morning, Sam slept in, and the smell of coffee and the laughter from downstairs was a nice way to wake up. She showered and dressed and joined her family in the kitchen.

Susan was helping her mom prepare breakfast. "Aunt Sam, how do you want your eggs?"

"Over easy. What can I do?"

Susan handed her a cup of coffee. "Sit down and rest while you can. The caterers will be here in a couple of hours, and we will put you to work filling trays." She followed up by getting Sam the half and half she liked in her coffee. "Here you go. The guys are off to play golf. I'm surprised you didn't go with them."

Before Sam could come up with a response, Julia intercepted, a little too forcefully. "Susan, Sam is here to visit and have a little down-time before she is off and running again."

Susan was taken aback with her mother's snappy remark. She held up her hand, her palm facing out in defense. "O-k-a-y... but I'm not sure what that was about, Mom."

A little embarrassed for how she had come across, Julia said, "Just let it drop." She busied herself at the counter. "Sam, toast?"

Sam avoided making eye contact with Susan's questioning face. "One piece please. I'll be right back; I left my phone upstairs."

As she exited the kitchen and headed toward the stairs, Sam could hear a couple of words of the exchange between her sister and Susan. Laura's name popped up. She hated that her sister avoided talking about Laura. Julia tiptoed around her death, trying to protect Sam from her memories. They didn't understand those memories made her happy — most of the time.

She had shared a lot of those memories with Dani the weekend they were together. Some good, some painful, but Dani wanted to hear them. She was a good listener and a straightforward talker. They had shared a lot about their pasts. Maybe they did, because it was easier and therapeutic, like talking to a shrink about feelings, with someone not so close to their lives. In Sam's case, someone who wandered into her world, and as quickly, was gone, until recently making a move back into her heart.

Breakfast dishes were cleaned, and they took their second cup of coffee out to the patio. Susan showed her pictures of her daughter, Katie, who was now almost eight and staying with her in-laws while they were in California. Sam took out her phone and showed them pictures of Garrett and Macy. Funny grandchildren stories were exchanged, and Sam shared how lucky she felt to have them in her life. She said that Garrett and Macy loved to hear wonderful stories about their grandma Laura, whom they had never really gotten to know. Sam hoped that talking about Laura, showed Julia she was okay and had moved on as best she could. It appeared to ease the tension around the subject of Laura.

Soon after their respite by the pool, the guys came back from golf and went to take showers. On their heels, arrived the caterers. Things got busy quickly. Sam put a few bottles of champagne in the outside beverage cooler for toasts to Ed and helped set up the champagne glasses. Some people had arrived a little early, and Julia was playing hostess and making introductions. Susan was close behind her mother, offering drinks. Sam shook a few hands and went into the quieter kitchen to help the servers plate the trays with food.

Susan came in and pointed through the kitchen window to the yard. She whispered into Sam's ear. "See that tall guy in the blue shirt? The one with the toupee. Damn thing looks like a dead animal was glued to his head." She laughed with abandon at her own joke. "He asked who you were and said you were a beautiful, tall drink of water. Whatever the hell that even means. He's a jerk that's married to a friend of Mom's. I had the delicious pleasure to inform him that he had the wrong plumbing to interest you. You would have loved his expression when that sank into his horny, little mind."

Sam had to smile at her niece. "God, I hope your mother didn't hear your conversation with him. She would be appalled."

"Don't worry, she was talking to his other half while he was ogling you. It always amuses me how you become a testosterone magnet when you walk into a room." She kissed Sam's cheek. "You only get more stunning as you get older."

Sam smiled at her niece. "You're a little biased."

Susan stated, emphatically, "No! Of course, I love you, but my observations are shared by everyone around you. You are a very stunning woman. You are the only one who doesn't see it. All my life, I have wished I looked like you. Unfortunately, I take after Dad's side of the family."

Sam took her niece's face in her hands and kissed her forehead. "I think you need to take a better look into the mirror. You were an adorable child that has blossomed into a beautiful woman, inside and out."

They hugged. Susan heard her name called. She rolled her eyes and scurried out to the patio.

Sam casually knew a few people who were attending the party. A sign had been placed on the front door, redirecting the guests to the gate at the side of the house, that lead into the pool and patio area.

Sam remained in the kitchen, out of the traffic of arriving guests. She could hear more talking and laughing from the open patio door, as the crowd got larger.

She watched the caterers artfully placing the food and garnishes on the tray, and soon Sam was copying their techniques.

She heard Julia's voice behind her. "I want you to meet my sister."

Sam placed the tray on the counter, so she could turn around.

"Sam, this is Dr Masters, a colleague of Ed's."

Sam and Dani stared at each other, both paralyzed from the shock. Feeling a little light-headed, Sam held out a slightly trembling hand. Dani took it and shook it firmly, as her legs felt like they may not support her.

Dani found her voice and said, "Nice to meet you."

Julia pulled Sam toward her and quietly said, "I'm sure these capable caterers have everything under control. Come join us outside."

Not yet totally recovered, Sam followed her sister and Dani outside. She watched the familiarity of Dani's sexy hips move as she walked ahead of her, and her mouth went dry. Her hands grabbed two bottles of beer out of the cooler on the counter.

As soon as they stepped outside, a woman came toward Julia, taking her arm. "There you are! I was looking for you. Joe's over here. This is such a great turnout. Come sit with us, and let's catch up." She pulled her away.

Sam handed Dani a bottle of beer. "I thought you might need this. I know I do."

Dani stared at Sam, not believing she was really standing there, looking at her. Sam thought she might faint from wanting her. Dani took the beer from Sam. Their hands touched in the exchange, and a shiver ran down Dani's back.

Sam took the lead. "Come, we'll find a table." She chose an empty table under a tree against the back wall, where it was more secluded. She opened the sun umbrella and sat down next to Dani.

"How long have you known Ed?"

Dani opened the beer and took a sip. "Going on five years. He is in radiology, and we do a lot of my consultation work together. Small world, isn't it?" As direct as Sam remembered her to be, Dani asked, "Did your heart stop for a moment, back there?"

Am I really sitting next to her? Sam thought. "My heart is just beginning to slow down. I can't stop looking at you. I'm afraid that if I blink, you might disappear."

Dani gave her that smile that instantly made Sam wet, and said, "You look amazing. I have daydreamed about you so often, I was sure, in my mind, I had made you sexier than you are. I was wrong. I remembered correctly, after all."

Sam closed her eyes briefly, thinking about the last time they made love in the shower. "Dani, don't."

Dani didn't skip a beat. "Why, Sam? Don't tell me you aren't feeling the same. Today didn't happen by chance, any more than Chicago did. People don't get second chances handed to them like this." Dani thought about her comment, as Laura came to mind. "Well, most people don't."

Sam turned to her with a set jaw. In a whisper, she said, "Dani, stop. I am not going to deny that I'm very aroused right now, but you know this can't go anywhere. There are way too many obstacles."

Dani became defensive, but very determined. Her voice rose. "Like what? Obstacles become obstacles only if you place them."

Sam was getting flustered. Her calm, controlled self, vanished instantly. "The obvious ones!" The volume of her voice also went up two notches. She became aware that her niece, a few yards away, was glancing in her direction with a puzzled look. Sam lowered her voice, and leaned in closer to say, "Shall we start with our age differences?"

Dani stated, between clenched teeth, "That certainly wasn't an issue in Chicago." Challengingly, she asked, "Anything else?"

Sam stared directly at her. Frustrated and momentarily lost for words, Sam's hands sprung open dramatically, as she leaned toward Dani, defiantly. Her voice now dripping with sarcasm, she said, "Oh. I don't know, maybe your marriage?" Trying to keep her voice lower, she continued. "Oh right… and you're straight. That might be an issue too." Sam's abrupt gesture and intense expression had gotten Susan's attention again, and now, her sister's, as well.

Dani wasn't finished yet and replied, "David and I are divorced, so unless you are in a relationship… are you in a relationship?"

Sam placed her hands in her lap, to restrain her gestures that were accompanying her raised voice. Much quieter, she answered, "No, I'm not in a relationship."

Dani proceeded. "I was very curious to know if my attraction was to you, or to having sex with a woman. So, I tried sex twice, with two separate women. Nothing."

That was so like Dani.

Sam momentarily let her guard down and laughed. She was amused. "Seriously? I have very much missed your boldness." This sudden change from anger to laughter received even more confused glances from Julia and Susan.

Matter-of-factly Dani said, "Well, that, at least, is positive and encouraging. Might as well get to the point. I can't get you out of my head since we met. Look me in the eye, and tell me it hasn't been the same for you."

Sam softened. She was on an emotional roller coaster. "I can't deny it. I look forward to your calls and texts during the day." She looked lovingly into Dani's gorgeous, green eyes. "You have to agree, given your logical, analytical mind, that there are issues that need to be discussed."

Dani was on the verge of tears. "I just can't bear the thought of losing you twice."

Sam was excited and scared at the same time. The prospect of them, once again, physically walking away from each other, seemed too painful to think about. *But how could this possibly work?*

It had been over a year since Chicago. They were oblivious to the party surrounding them. Two hours later, Julia approached them. "My, you two have been talking a while. Looks like it was some serious subject going on over here."

Dani looked up at Julia and completely ignored her comment. "Julia, it was so kind of you to include me today. I'm sorry, but I have to check in at the hospital. Is Ed around? I need to say goodbye."

Actually, since the moment she had arrived, she had only been with Sam. That did not go unnoticed by Sam's sister.

Julia realized that no light was going to be shared, by Dani or Sam, about their animated conversation. "He's in the house, watching a game with the guys."

Sam stood. "Let me show you where the den is." She led Dani away from a bewildered Julia.

They hadn't made it to the upstairs den, when Sam pulled Dani into the guest bathroom and locked the door. So much for her earlier reservations. She took Dani into her arms, and the kiss that followed was familiar and as passionate as the first night they had been together. Dani couldn't stop there; she crushed her hand into Sam's breast and moaned into her ear. "God, I've missed you so badly."

Sam didn't need to be told twice. She responded by sliding her hand into Dani's lacy panties. Dani instantly began rubbing herself against Sam's probing fingers. Sam's breathing quickened, as she felt her own underwear dampen with every encouragement she was giving to Dani. She could tell that Dani was about to come and placed her mouth over hers to muffle the scream she anticipated would soon come from deep inside her.

"This isn't enough," said Dani, in a raspy voice.

Sam couldn't agree more. "I know." She whispered and kissed Dani's neck. Her perfume was so familiar and intoxicating. She gently sucked on her ear, that place where Sam drove her into overdrive.

"Jesus, I want you."

There was a quiet knock at the door. Dani was barely able to speak. Breathlessly, she said, "Be out in a few minutes."

The male voice responded. "No problem, I'll use the downstairs bathroom."

They pulled themselves together the best they could. Sam opened the door slightly and peeked out. No one was in the hallway, as they emerged from their hideaway.

"I'll text you later, from the hospital."

Sam nodded, and they looked longingly at each other, before Dani made her way to the den to talk to Ed.

Sam made her way downstairs and went directly to the kitchen to avoid her sister and niece. Her head was spinning and all she could think was, *what just happened?* Not just upstairs, but the last few hours. *Now what?*

Chapter 4

Sam's phone vibrated. Dani hadn't waited, and she'd texted Sam from the car, ten minutes after she'd had left the house. 'Can you come to the hospital for lunch tomorrow?'

Sam texted back. 'I'll get back to you.'

The guests didn't seem to be in any hurry to leave. A few had even brought their swimsuits, and they were enjoying the pool.

Susan entered the kitchen. "Aunt Sam, come join us outside."

Her behavior was already suspicious, so she went with Susan to the backyard. There was a group of people sitting around a table, and Susan pulled a chair out for her aunt.

Their friends were laughing and recalling stories and memories of interactions with Ed, and the good times they had shared over the years. Julia glanced at Sam and forced a curious and awkward smile. Sam knew she would be questioned later about Dani and their strange, lengthy and curious animated discussion. Sam smiled back and tried to fit in with the laughing and teasing that was taking place.

The distraction was not enough. Sam was deep in thought about Dani. She glanced up and caught Julia staring at her. Her sister was easily read, and Sam knew she was running scenarios through her mind about Dani and wondering what had gone on between them, earlier in the day.

The day was turning into evening, and Sam wanted to get back to Dani with an answer about tomorrow. There were only a few people left, and finally they were saying their goodbyes.

Ed and his son-in-law remained in the backyard, folding up the rented tables and chairs and stacking them for the service to pick them up in the morning.

Julia, Sam and Susan where bagging paper cups and after-party litter in the kitchen, when Susan asked, "Aunt Sam, what was that about with Dr Masters?" She smiled, and with a sexy voice, she continued. "I might be wrong, but I'm pretty sure there were some interesting sparks flying between you two."

Julia whipped around, facing her daughter. With a look that could take down a bull, she barked, "Susan!"

Susan stepped back in mock defense. "Jesus, Mom. I'm just saying."

Julia turned to look how Sam had reacted to her daughter's comment. Sam had a poker face that she was unable to read. Curious about the serious discussion that had occupied her sister's and Dr Master's afternoon, she asked, "Sam, had you met Dr Masters before? It seemed like you knew each other."

Sam pushed a handful of soiled napkins she was holding, into the trash bag. "We met in Chicago. She was attending a medical convention at the hotel I was staying at." Sam quickly switched the conversation to a question. "If you don't have anything planned for tomorrow, could I borrow one of the cars? We wanted to meet for lunch."

Susan beamed as if she had won the lottery. "Damn, I was right! Score! Aunt Samantha!"

Julia's instant anger erupted. "Enough, Susan! Daniella is your age, for God's sake." She then turned to her sister, anticipating confirmation that Susan was way off base and out of line. What she met was Sam's look that hadn't changed, and only confirmed Susan's assumption.

Julia's eyes widened in astonishment. "Sam? Sam, you didn't." When Sam did not answer, she became angry and practically bit her head off. "Society has boundaries, even for you!"

Anger surfaced instantly, as Sam leaned into Julia's personal space. "Excuse me. What the hell does that mean?"

Julia was so outraged, that the words left her mouth before she could think them through. "It took me forever to shake the image of you and Laura in bed, but this…" Julia heard her own words and was so ashamed, that she fumbled, trying to take them back. "Oh my god, I'm so sorry… Sam, that came out so wrong."

Sam felt like she had been slugged in the stomach. She stood there, paralyzed.

Susan's jaw was set in anger, at her mother's hurtful words. She aggressively grabbed her handbag from the kitchen counter. She pulled out a set of car keys and thrust them toward her aunt. "Here. Take our rental car," she said, as she shot dagger-like eyes toward her mother.

Sam's hand shook, as she took the keys from her niece and turned to leave the room.

Julia desperately tried to make things right. Pleadingly, she said to Sam's back, "Samantha. Sammie, you know I loved Laura."

She started to go after Sam, but Susan grabbed her mother's arm and pulled her back. Gently she said, "Mom, no. Give her some time. Leave her alone."

Julia sat down at the kitchen counter, held her face in her hands and cried.

Sam heard her sister crying, as she started up the stairs to the guestroom. In that short distance, her own tears streamed down her face in release. Suddenly, more invisible boundaries had been stripped away.

It took a lot to make her cry. Sam sobbed into her pillow as quietly as she could. The afternoon had been overwhelming, and she hadn't yet been able to sort out all the emotions and confusions swimming around in her pounding head. Now she was slammed with her sister's comments. She picked up her phone and texted, 'What time tomorrow?'

Her phone rang right away. It was Dani. "Hi." She chuckled. "How about right now? I've been waiting all afternoon for your call. I can't wait to see you."

There was silence from Sam. Dani knew something was wrong. "Honey, are you okay?"

Sam had only wanted a text response and wasn't ready to talk to Dani about what happened in the kitchen just now. She really wasn't even sure herself. Through a tightened throat, she quietly said, "No."

Dani's heart sank. "I'll leave now and come get you."

Sam's response was harsh. "No!" She regained control. "I'm sorry. Can we talk about it tomorrow, please?"

Dani could hear the pain in Sam's voice. "Of course. I will be finished with rounds around eleven. Just have me paged. It's going to be okay, I promise."

Sam couldn't even respond, and she just hung up.

In the master bedroom, Julia paced and cried, as she told Ed what had happened. Ed tried to comfort his wife the best he could. Finally, to get her to calm down, he took her hand and lead her to the chair in their private sitting room of their bedroom. He pulled the second chair closer and sat down facing her. Once again, he took her hand in his. With her free hand, she dabbed at her eyes with a tissue.

He gently lifted her chin. "Look at me, honey."

She looked up into his sympathetic face.

He smiled. "It's going to be all right. I would like to understand if you are more upset about what you said to Sam, or about them having had a sexual relationship?"

She shrugged. "Both. I hurt her, and I'm so sorry. I need to tell her that I'm so damn sorry. I know how much she loved Laura. I need to just go into the guestroom and tell her and beg her to forgive me." She started to cry again, softly.

"Ed stated, calmly, "You can't tell her anything until you understand why you reacted the way you did. Honey, why are you so angry?"

With an outraged face, she hissed, "Jesus, Ed! Daniella is our kids' ages. Why can't Sam see how that is so wrong? The human mind needs boundaries, or there would be no order in the world. How would her girls take this news? They would be devastated."

"Julia, just because you think that their relationship is wrong, does not mean everyone else will, too. Does order in your world mean that we should bully everyone into categories? I know—"

Julie didn't wait for him to continue his thought. "Ed, really? You are okay with their behavior?"

"Their behavior is not for us to judge," he stated, harshly. "I know Dani and I know Sam. They are remarkable women, who have both faced judgments all their lives. Your comments are way too premature, anyway. It sounds like they are still sorting out their feelings about each other. Step back. I should think you would want to be there for Sam, so she can confide in you about her feelings." He softened his accusations. "Honey, I know you, too, and this is not who you are. What's going on in your head?"

She patted her husband's hand. "You're right, of course. I just wish Sam... I wish she didn't make her life so complicated. When she came out, I didn't know how to introduce them to our friends. Then she started to write lesbian books, and I had people asking personal questions about her childhood."

Ed's eyebrows raised. His tone became the tone he had used when Susan was a child. "It sounds to me like you wish Sam didn't make *your* life so complicated."

Momentarily, Julia was taken aback. She slowly nodded. "You're right. This isn't about me. It's about Sam."

Sam didn't leave the guest room for the rest of the evening. She laid on the bed, staring at the ceiling. *What am I doing? My life is uncomplicated. I have the kids, my work. What the hell am I thinking? I'm letting my hormones run my life. We are not teenagers.* That thought made her chuckle. *Shit, that is the problem. I'm almost seventy years old, and I'm obsessed with a woman half my age. For all I know, a straight woman who doesn't know she's straight!* Her thoughts turned to her sister, which made her more depressed than angry. *What the hell does Julia know about boundaries? She didn't have to live half of her life hiding who she was.*

She didn't have to marry because she wanted children, and that's how the world worked back then!

She got little sleep, as did her sister, as they laid in separate rooms, thinking their separate thoughts and feeling as though it would never be the same between them, again.

Sam was up, dressed and out of the house, before the sun was up. She didn't want any interactions with her sister, until she knew what she wanted. The pain was still too fresh. She took her laptop and the book she had been reading and found a twenty-four hour I Hop. Working didn't happen, and she couldn't concentrate long enough to read her book. She ate breakfast and watched the people around her. It surprised her how many people were in the restaurant at such an early hour.

The couple at the corner table had a toddler, who was delighted with her game of tossing silverware on the floor for her parents to fetch. There was a man who looked homeless. He was drinking coffee and looking at the newspaper that had been left in his booth. Sam wondered what complications in their lives they struggled with.

The restaurant was not far from the cemetery where her parents and brother were buried. She hadn't been there for a while and found herself parking near their grave site. It was a beautiful location in the Lafayette hills. She sat on the bench overlooking the valley and watched the sun come up.

She hadn't had a bad childhood. She, Julia and their brother had not gone without food or shelter. They had known they were loved by their parents, but Sam's secret had always placed a barrier that could not be crossed. She had known at thirteen that she was gay, and in her mind, that was bad. That could only bring shame to her family. Her behavior had been deviant, she had learned that from the books she had secretly read about homosexuality, back then. That had not been a subject to be explored with anyone. Sam had dated in high school, because she was expected to. She had gone to college where her parents hoped their daughters would find educated husbands. Girls could be teachers, secretaries or nurses, but only until they started a family. That was life in the fifties and sixties.

Sam was distracted from these thoughts, as a deer appeared from the trees, with a fawn. They stared at her for a few seconds, decided she was not a threat and munched leisurely on the grass. Sam sat and watched, until a noise startled them, and they disappeared into the brush.

She picked up two small stones from the path and placed one on each of her parents' grave sites. It was Jewish custom, which announced that someone who cared for or loved the deceased, was remembered with a visit. Through the years, she had often wondered what her mother's reaction would have been if she had come out to her. After Julia's reaction, sadly, she knew the answer. Julia was cut from their mother's cloth. Deep inside, she had always known the answer.

She stood over her mother's grave. Sam was convinced that her mother, too, would have been disturbed and disgusted by the thought of her in bed with Laura, the love of her life. Her mother and Julia had always mirrored each other's thoughts, judgements and expectations.

She got back in the car and drove out of the cemetery. Traffic was always congested in the Bay Area, no matter what time of day. She headed for the hospital in Walnut Creek.

Sam was always on time. All morning she had managed her time well and parked in the hospital garage fifteen minutes early. She entered the lobby and had Dani paged. Twenty minutes later, Dani stepped out of the elevator. Sam's heart raced, like it did yesterday, as it did whenever she was with her or heard her voice. The concern over last night's discussion vanished when Dani saw Sam's smile.

Dani suggested, "Why don't we take my car, and I can bring you back here later, since I'll need to come back again this evening."

"Do you live here at the hospital?"

Dani chuckled. "Let's just say I spend little time in my apartment, where I'm taking you right now. Unless, of course, you're hungry."

"I had a big breakfast."

Dani's apartment was just a few minutes from the hospital. It had minimal furniture and no decorations or photos on the walls. It was obvious that Dani only slept there and did, indeed, spend most of her life at the hospital.

Sam asked, "Have you eaten?"

"No, haven't had time."

Sam went into the kitchen and opened the refrigerator. There was a wilted salad and a bottle of French dressing, peanut butter, a loaf of bread and eggs. "You weren't kidding, you are rarely home. Where is the frying pan?"

Dani reached under the stove, into the cabinet. She handed Sam a brand-new pan. "I would much prefer being in the bedroom."

Sam abandoned the frying pan, putting it on the counter, and told her to sit down at the small kitchen table. "We have to talk."

Dani could see that Sam was still upset from what took place at Ed's house after she had left. "Start from the beginning."

Sam told her everything that was exchanged between herself and Julia. "Needless to say, I didn't sleep all night and had nothing, but time, to think." She paused, and Dani nodded for her to continue. "Dani, what are we doing? The sexual attraction cannot be denied. I love talking to you about anything and everything. I miss you when we aren't together…" She left the comment unfinished.

Dani said, "But what, Sam?"

"But the obvious. Your parents and I are probably the same age. Are they going to react the way Julia did last night? Are they going to be thrilled that their daughter is sleeping with an old, white, Jewish woman?"

Dani didn't laugh, nor did she hesitate. "No. They are going to be very upset. They are going to tell me that this gay thing is a strange stage I'm going through. You and I know it isn't. Then they will try to shame and guilt-trip me." She stopped to laugh and added, "So, they have more in common with your Jewish heritage than you think."

Sam ignored the humor in her teasing. Instead, she asked, "*Is* this *a stage* you are going through? Dani, I don't want our families' lives turned upside down if you are searching to find out who you are."

Dani took her hand. "Sam, rain is wet, fire is hot; it's as simple as that. I am who I want to be, only when I'm with you. I am not searching; I have found who makes me happy and complete. I saw you yesterday, and I knew I couldn't walk away again."

Dani hadn't expected Sam to be so conflicted today. Sam was unshakable, not this vulnerable woman before her.

Feeling the heavy weight of the situation, Sam said, "You realize, that with a commitment, you will definitely get the short end of the deal. Both my parents only lived to their late seventies."

Dani placed her hands on Sam's shoulders, turning them to face her. "Honey, I'm not going to tell you all the clichés about 'age doesn't matter'. I will be devastated if you die tomorrow or twenty years from now, but I will never recover if you walk away from this second chance that we have right now."

Sam smirked. "*This gay thing* is very new for you, so you are probably unfamiliar with standard lesbian jokes. Officially, this is only our second date. So... what do lesbians do on their second date?" She didn't wait for Dani's guess. "They move in together. Aren't we moving way too fast?"

Dani smiled. "Then I definitely like ..." She made air quotation marks with her fingers. "This gay thing." Sounds wonderful to me. Seriously, you have got to stop feeling what Julia is trying to make you feel. Jesus, I am not some adolescent that is being sexually taken advantage of. I remember a long discussion we had the second night together in Chicago. I recall you telling me that when you were growing up, you always felt ashamed of who you were and that you never fit in. Those days, you said, finally ended when Laura came into your life. Don't let anyone make you feel that way again. Not your family or mine. This is about our lives."

Sam kissed her hand. "How did you get so fucking smart?"

Sam squeezed her hand. "I remember that conversation, because I understood how alone you felt. I grew up in an upscale, black community. When I was around other black kids, I never felt I belonged. I tried to talk their jive, and they looked at me like I came from another planet. If I spoke that way at home, I was told that educated black people didn't talk like that. When I was accepted to med school, I was told by white students it was because the school had a diversity quota to meet. I had to compete for respect from the good-ol'-boys in med school. I, too, did what was expected of me and married David. It never felt right. I never felt comfortable with anyone until I met you. You could have been black, male, straight or my age. All I know is that I fell in love with the person I am meant to be with." She tugged at Sam's sleeve. "Can we go to bed now and finish what we started yesterday in Julia's lovely guest bathroom?" Trying to lighten the mood, she added, "We very well may not have much time left together. You can die of old age, or I could be attacked by a crazed patient at the hospital."

Sam laughed but still needed to explore further concerns. "Dani, I am a person who spends a great deal of time in solitude writing. I like that world, and I don't want you to come to feel excluded. I have schedules for deadlines and travel. Your career takes up most of your time at the hospital." Sam waved her hand, as she surveyed the room. "You are here, and I'm in Tucson. How is all this going to work?"

Dani's shoulders dropped, hoping that the discussion had been settled. "So, we both have busy lives. Stop putting obstacles in our way. I love that we always have something to share and talk about. I'm always excited to hear about your next book and your family. I love to watch how engaged you are when I tell you about a case or a surgery." Dani leaned forward and took Sam's face in her hands. "We will find our 'comfortable' together, whatever that will turn out to be. I love to listen to you tell me about how you love your house and garden. Baby, in all of my adult life, I have never been in a place that felt like a home. I've never hung a picture or bought a plant." She waved her hand to encircle the sterile room. "I want a home with you. I want to look forward to coming home to you. I don't care if home turns out to be here or in Tucson or anywhere else."

Sam's smile spread across her face. "Based on last night and coming attractions from our families, we may end up god knows where."

The rest of the afternoon was spent in bed, reinforcing the rightness and joy of being together. They made love, again, in the shower, as they had in Chicago before having to say goodbye.

On the way back to the hospital, they checked each other's calendars to determine when Dani was free to come to Tucson. Dani booked a flight from her phone. They were both spending Thanksgiving with family. Dani in Atlanta and Sam in Tucson. Dani would arrive in Tucson two days after Thanksgiving. Sam had two weeks to prepare her family's Thanksgiving and for Dani's introduction.

Dani dropped her off in the hospital garage to get Susan's rental. They shared a long, passionate kiss.

Sam was feeling strong about their decision to move forward. She felt nervous, but confident, about breaking the news to the girls when she got back home.

She wasn't as confident with what was awaiting her at Ed and Julie's house.

Sam parked the car and sat for a few minutes, preparing herself for whatever awaited her in her sister's house. She entered and heard conversation coming from the dining room. Sam walked in and handed Susan the car keys. The family had just started dinner. There was an awkward silence. Sam took a seat where a plate and silverware had been set for her. Ed handed her the platter of meat, and Julia pushed the vegetables toward her. They all ate in uncomfortable silence, for a while.

Finally, it was Julia's son-in-law, Scott, who cleared his throat and broke the silence with a non-confrontational question. "Sam, do you have another book signing coming up soon?"

She cut a piece of the chicken and took a bite. She chewed slowly and swallowed. "I'm finishing up a book, now. With the holidays coming up, there will be an extended break for a few weeks or so before traveling again."

Julia ventured cautiously, "Ed and I are going to Susan and Scott's for Thanksgiving. It's been a while since we've seen Katie. What are your plans?"

Expressionlessly, she looked at her sister, not really wanting to talk to her, yet. "As usual, I'm cooking this year. A friend is joining us." Sam watched as Julia's left eyebrow curiously raised. Sam unkindly enjoyed letting her wonder, momentarily, if that guest might be Dani. "Connie lost her husband recently, and I didn't want her to be alone during the holidays. She will be joining us for the Chanukah party, as well."

Maybe it was just her imagination, but Sam sensed a flicker of relief cross Julia's face.

Julia sipped her wine. "Oh, that's nice. Didn't I meet Connie a few years back?"

That was the sad moment that Sam realized just how out of touch her sister was in her life. Annoyed, she said, "I'm sure you have, a few times over the years. I've known her forever. Her kids grew up with Addie, and later, Clancy." Sam suddenly felt removed from Julia's world. Her sister had met Connie a number of times. At least, then, Julie had known she was Sam's best friend.

Julia nodded her head. "Yes, of course. Her husband was an accountant. Addie worked for him. I'm so sorry to hear about his death. Does Connie work?"

"She is retired from teaching at the U of A. She has been selling real estate for the last ten years." Sam was not in the mood for small talk with her sister. The painful betrayal was still fresh from last night, and now, her sister's vague memory of Connie and their friendship, was reinforcing her hurt feelings. "Well, it's been a long day, and I'm going to pack. I have an early flight in the morning."

She and Ed took their plates to the sink. He put his hand on Sam's shoulder. "I'm taking you to the airport tomorrow," he said.

Sam stood next to him, rinsed their plates and put them in the dishwasher. She looked up at him. "Thanks, Ed. We haven't had much time to visit. We can catch up in the morning."

He patted her on the back. "Good."

She wasn't sure what Ed felt about his friend's new relationship with his sister-in-law. Yesterday afternoon, Dani had said she respected him and always enjoyed their friendship. Sam had always found him to be straightforward and open-minded with his opinions. Would he be as removed from her life as Julia was? *Well, we will see,* she thought, as she went to the guest room to pack.

A few minutes later, there was a soft knock at the door. Sam rolled her eyes in anticipation of the inevitable second confrontation with her sister.

"May I come in?"

Sam opened the door, turned and returned to the open suitcase on the bed. She folded a blouse and placed it neatly on top of a pair of slacks. Julia sat down on the chair next to the bed. Quietly, she said, "I have to apologize for my comment last night."

Sam's biting sarcasm came to the forefront. "Which one? The one about Dani, or the one about Laura?"

Julia sheepishly looked at the carpet and then into Sam's glaring and hurt face. "I deserved that." She balled her hand in a fist, like she always did when she found herself in a difficult situation. "Sam, you know I loved Laura. Yesterday, those words came out without me thinking."

Sam sat down on the bed. "My experience has been that those are the times when the real truth is revealed. How many of the twenty plus years did it take you to get used to the idea of me and Laura in bed, or has it yet?"

Julia slowly released the breath she had been holding. "Sammie, it was Ed that pointed out to me my own selfish feelings. It was not your relationship with Laura. I was concerned about what our friends would think. As I got to know Laura, I saw how much you loved each other. Then, when the two of you would visit, I worried about the two of you showing affection toward each other in mixed company." Tears rolled down her cheek. "I'm so ashamed. I'm so sorry."

Whenever Sam and Julia had disagreements or arguments, it was usually Sam that comforted her and made everything all right again. This time, Sam did not want to be the understanding one, comforting her sister. She remained seated on the bed. "Julia, I don't see that your reaction to Dani and my relationship is any different. The gay issue is uncomfortable for you, and now you have Dani's age to explain to your friends as well. You made that point perfectly clear."

Julia reached for the tissue on the nightstand and wiped her eyes and nose. "Sam, you have to admit that this new situation is…"

Sam watched, as Julia hesitated to choose her next word carefully. "Unorthodox."

Sam's discussion with Dani had reinforced that she was no longer at a place in her life that she felt the needed to explain her choices for others to approve. All her life, Julia had had the ability, like their mother, to instinctively zero in on Sam's vulnerable spots. Then, they would scratch at them until they became angry and inflamed. Those feelings were becoming very familiar. Most of her life, she had had to struggle to accept her sexual preference, herself. Like Dani had pointed out to her earlier, she was finally comfortable with who she was, and she was not about to defend herself to her sister. This is where she was going to make her stand. "I'm sorry you are having a difficult time with *your* issue; frankly, it is no longer mine. You are officially off the hook with everything. I will no longer be your problem." Sam could see that her sister was taken aback, and she was about to speak in anger.

Sam held her hand up to silence her. "You might want to think before you speak *this time*."

Julia did just that. "I'm not sure what you mean by that. We are sisters. We always have been, and we always will be. We are sisters and we will always love each other." Shaking slightly, she stood. In her proper manner, she said, "I think you, too, should give this discussion some thought before any pronouncements are made in haste." She left the room, closing the door silently behind her.

Sam listened to Julia's footsteps descending downstairs. She sat on the bed, wondering if Julia's love was like religion, keeping faith with the invisible. Loving with closed eyes and heart. Would this love be tested, again, in Tucson with her girls?

The following morning, she and Ed were up early to leave for the airport. Susan had made sure her dad had awakened her, so that she could see her aunt Sam before they left. She gave Sam a reassuring smile and a big hug. "Mom will get over it. Don't worry. Have a safe trip home. I love you, Aunt Sam."

Sam hugged back, tightly. "Love you, too."

Sam hoped that her daughters' reactions would be the same as Susan's. Maybe this generation was ready not to judge too quickly.

Ed put her suitcase in the car, and they left for the airport. He didn't waste any time. "I'm sorry that you and Julia have hurt each other."

Sam was in defense mode. "I don't recall hurting her."

He smiled and looked at her out of the corner of his eye. Her jaw was set. He continued, with a laugh, "I always find it interesting how siblings revert back to their childhood interactions, as adults. You know your sister loves you very much. I have gotten the blow-by-blow from her, and she is miserable, as I'm sure you are, as well. Things were said in anger, and you both need time to recover and move on."

Sam dismissed his comment. She spoke to him directly. "Ed, how do you feel about Dani and me?"

There was no hesitation. "I have known Dani for over five years now, and she and I have become good friends. She is a strong, tough woman. I respect her greatly. She called me yesterday morning, before you met her at the hospital. She was worried about you. She, like you, wanted to know, as she put it, how I felt about the big surprise."

Sam was quietly shocked that Dani had called him, but she remained silent.

He continued. "I told her the same thing I'm about to tell you. This week will only be the beginning of the issues the two of you will have to face. There will be looks, comments and stares." He patted Sam on the leg. "But then, that is not something you haven't already experienced since coming out. You have all the history and baggage, as you witnessed this weekend. You have already done this once." He laughed. "This is all new for Daniella, yet, knowing Dani, I think she will take it in her stride and, frankly, handle it all a lot better than you.

Sam turned to him. "Ed, for you, does the age difference…"

He replied, "When Dani came back from the Chicago conference, something had changed in her. She was different. I approached her about what happened. She said she had fallen in love with a woman. She was struggling; not about her attraction to a woman, but she was afraid that she had walked away from what could be her chance at real happiness. Dani is not a flighty person, as you well know. I knew it was real. She did not mention your age, nor your name. Besides you two being dumfounded at seeing each other at our house, I was shocked to learn it was you that Dani and I had been discussing for months. I know you, and I know Dani. Your ages do not define either one of you."

Sam took his free hand, squeezed it firmly and then released it. She was so emotional, she could barely hold back the silent tears, that she characteristically didn't allow others to see. She had cried now for the second time in less than a day.

He could see that she was unable to speak, and that she was uncomfortable being so vulnerable. "I hope that this relationship works out. You are both overdue for some happiness."

Chapter 5

Dani arrived at her parents' house the night before Thanksgiving. Each year, her family and the Masters', David's family, had always celebrated the holidays together. It was a tradition since she and David were children. She had not thought to ask her mother if they would be at the house for Thanksgiving this year. After unpacking her suitcase, she went downstairs to the kitchen. Her mother's part-time maid, Angela, was preparing food for their holiday celebrations. She had always felt comfortable with Angela in the kitchen. Dani had gotten her cooking skills from her mother, which involved a frozen box and a microwave.

Dani poured herself a cup of coffee, patted Angela's back affectionately and took her coffee to the family room to sit in one of her mother's uncomfortable designer chairs. Her Dad was in his comfortable recliner that he insisted on keeping, despite her mother's disapproval during her latest house makeover. He rarely demanded anything of his wife, but when he did, it was final.

Dani's mother joined them. "Mom, are the Masters coming tomorrow?"

Her mother looked at her as if she had just grown a second head. "Dani, you don't think that would be the most awkward, not to say the most inappropriate, situation for all of us? Unfortunately, that is no longer a tradition we are able to share, after you divorced David." She sneered, and with disgust in her voice, finished her statement with, "Now they will be going to David's house for the holidays."

Dani looked at her father for a defending remark on her behalf. It was not forthcoming. She answered her mother, "We divorced each other. It was amicable and the right thing to do. We have been through this ad nauseum. It's getting old."

Her mother pursed her lips in annoyance and backed down from Dani's strong response. Sometimes her mother was intimidated by Dani's strength but always hid it the best way she could, which was usually by diversion or annoyance. "They are spending Thanksgiving with David. They left yesterday. We are meeting them in Florida for a week, after they leave him."

Dani nodded, giving herself a second to calm down from her mother's attack. Dani was sure she and David would not have been hesitant in being together for the holidays. It was obvious to her that her parents were the ones deciding to go against tradition. Keeping that thought to herself, she said, "That's nice. So, it's just us tomorrow?"

Her father finally spoke. "Your brother and *his wife* are coming."

Darla was always referred to as *his wife*. She was not approved by either one of Dani's parents. Charles, Dani's younger brother, and Darla were married four years ago. It was clear that Dani's parents hadn't moved on from the disappointment of that union.

Wait until I tell them about Sam.

Her mother announced, "At least one of our children is giving us a grandchild. She's six months pregnant with our grandson." She made it sound as if Darla was only the vessel used to produce them a grandchild. Her mother hadn't needed to add that she wished it was a grandchild of David's and hers. The message was loud and clear.

Dani instantly felt sorry for Darla. Her child's life was, no doubt, already being planned out by her in-laws. Dani didn't know Darla very well, but she was sure, from the few times they had met, that she was not strong enough to fight for the prize of motherhood when Dani's parents moved in to take over. Charles would be of no help to his wife. Their mother controlled his every thought. They still lived in the same part of town, close enough for his mother to constantly run their lives.

Dani's father was a successful attorney. He contently took a back seat to his wife. He, for the most part, distanced himself from his family. He would occasionally have enough of his wife's barrage of judgements and snooty comments, and lose his temper, which would back his wife down for a while. She would bide her time, only to resurface when she felt he was over it. That was usually the average time it took for a good shopping afternoon away from the house, for her mother.

Charles bared the brunt of their father's anger, when he did not go along with the idea of law school and someday taking over his father's practice. Luckily Charles was talented and became the CEO of his own web design firm. That was his saving grace, until he married a woman beneath his station in life, according to Dani's parents. Frankly, Dani was surprised Charles had gone through with the marriage.

Dani was luckier and didn't have to fight her parents' disapproval of careers. She showed an interest in science at an early age. The right medical school was locked in for her, before she was finished with junior high school. Apparently, being a doctor was prestigious enough for her parents. Dani loved her career but wondered what life would have been like in this house had she chosen to be a teacher, or god forbid, a secretary. She already knew how they were going to react to the older, white, Jewish author of lesbian novels. The thought brought a sadistic smile to her face.

Dani had no idea what help she could be in the kitchen the next morning, but it was better than listening to her mother's comment about the neighbors across the street needing to have their gardener trim their hedges. They were apparently an eye sore that tarnished the whole block, bringing down resale prices for everyone. Dani had made the fatal mistake of sarcastically asking her mother if they were planning on selling the house prior to the neighborhood turning into a slum. Her mother had found no humor in her inquiry, but she did get a glimpse of a smile on her father's face.

Angela had worked for their family for as long as Dani could remember. She rarely spoke unless spoken to. Her mother had made it clear early on that Angela was 'the help'. Even after all these years, it remained the same arrangement in her mother's mind.

Angela smiled at Dani when she came into the kitchen. "It's nice you were able to get away from your work. It is good to see you."

"It's good to see you too, Angela. How is your mother?"

"She is eighty-nine now, but as spunky as ever. She is looking forward to me bringing her some of this Thanksgiving dinner. Your Dad is so nice. He always makes sure I don't leave without taking food home to her."

Dani felt a rush of sadness. For all the years she had worked for this family, Angela was never considered *part of* the family. Dani realized she really wasn't, either. There was little, to no, affection, growing up here, never the feeling of comfort and closeness she craved. She had buried the need under study and hard work.

Suddenly, an urge to leave straight away and fly immediately to Sam's arms overtook her thoughts. It was with Sam that she felt comfort and ease. She would deal with the repercussions of her announcement today, and then start her new life with Sam.

Charles and Darla arrived with a pie in hand. Charles had his father's good looks. He was tall, handsome and fit. Years of high school and collegiate swimming gave him his muscular, broad shoulders. He handed the pie to his mother and kissed her cheek. He then turned to Dani with the same charming smile as his sister, the same smile inherited by their very attractive mother, who didn't display it often.

He gave Dani a tight hug, then gently pushed her away to look her over. "Hey there, Doctor. You are looking good."

"So are you, you handsome devil." She gave his cheek a kiss and turned to Darla for a hug. Her large belly felt tight and firm against Dani. Darla was an attractive petite woman with a short-cropped afro. She looked lovely in her stylish maternity dress. "I hear and see I'm soon to be an aunt. Congratulations. How exciting!"

Darla's face lit up. Dani wasn't sure if it was from the acknowledgment of the baby, or that a member of her husband's family had warmly greeted her. "Thank you, Dani. We are very excited. How have you been?"

Dani took her hand and lead her to the couch. "Busy at the hospital the last few months. Come, let's catch up."

They passed by her mother, who had neglected to greet her daughter-in-law. Dani sat talking with Darla, while her mother made it clear that she wasn't interested in joining in their conversation. She led Charles off to the far side of the large, formal family room to join her husband. The red sea had been parted, and Dani didn't miss the brief hurt on Darla's face.

Angela made an announcement that their meal would be served in about fifteen minutes and returned to the kitchen. The time passed too quickly before dinner. Dani was enjoying the time, finally, getting to know her sister-in-law.

When they were seated in the ornate dining room, food was passed around, platter after platter.

Dani opened the conversation. "Darla, you were telling me about your work. Do you enjoy being a medical assistant?"

Her sister-in-law looked around the table, as if to determine whether she had permission to speak. After a brief hesitation, she said, "I do. It's rewarding work, and I enjoy interacting with patients. Actually, I will be going on maternity leave in two months, and I'm presently training my replacement while I'm gone. I find I like training as well. I hope to…"

She was suddenly and rudely cut off by Dani's father. "Charles, pass the cornbread please." He held out his large hand for the dish, and without missing a beat, he addressed his son. "Your mother told me you got a big contract with a large firm."

A flash of anger rushed over Dani. "Father! Darla was speaking."

There was instant silence. Her father's jaw set like it did when she had been a willful child.

It was her mother that next spoke. "Daniella, do not take that disrespectful tone with your father. Apologize immediately!"

Dani did not back down. "I'm not the one who should be apologizing." She glanced at her brother, who seemed to be in shock. "Charles, do you always sit quietly by when your wife is being disrespected?"

In an attempt to show who was head of his household, Dani's father slammed his knife down next to his plate. "Enough! Once again, you managed to turn this family upside down. First you shame our family by divorcing David, and now you feel you have the right to attack me and your brother."

Dani took her napkin from her lap and placed it on the table. She took a deep breath and blew it out slowly, calming herself the best she could. "Well, it looks like we are, once again, on the subject of David, shame and disrespect." She continued. "I guess it's time I share my news. I'm in a serious relationship with a woman named Samantha."

Her mother's napkin remained suspended midway to her lips. Charles eyes looked like they couldn't be contained within their sockets. Her father's jaw was still clenched. Darla had a faint smile on her face.

Charles was first to speak. Thinking she had made the statement as a joke to break the tension, he forced a smile and asked, "You're kidding, right?"

Unflustered, she continued. "She lives in Tucson. She is a lesbian writer. She has two daughters and two grandchildren. I'm flying to Tucson to meet her family, when I leave here the day after tomorrow." She returned her napkin to her lap and took a bite of her collard greens.

Her father was stunned into silence.

Her mother shot back at her, "Have you gone completely mad! What the hell is the matter with you? A woman, and she has grandchildren! My god, how old is she?"

Dani's announcement had dissipated all her built-up tension, and now she was calm. There was no time like the present to give them all the facts. "She is your age. She is white, Jewish, and a strong, stately, beautiful woman, inside and out."

Dani's mother buried her face in her hands.

Her father seemed to have calmed down from his recent rage. It was replaced with concern. "Dani, you have always been immersed in academics. You realize it is too late in life for childish rebellion? You missed that opportunity during your teens. You have always been a driven kid, who never gave us trouble. The time for figuring out who you think you are, should have taken place years ago. Are you doing this to shock us, or hurt us?"

Dani saw that he was really confused. "Father, this has nothing to do with you or Mom. I am not experimenting. I simply fell in love. I want my family to accept that fact and be happy for me."

Her mother was not about to accept anything about Dani's new relationship. "Can you not see that this woman is using you to relive her youth? She is flattered that a younger, successful woman is interested in her." Convinced she was on to something, she stated emphatically, "That's what this is, and you are too smart to fall for this nonsense."

Calmly, she responded, "Mother, you haven't met Sam, and yet, you have no problem telling me who she is. Perhaps I should introduce myself to you. I'm not easily gullible, nor am I flighty. I am not, nor ever will be, subject to being used. If you must know, I was the one that made the first move with Sam, and she was the one with the doubts."

Dani's mother pursed her lips and said, "Well, perhaps you should have listened to her."

Dani knew that this confrontation was not going to get any better. "I see there is no reason to continue with this discussion." She started to push her chair away from the table, when her father asked her to wait and pointed to her chair. Only out of curiosity, did Dani sit back down.

"I need to ask you this. Did this relationship ruin your marriage?"

She closed her eyes, in exasperation of rehashing the divorce. "No, Father. David and I should have never gotten married. He was my childhood best friend, and we grew up together. We married because it was convenient, and easier to do what was expected of us, by you, mom and his parents. David is a great guy, but from the beginning, we really never had a marriage. It was a mutual decision to part. Can we *please,* finally, put that to rest?" She turned and gestured to Darla. "Charles and Darla are married and are expecting your grandchild. Please open your arms, and welcome the chance to love *all three,* and be happy. That is all I want for myself — to be happy."

Having heard the loud conversation from the kitchen, Angela sheepishly served desserts and coffee. They ate silently. After dinner was over, Charles asked to speak to his sister alone. A smile spread across their mother's face in anticipation that he would be the one to talk some sense into her. They went into the family room.

He didn't waste any time. "Your comment to me really stung. I want them to respect and be kinder to Darla. I love her, but I'm not strong like you. I don't know how to stand up to them."

He looked so miserable. Dani was shocked by his confession. She placed her hand over his, resting on his lap. "I'm not so sure I'm the one to give you advice."

She chuckled. "It took David and me seven years to finally divorce, and I'm about to begin with another tough journey with our parents and Sam's family."

He looked up at her pleadingly.

"Listen, if you want them to respect Darla, you first have to respect her and yourself." Her voice softened. "Charles, you are no longer mother's little boy. You are a successful grown-ass man with a lovely wife. That is where your loyalty should be; with her and your soon-to-be son. You need to take charge of this before my nephew is born, because this will be twice as hard when mom and dad take over raising your son, and you know they will if you don't stop them."

"I know you're right. I just don't know where to start."

Dani nodded toward the silent dining room where Darla and their parents sat uncomfortably, ignoring each other. "Start with your wife. Talk to her, share how you feel. Then make a strong alliance." Dani patted his hand and smiled. "She has to really love you to put up with our parents. Decide how both of you want to raise your son and stick together. Set down some ground rules. I'm no expert, but grandparents are supposed to have fun and spoil, not raise and take over their grandchildren's lives."

"Thank you. I mean it. I hope you and Sam find that happiness you're looking for."

Dani was touched by his remark. This was the closest they had been to each other in a very long time.

"I might need a pep talk now and then."

Dani kissed his cheek. "You know my number."

He laughed. "Actually, I don't."

Dani rolled her eyes. "I'll text you."

The evening finally ended, as well as their discussion about Sam. Darla and Charles went home. Dani said goodnight to her parents and went upstairs to her room.

Chapter 6

The same day, Sam and her family were having Thanksgiving together, as well. Sam loved preparing the meal. Her daughters and Connie made side dishes, and there was enough food for an army. Her son-in-law, Josh, was watching the game with Clancy's boyfriend, Matt. He and Clancy had been together a little over a year now. Sam liked him. Garrett and Macy were in the playroom that Sam and the girls had made for them. Connie and the girls were at the dining room table, putting away another piece of pie with coffee. Sam couldn't put off telling them about Dani, any longer. She would be arriving in two days.

She was more concerned about Clancy's reaction. She had taken her mother's death silently and hard. Sam could hear the guys rehashing the end of the game. She asked the men to join them at the table. Josh sliced himself another piece of pie and sat down next to Addie.

"Now that everyone is here, I have some news I'd like to share." She smiled to show them it was good news — she hoped. "I'm seeing someone, and it's looking serious. Her name is Daniella." Everyone remained quiet, shocked at the news. Sam glanced at Clancy's face first, for a reaction. She couldn't read her placid look. She continued. "She and your uncle Ed were colleagues before he retired."

That got Clancy's attention. Her question was accompanied by a hurt look. With slight accusation, she asked, "So, you knew her when Mom was alive?"

Being sensitive to her stepdaughter, Sam treaded lightly. "No, sweetheart. I've known Dani just over a year."

It was hard for Clancy to look her in the eyes.

Wanting to make it perfectly clear, she said, "Clancy, look at me, please."

Clancy looked up at her through watery eyes.

She reached over and took Clancy's hand. "Your mother has been gone thirty-six months and one week. From my heart, I can tell you that almost each day since, I have missed her."

Clancy let go of her hurt instantly. "I know, Mom. I didn't mean…"

Sam squeezed her hand. "No, it's okay, baby. It's time for me to move on, but your mother will never be out of my heart."

Clancy just nodded. Addie wiped her own tearful eyes with her napkin.

Wanting to lighten the mood, Josh asked, "So, Mom, is she retired too?"

Now that she knew Clancy would be okay, she felt more confident, but still nervous about telling them the rest of the news. "No. She is younger than me. She is a neurosurgeon and works at the same hospital where your Uncle Ed worked, in Walnut Creek."

Addie didn't seem to be as interested in Dani's career as she was on the word 'younger'. "Well, how old is she then?"

"She is a couple of years older than you guys." Sam turned to Addie, whose face looked shocked. Slightly defensive after Clancy's initial reaction, she asked, "Is that an issue for you, Addie?" She looked around the table. Frankly, everyone looked uncomfortable.

With skepticism in her voice, Addie asked, "What could she possibly see in a relationship with you? Perhaps you are just flattered by her interest in you."

Josh, outraged, turned to his wife. "Addie!"

Sam's sarcasm was tinged with anger. "Well, thank you for that glowing synopsis of me, my character and my attributes. But then, I'm not surprised. Your Aunt Julia has also made her judgment and assumptions quite clear, as well."

"Mother, you know that didn't come out right." She didn't attempt to correct or explain, and she moved on, to hear more. "So, Uncle Ed and Aunt Julia disapprove?"

Everyone at the table, including Addie, could see the anger flash across Sam's face. "My relationship with Dani is not up to you or your Aunt Julia's approval. For your information, your Uncle Ed has given us his blessing, which was also not needed, but it was nice to hear that he was happy for us." Now she was pissed. Stepping out of her usual calm, demeaner she angrily stated, "My god, you haven't even met her yet!"

Connie, Sam's longtime friend, attempted to cut through the growing tension. She smiled. "She is a neurosurgeon; how interesting. Tell us some more about her."

Sam was grateful for Connie's interjection, giving herself time to release a deep breath, and begin to control her anger from her daughter's comments. "Dani grew up in a black community in Atlanta—"

Before she could finish her sentence, it was Addie who spoke, once again. "She's black?" It was more a statement than a question.

Sam bore holes into her daughter's eyes. She released her clenched jaw, and trying to calm down, she dramatically addressed her daughter. "Adeline, if Laura and I hadn't been the parents that raised you, I swear I would think…"

"Mother! Mother, stop." Addie held her hands up. "You know me too well to even think I meant anything by that question! I was just surprised, that's all."

"Quite frankly, Addie, I'm not sure I know you at all today. It's also clear you don't know much about your mother. I am not senile, yet. I am sound of mind and do not need you to protect me from myself. I can make decisions for myself without your approval." Sam stopped and addressed everyone at the table. After Addie's reaction, she said, almost challengingly, "I haven't heard from the rest of my family, yet. I wanted to share my news with all of the people I love and care about. Unless you have an opinion you would like to share here, I only ask that you be polite and welcome her on Saturday. She will be coming to meet all of you."

There was silence, and then Addie cleared her throat to speak.

Sam jabbed the air with a pointed finger at her, before she started to talk. She gave her fair warning. "As for you, my dear, you are walking on thin ice, so before you speak... think."

"I just want to apologize if I came off as judgmental. We love you very much. It was just my instinct to want to protect you. I'm sorry I upset you."

Sam nodded. "I accept your apology, and I do not need your protection."

Matt hated any kind of confrontation. He chimed in, wanting the uncomfortable conversation to end. "So, we are all back here Saturday for Thanksgiving leftovers?"

Picking up on Matt's nervousness, Clancy said, "No, we are splitting up all this food and we each are taking some home. We will finish it off before Saturday, so that Mom can make her lasagna. I don't want to see turkey again until next Thanksgiving."

Sam was very grateful that Clancy was the one to put everyone back on calmer ground.

Relieved of tension, Sam addressed Connie, "You are in charge of dessert."

Addie and Clancy exchanged looks. They were close, and very accurate in reading each other. Clancy's direct message to Addie to back off was read immediately. Putting a period on her silent message, she pointed toward Addie. "You bring garlic bread; I'll bring salad."

Sam was beginning to feel the weariness from all the emotions she had been dealing with since coming home from California. She tried to cover up the stress that she knew her face was showing. It didn't go unnoticed by her son-in-law, Josh. He winked at her and gave her a small smile.

The girls took over in the kitchen to make packages of food to distribute. The boys went into the playroom to check on the kids.

Sam and Connie remained at the table to talk. Connie padded her best friend on the shoulder. "You surprised me with your news tonight. Is this the mysterious woman you met in Chicago? If so, I'm glad you decided to start living again, and that makes me very happy. I was worried about you for some time now." She laughed. "Maybe it's time for me to find a younger stud to hook up with." She nudged Sam's shoulder. "Am I going to like this younger woman?"

Sam smiled. "Yes, she is the one I told you about, although I left out the part about her age. I think you will. She's amazing. I must sound smitten, but she is. She is so smart and confident." Sam shrugged playfully. "It doesn't hurt that she is also stunning."

Connie blinked her eyes, teasingly. "Why, Samantha, I am intrigued, indeed."

More seriously, Sam said, "Actually, she is a lot like you. She is direct and doesn't play games."

Connie wiggled her eyebrows. "Stunning like me, too? If I wasn't straight, I might want to steal her from you."

Sam chuckled and said, sarcastically, "She has your sense of humor as well."

Connie took Sam's face in her hands. "I can't wait to meet her." She kissed Sam's forehead. "You need to relax, because we all love you, and it's going to be all right." She released Sam's face. "I know this was tough for you."

Sam lowered her voice. "I was mostly worried about Clancy's reaction. You think she's okay?"

Connie stated, strongly, "I do. And if you need me to slap Addie around, just give me the word."

Everyone went home, and Sam was finally able to check in with Dani. She texted to see if it was okay for her to call.

Dani instantly called her back. "Hi, darling. So… how did it go?"

Sam sighed. "It was a little rough, but I think it's going to be okay. The verdict is still out. How about you?"

Dani laughed. "It was a fucking disaster, just as I predicted. It's over, and that's the good news."

Sam replied, "I'm sorry, babe. I'm also sorry to say, it's not over yet. We haven't met each other's families."

Dani's voice deepened dramatically. "I am woman, I am strong!" After Sam laughed, she said, "I don't want to meet your family on Saturday until I have had time to ravage your body. That is the only confidence I need."

Sam smiled to herself. "That sounds like heaven. It's a date."

"No," Dani said. That's not a date, it's forever."

It was busy at the airport. Everyone was returning home from family Thanksgiving celebrations. Sam's eyes lit up when she saw Dani through the crowd of faces. She waved and got her attention and was rewarded with Dani's heart-stopping smile. She was rewarded, once more, when she was embraced, and they kissed. At that moment, Sam didn't care about tonight's dinner or her family's reaction to Dani.

Sam held her at arm's length and declared, "You are the most beautiful woman in this airport and, probably, worldwide."

Dani chuckled. "Well, my dear, have you been waiting here and checking out all the women?"

"Yep. And you're the one, for sure. Let's get your bags and get out of here."

Dani had taken the red eye, so that they could have the day together before facing family. They only had three days together, before Dani had to be back at work. Sam pulled into the garage, and Dani took her luggage into the house. The entry and large family room were casually decorated with comfortable furnishings. It opened to the large open kitchen, with a lovely view of the garden, patio and pool beyond. It was so unlike the stuffy, formal house of her parents'.

Dani put her suitcase down on the floor and stood looking around. Her shoulders relaxed, and with a sigh, she said, "My god, Sam, this is so you." She shook her head in disbelief. "This is a home. Your home. It's perfect."

Seeing Dani's emotional reaction, Sam understood instantly. Dani never felt like she had a comfortable place to call home. She had never been comfortable in her parents' formal, austere house growing up, and as she had seen first-hand, she and David had lived in an apartment with bare, white walls and little furniture.

Sam took her into her arms and kissed her gently. "This is your home now, too. Come, I'll show you the rest of the house."

Dani stood in Sam's office. "I tried picturing you at home, writing. The office is better than I envisioned, and I can see you here perfectly." She picked up a photograph from the credenza behind Sam's desk, knowing it had to be Garrett and Macy. They were playing on a swing set. "They are so cute."

Sam took a picture of the family, off the shelf. She pointed out each member of the group, introducing who Dani would be meeting that night.

Sam walked to the large, comfortable master bedroom and sitting area. Sam explained. "Sometimes I like to write in here as well. It's peaceful and quiet." She added, "This is our room." That made Dani tear up.

Dani sat on the bed and patted the comforter. Sam sat down, only long enough to pull her onto the bed next to her. That was as far as Dani got of the tour of the rest of the house. That would have to wait until later.

Dani showered and changed into fresh clothes, while Sam busied herself in the kitchen. Dani reappeared and announced that she had finished checking out the rest of the cozy rooms, and that she loved the kid's colorful playroom and the welcoming guestroom. "This house, like your books, are so you. Warm and comfortable."

Sam had placed the dishes and silverware in the dining room. Dani began setting the table. Sam opened the cabinet and directed her to where the glasses were kept. "We got a little side tracked in the bedroom." She smiled at the memory, fresh in her mind. "So, tell me all about Thanksgiving."

Dani sighed. "It went as I suspected it would. My mother was appalled, and my father... actually, I'm not sure where he stands, other than needing to be sure you were not the cause of the divorce. They are like pit bulls when it comes to David and his family.

There is some pleasant news to report. I got a little time to spend getting reconnected with my brother. We used to be close, but through the years, we just never kept in touch. He married four years ago, and he and Darla are expecting their first child. I know very little about her, but she seems very nice, and I'd like to get to know her better. Although she said nothing about it, she needs my brother to step it up defending her to my parents and making them respect her. She's almost invisible to them, and they are very disrespectful toward her. I hate to tell you, but I have no doubt you will get more of the same when you meet them." She raised her nose into the air and with a snooty voice, said, "They think Charles married beneath him. My brother needs a wake-up call before our parents not only ruin their lives, but take over raising my soon-to-be nephew, as well. Charles is five years younger than me and has always been mother's little prince. He is aware of the problem. I just hope he steps up and does something about it before the baby is born."

"That's a shame. Is Darla close to her family?"

Dani shrugged her shoulders. "I really know nothing about her family. Sad, isn't it? Whenever you talk about your family, I can see you light up. I know you love them very much, and I hope they accept me into the fold. Please know, that whatever happens tonight, I never want to keep them from you. Are you nervous about tonight?"

Sam was touched. "Thank you, baby. Yes, I am a little nervous. I'm counting on them to come through for us tonight, but it's been a shock to them. I really think they never expected that I could fall in love again." She smiled at Dani. "I guess I didn't either."

Dani kissed her and said, "I just feel so lucky it was with me."

Connie was first to arrive. She put the desserts on the counter and shook Dani's hand; more like pumped it. She suddenly decided to pull her in for a hug. Dani looked startled, which made Sam smile at her over Connie's shoulder. She released her and announced, "Sam wasn't biased at all; you are indeed gorgeous."

Sam had rarely seen Dani at a loss for words, but then, most people were run over by Connie's overpowering personality. Sam didn't doubt that Dani could hold her own.

"I'm Connie. Sam and I have been friends for over forty years. Sam's girls and my boys grew up together."

Sam knew better then to interrupt Connie when she was on a roll. As Connie continued to introduce herself, Sam thought about their forty-year friendship. *Shit, Dani was five when Connie and I became friends. Her girls had just been toddlers.* That was a sobering thought.

Finally, Connie took a breath, giving Dani a chance to say hello. On the heels of Connie's lengthy introduction and history, Addie, Josh and Macy arrived. Macy ran to her grandmother, wearing a princess tierra and holding a wand. "Softa, I'm princess Macy."

Sam curtsied and said, "Your highness, so good to see you. May I have a kiss?"

Macy crunched up her face. "I'm not a 'your highness', I'm a princess."

Sam bent over and got her kiss. "Princess Macy, this is Dani."

Macy giggled when Dani curtsied as well. "Pleased to meet you. Are these your parents?"

Addie and Josh kissed Sam's cheek. Dani was soon to learn that it was a family tradition upon entering their mother's house.

Addie held her hand out. "Nice to meet you."

Dani took and shook her hand and then reached for Josh's hand, as well.

Dani smiled at Addie. "You look like your mother." She added, "That is a compliment."

Addie reacted to the statement with a nervous laugh. "I feel I, too, should curtsy, thank you."

Sam kept an ambiguous face, as she locked eyes with her daughter. She appreciated that her family would have to adjust to this huge change in their lives, and she hoped that they would be supportive.

Macy was off running to the front door to greet her cousin, Garrett. Clancy and Matt came into the kitchen with their contribution to dinner and placed it on the counter. Clancy kissed Sam and said hello to Dani. She introduced herself and Matt, although Dani already knew who they were, from the pictures in Sam's office.

Garrett stared at Dani for a few minutes after kissing Sam and decided she was okay to talk to. "I'm Garrett. I'm this many." He held up four fingers. He didn't wait for confirmation, and he and Macy went off to the playroom.

Dani chuckled. "They are adorable."

Both moms said thank you at the same time.

Sam said that she had put the lasagna in the oven and then added, "Well Dani, I think you have met everyone, now. Why don't we all sit and talk?"

Everyone found a seat in the family room. Addie decided to act as if life had not changed, with Dani's introduction to the family dynamic. She turned to Connie. "I enrolled Macy into daycare. It will only be half-days for a while, but I think it's time I come back to full-time work. She needs it, and so do I. Josh will pick her up from there in the afternoons."

Connie nodded vigorously. "Thank god. The newest guy is a nightmare. I am so tired of the revolving door. I'm too busy with my own real estate sales to worry about Martin's business, too. When can you start back?"

"In a month, maybe. I'd like to see how she adjusts first."

"Excellent."

Addie included Dani into the conversation by explaining, "I took time off after Macy was born. I've been only doing some part-time work remotely. I am Aunt Connie's office manager for Uncle Martin's accounting firm."

Connie explained further. "It's mine in name. After Martin died, like Addie said, she was only able to work part-time. She is the one that runs the business. I'm a retired art history professor and haven't a clue about accounting. I sell real-estate now."

Dani felt included in the conversation and couldn't help thinking of how Darla had been ignored at Thanksgiving. "I'm sorry to hear about your husband."

"Thank you." With a curt, stoic nod, she continued, "I miss him. He was having mini strokes and then a massive one took him, three months later."

The doctor in her was curious. "Was he having memory losses after the first mini stroke?"

Connie nodded. "Oh right, that's your area. Yes, he was. Each mini stroke took more and more of his memory."

Dani explained, in layman terms, the part of his brain that had been affecting his cognitive capacity. "As we age, cell deterioration is also part of the process..."

As Dani continued keeping everyone fascinatingly engaged. Sam was thinking about yesterday, how it took her a few minutes to find her keys before leaving for the airport. She was very aware, as she shifted position in the chair, that it was to help release the ache in her arthritic hip. *I'm so fucking old! Jesus, this is depressing.*

The conversation turned. The family was now sharing with Dani their careers and interests. Clancy wrote grants for government funding. Dani asked her questions about how she had qualified for that type of job. She was interested in what kind of web work Josh was involved with, saying that her brother Charles had a web building company. Everyone seemed to be enjoying themselves and feeling comfortable with each other. Sam could finally relax, but she was feeling uneasy. *All is going well; isn't that what I prayed for?* But the feeling didn't leave her.

Clancy was the one to say that she thought she smelled the lasagna. They called the kids and sat down for dinner. Conversation continued to flow easily, peppered with laughter and gentle teasing, which was typical of their family interactions. Dani seemed to enjoy the banter.

Sam had purposely seated herself across from Dani at the table. She didn't want the kids uncomfortable, if she unintentionally touched Dani affectionately. Every so often, she and Dani would make eye contact and exchange smiles. Sam could tell how happy Dani was with the way her family had accepted her.

As dinner and the evening progressed, Dani and her kids began to talk about popular singers that Sam had never heard of before. From the look on Connie's face, she, too, was in the dark. Sam was beginning to feel a hundred years old, and her and Dani's age difference began to needle at her. Sam didn't want a third daughter, and that was how she was suddenly feeling.

Clancy and Addie volunteered to show Dani the Tucson sights the next day, while Sam finished the synopsis she had to get to her publisher. Sam was already looking forward to the next day and the quiet haven of her office.

The last family member left, and Sam was drained, physically and emotionally, from the long day. Dani was still excited about how the evening had gone. She took Sam in her arms and looked like she could cry from happiness. "Baby, I cannot believe what an amazing day this has been."

Sam hugged her back. *This, obviously, is not the time to talk to her about my feelings.*

The following day, the girls took Dani out for a tour of Tucson and lunch. Sam went into her office to work. She was into the first paragraph of her piece, and she had lost her focus twice. Last night had upset her more than she wanted to acknowledge. In bed last night, Dani's reassuring touch was all she needed to let it all go away. Sam had convinced herself that it was just all the chaos and stress of the past week that had gotten to her. Morning came, and once again, she felt unsettled with last night's feelings. Sam picked up her cell and called Connie.

Sam barely waited for Connie's hello. "So, have you ever heard of Run-DMC?"

"Shit, I'm impressed you remembered the rapper's name overnight."

"Connie, what the fuck am I doing?"

"Girl, what's going on in your head?"

Sam leaned back in her chair. "Last night, I felt a hundred years old. I barely have the energy for Garrett and Macy, for god's sake!"

"After not seeing her for a while, did you feel old in bed last night? Sorry, couldn't resist." She chuckled. "Listen, Dani is incredible, just like you described her to me. The kids like her, and she likes them. Isn't that what you wanted?"

"Yes, of course." She hesitated a moment and then continued. "I just felt like I had a third daughter, last night. Our differences were so much more apparent. When we are alone, I don't feel that way. Last night I felt, again, like we were two people born at the wrong times."

"Did you tell Dani how you feel?"

"No, she was so happy. She doesn't have the same relationships, at all, with her family. I have to be honest with myself right now. I love us together, but I don't know how to fit *us* in with everyone else around."

"It sounds to me that it's time to talk to her about your feelings. If the two of you are meant to be together, now is the time to work out the kinks."

"As always, thanks for the ear."

When the girls got back, Dani kissed Sam and proclaimed how she had enjoyed seeing Tucson. Sam was acutely aware of her daughters' reaction to Dani's brief kiss on the lips. Unless her girls were very good actresses, they seemed okay with it. Maybe they considered the kiss to be like theirs when coming into the house, although Sam was acutely aware that Dani's kiss had been to her mouth.

They sat in the living room, and Dani curled up next to Sam on the couch and held her hand. Sam didn't detect her kids being uncomfortable with the open affection, but her mind went straight to what they might be thinking. Her daughters and Dani shared the details of their morning and lunch. Sam kept looking for signs of disapproval from Addie and Clancy. All seemed fine, but it was Sam that was the one still feeling uncomfortable. Finally, the girls left, and Sam knew she could no longer put off the discussion.

She took Dani's hand and lead her back to the sofa. "I… we need to talk about something."

Sam was completely honest about how she had felt the night before and added that she knew this was completely her problem. Then she asked Dani to help her sort out how to mix the 'us' with the world around them. "You seem to have no problem doing so."

Dani smiled lovingly at Sam. "Your uneasiness last night and today did not go unnoticed by me. I know you felt the full impact of the generational gaps between us." Dani caressed her cheek with her hand. "I did as well. There is a difference for me, but it doesn't change who we are. Baby, you need to reread some of your own books. *That* Sam is amazingly funny, intelligent and has the most loving heart I have ever known. You are confident and strong. You just need to get in touch with her again." Dani kissed her and continued. "By the way,

I feel very comfortable around your girls. However, today was an eye opener for me as well."

Sam looked intrigued. "Really? In what way?"

"They felt I needed to know that you push yourself too hard sometimes, and that you need to take better care of yourself. They are very protective of you. Mostly Addie. Although the thought is caring and comes from love, it's not something I'm personally familiar with. I think you are constantly being reminded by your girls of your limitations in regard to your age. I know you have arthritis in your hip and hands." Dani laughed. "I know something they don't know. You are self-conscience about the slightly creeping skin starting to appear on your very sexy thighs and chest." Dani raised her eyebrows, sexily. "For me, that crepe wrapping is the first exciting introduction to the gifts within. I also cannot resist your slightly less-than-firm, delicious breasts, that perfectly mold to my eager hands and mouth. I sound like one of your books, but that is who you are to me." She leaned over and kissed her. "You are not twenty-five, and that is a physical fact. I did not fall in love with an older woman, I fell in love with you. But you are right; it is your problem, and you need to fix it. I purposely kissed you and held your hand in front of them to see how they would react. They are fine with us; you need to be fine with you."

Sam felt instantly better. She smirked and said, "You didn't mention my saggy ass."

Dani chuckled. "Yes, I love it too. Seriously, to answer your question. We are *us* when we are in the company of your family and friends, or mine. No excuses, because we know who we are and who we are together. I saw the coming attraction with telling my family about you. I'm not naive in believing we aren't going to get looks and, worse yet, comments. Julia being one example."

Sam nodded. "It might take a little practice, so be patient with me. It's interesting; your comments reminded me of something Ed had said to me. He said that he felt our relationship would be harder for me. I think part of my problem is that the judgmental experiences from my past are haunting me. I might have transferred them to our age issues. I promise to remember that *us* is still *us*, no matter whose company we are in at the time. Before I forget — because I'm old — how did you respond to the girls' concerns about their mother?"

Dani laughed at the age reference. "I didn't. I wasn't about to lecture them on how they should be daughters. They, so far, seem to like me; I'm not about to press my luck. I've yet to see the havoc I might have caused with my advice to Charles on how to be a son to my parents." She took Sam's hand and kissed it. "So, when you are tired or your hip hurts, and my head is elsewhere, which is often the case, tell me, so I don't have to hear about it from the girls."

"My hip isn't hurting right now. Before I completely fall apart, maybe we should adjourn to the bedroom."

Chapter 7

Dani returned to California and became immersed in work. Her caseloads were heavy, and she returned to her apartment only to sleep and have the downtime to miss Sam. They spoke or face timed as often as possible.

Sam was busy writing and preparing for Christmas and Hanukah for the kids. Dani was disappointed that her schedule didn't allow for her to join them, as she now explained to Sam on the phone. "Most of my working patients try to get their surgeries done just prior or during the holidays, so that they have more time to recover before returning to work. I really wanted to come down, but I can't see that happening. I miss you so much." She sighed and added, "At least it's the perfect reason I don't have to be in Atlanta. Holidays with my family are not fun."

Sam frowned. "I miss you, too. I understand, but I hate you being there and me here." Sam's next comment brought a big smile to Dani's face. "My fingers get tired from working where your incredible mouth should be."

In a very sexy voice, Dani replied, "Oh yeah? Are we going to have some phone sex right now? Tell me, what are those long fingers doing right this minute?"

With a jokingly accusing voice, she said, "You're not listening to me! I need you to take over. My fingers are arthritic and not doing the job, woman!" Sam loved Dani's hearty laugh. "Don't laugh. See what you've done to me. Having fallen in love with you, makes time crawl when we are not together. I feel like the distance is a constant interruption to our life together."

"Read a love scene from one of your books. That always gets me off, but you're right, it just leaves me hungrier for you, too."

Sam sighed. "It's the pits. I have to be in Denver the second week in January. Maybe you can get away and join me?"

"I'll try. I don't think I'll ever adjust to not being with you. When I was in Tucson, one night I woke up, and you weren't in bed. I got up and saw you working in the office. You were so focused. I sat in the family room and just watched you." Dani sighed contently. "It was so comforting knowing you were nearby. We didn't have to even speak. I love that feeling."

Unfortunately, in January, Dani couldn't get away. Sam returned from Denver, and their frustration continued another few weeks. Dani checked in with Sam and announced that Darla had had her baby. They named him Charles Jr. Little CJ and mother were doing fine.

"She and Charles are exhausted from little sleep, but very happy," Dani told Sam. "Charles wanted to talk my ears off, he was so happy. He is making little progress with changing up some of my parents' behaviors when it comes to Darla." She chuckled. "His attempts must be really tightening my mother's ass." Dani's comment about her mother was just how Sam pictured Dani's mother. Dani continued. "Charles wants us *both* to come out to visit. They are looking forward to meeting you and want us to stay at their house. I can't tell you how happy that makes me. Of course, you will get to meet mommy dearest and dad. Do you think we can do this in the next few weeks? Just a long weekend should do it. Maybe I could even extend time in Tucson, after. Do you think you can plan a week that will work for us? I'll send you my available slots, and we can compare and get flights."

Their available times didn't mesh until the end of March. Sam stepped off the plane in Atlanta and made her way over to Dani's terminal to meet her incoming connecting flight from Sacramento an hour later. They hadn't been together since Thanksgiving, and they both clung to each other like it had been forever. Dani announced, "I booked us a hotel tonight; they don't expect us until tomorrow. We need some just *us* time."

Sam nodded her head. "Good. That will work. I don't want your brother rushing in when he hears his sister screaming from his guest room. I have every intention of making that happen tonight."

Dani closed her eyes briefly and sighed. "I can't wait."

The night's activities did not disappoint either one of them. They couldn't get enough of each other. The morning came too soon. From the hotel bed, Dani watched Sam dress. "What's with that face? Is something wrong?"

Sam sat down on the bed. In a frustrated gesture, she ran her hands through her hair before leaning over to kiss her. "I hate this. I hate having to know our time is so limited, and each moment has to be scheduled before we have to leave each other again. I hate the thought that in a few days we will be leaving separately, for god knows how long, this time."

Dani pouted and said, sadly, "I know. Me too." Then her face brightened, and it looked like she was about to say more but was interrupted by the room phone ringing. She reached over and picked it up. "Hello. Yes, Charles, we got in yesterday. We are showering and grabbing a quick breakfast." She listened for a few moments. "That will be fine. Yes, of course. Me too, bye."

Sam was putting on her shoes, when Dani ended the call. "Now it's you who looks upset."

"He is excited about us being here. He said our parents decided that they would only have us over for dessert, rather than dinner. Although he didn't say so, I'm sure he had to twist their arms to agree to that. Honey, I'm afraid this meeting with them will go as I expected."

Sam tied the shoelaces on her sneakers. "I'll put my big girl pants on; don't worry about it." Even as she made light of the situation, she was dreading the encounter. All the family stress shit was back.

Dani punched her brother's address into the rental car's GPS. "They have lived in their house since they married, no more than five years ago, and I have never been there. Sad, isn't it?"

He lives a mile and a half from my parents. I suspect that, once my parents approved the house and location, they never set foot in it again. Charles and Darla are expected to come to my parents."

Sam knew how hopeful Dani was for this trip. "Well, hopefully this will be the beginning of a new chapter for you and your brother."

It was mid-afternoon when they arrived at her brother's house. Charles must have been eagerly awaiting their arrival, because he appeared alongside their rental car before Dani could get their luggage out of the trunk. He gave his sister a big welcome hug and proceeded to hug Sam, as well. Charles stood only two inches taller than Sam. She wasn't surprised to see how handsome he was. Afterall, he was Dani's brother. Dani had had no pictures to share with Sam of her family. Based on her sibling's looks, Sam was sure the parents would be amazingly attractive people.

"Sam, I'm so very happy to meet you." He reached into the trunk, grabbed their bags and lead them up a long cobble-stone path. The path dissected a lush well-kept yard, ending at a stately, brick colonial, set back from the street. "Darla is nursing CJ and will be down shortly. I'll just get you settled in."

The austere outside of the house did not fit the inside. Although the entry room was large, it was furnished casually. Charles led them down the hall to the guest room, which was pleasantly comfortable.

He placed their luggage on the bed. "Come, let's get some coffee. Have you eaten anything? I started to make a sandwich. Want one?"

Sam felt instantly comfortable. From the look on Dani's face, her brother's home was a surprise to her. She addressed her brother. "Charles, you have a lovely home. It feels so livable."

"Thanks. Darla wasn't too thrilled about its location." He laughed. "Not only the close proximity to Mom and Dad, but she said the house was too large and felt ostentatious. She didn't want to fill it with overstuffed furniture just to fill it. I think she did a great job decorating the inside. I really love what she did in my office. Come, I'll show you the rest of the house."

Dani patted her brother's shoulder. "Let me guess, Mom and Dad chose the house, right?"

He looked guilty. "Yeah, Mom did. She said Darla must have furnished the place from Target or Wayfair." He explained to Sam. "Mother's comment was not a compliment." He laughed. "Actually, most of the stuff is from Wayfair. Darla doesn't see any reason to spend a lot of money to impress anyone and not be comfortable in our own home."

Sam decided that she liked her before they even met.

Dani asked, "You've been here since you got married; do the folks come over much?"

Charles knew where Dani was heading. He smiled and admitted, "Counting coming over to see CJ when we brought him home, they have been here three times. Once when Darla invited them for dinner, about a month after we settled in, after we got married. The second time was when a water pipe broke while we were in Florida, and a neighbor called us. Dad had to come over to take care of it until we could get home."

Dani just shook her head. "I'm really sorry, bro."

"Since I started taking your advice, it hasn't been easy. I can see that, in the long run, it will be for the best. Things have got to change. Come on, I'm hungry."

When they entered the large gourmet kitchen, Darla was standing at the counter. "I see Charles started making sandwiches. I heard your voices and just finished them up. I'm starving." She walked toward Dani for a hug. "I need nourishment to keep up with nursing your nephew. He's voracious." She turned to Sam. "Welcome, and thank you for coming to meet us, Sam."

Sam smiled at her. "I wouldn't miss holding a new baby and meeting the family. Thank you for the invitation."

Dani interjected, "Speaking of my nephew, where is he, already?"

Darla pointed to the baby carrier on the dining room table. Sam and Dani walked over and peeked in. Sam pushed Dani's hand away when she started to pick him up. "He's sleeping. Unless you want to nurse him again to settle him back down, I'd wait until he wakes up."

Darla and Charles laughed. Sam smiled. "I've done this a few times. Oh my god. He is so adorable! Look at that head of hair! When he does wake up, Dani is going to have to fight me to hold him."

They sat down to eat their sandwiches with potato chips and southern iced sweet tea. Dani said, "I'm afraid I haven't taken the time to get to know you, Darla. I'm looking forward to this visit to do so. Tell us about your family."

She nodded. "My mother died, very young, from lung cancer. I'm an only child. I never knew my father. I was raised by my grandmother from the age of five." She smiled. "She was the best. I have only wonderful memories growing up in her little house. When I bake cookies, I always think of her. Her house always smelled like delicious food. She loved to cook and bake."

Sam could relate to herself, cooking with Macy and Garrett. "Is your grandmother still alive?"

Darla slowly shook her head. "No. She died just before Charles and I met. She was still living in her house and was ninety-seven when she died. I miss her every day. She would be beside herself, loving on CJ."

As if on cue, the baby made a squeaky little noise and stirred in his carrier. Dani's eyes opened wide. "Is he up now?"

David smiled at his sister and stood up to take a look. He returned to them with little Charles Junior swaddled in a soft blanket. He handed him to Dani. She looked down at his little face and beamed with pride for her brother. The baby took her finger in his tight little fist and look up at her smiling face. Quietly, so not to startle him, she said, "Oh my god, I think my heart is melting." She then looked up at her brother. "Please move to the west coast. I so want to spoil this child."

Charles and Darla made eye contact and smiled at each other. It was Darla who spoke, as Dani continued to stare, in awe, at her nephew. "I'm not sure how much Charles has shared with you about our recent relationship changes with your parents. It isn't good. Charles has been very thoughtful and careful about expressing our concerns about their interference with our wishes and choices for CJ. They have been less than receptive."

"I'm afraid I've been the one most to blame for not stepping up sooner." Charles spoke now. "We have to take a stand." He took his wife's hand. "This lady here has put up with a lot from Mom and Dad... and me, for allowing it. She has hated this house since mom found it and insisted we purchase it. We think it's time we sell the house and start fresh. It would be easier doing that away from Mother. I'm thinking of opening an office on the west coast. The distance can only improve the situation and force the folks to make the necessary changes if they want to see their grandson. They aren't there yet, and we have to make the change that is best for our family. We love the idea about being closer to you; we want family for us and CJ."

Dani was shocked and thrilled about the prospect. "Have you decided on a location yet?"

"No. I'm still researching a few state business tax advantages in different locations. I haven't told Mom or Dad about any of this yet."

Dani suddenly handed the baby to Sam. Excitedly, she stood up, as if to make her announcement official. "Listen, I have some news too. I haven't even shared it with Sam yet. I was going to tell her this morning when you called." She turned to Sam. "Honey, I waited to tell you in person. I've been doing some research, too. I'm tired of us being away from each other. So, I inquired about a practice in Tucson that needs another surgeon on staff. They want to meet with me. I'm coming back with you to Tucson for the interview."

Sam was floored at the news, and as it sank in, a smile spread across her face. "This is already the best trip ever. Baby, this is so amazing."

Overjoyed with Sam's surprised face, Dani, a little too enthusiastically, wrapped her arms around Sam and the baby, kissing her cheek.

Sam cushioned the baby from the crush. "Don't squish CJ."

Dani stepped away.

Sam looked at Charles. "Okay, so start checking out Tucson. Let's make this happen."

The rest of the evening was filled with laughter and learning about each other. Dani was excited at the prospect of living closer to Darla and her brother.

Later in bed, they worked off some of the excitement and nervousness about the upcoming interview and tomorrow's meeting with Dani's parents. Sam had to place her hand over Dani's mouth as she was about to come, and whispered in her ear, "Can't have Charles rushing in here."

With a smile on her face, Dani moaned quietly as she came.

After showing Sam some of the highlights of Atlanta, Dani and Sam took Charles and Darla out for dinner to thank them for their welcoming hospitality. After that, they were going over to Dani's parents for dessert. In spite of all the talk about the folks, Sam was determined to keep an open mind.

As they were about to leave the restaurant, Dani's cell rang. Darla and Charles went to the car to get CJ secured in his car seat. Sam lingered nearby while Dani spoke on the phone. When she had finished, Sam asked, "The hospital?"

"No, it was Ed."

Sam was taken aback. "My Ed?"

Dani smiled. "No, darling, our Ed. He wanted to know how our visit is going." She looked at Sam's startled face and filled in the blanks. "He knew I was nervous about this meeting with my parents and wanted to know if it had taken place yet."

Although Sam knew that he and Dani were friends, it never occurred to her that they kept in touch frequently.

Dani studied her face a moment longer. "You know, he worries about you too. He wishes that you and Julia would work out your issues. He feels it has been too long not to talk to each other."

Sam was not sure why the comment annoyed her, but it did. She felt a little betrayed and wasn't sure why. A little too sarcastically, she said, "Well, what other advice do the two of you have for me?"

Dani gave her an admonishing look. "Samantha, really?" She took Sam's hand. "I told him from the beginning that we should not interfere; it is between you and Julia. Honey, I know we are nervous about today, but you did ask who it was on the phone."

Defeatedly, Sam nodded. "Fine. One crisis at a time."

She was obviously upset as she took off toward the car. Hurrying to keep up, Dani followed her.

Sam forced herself to calm down on the way to the parents' house. She knew she had overreacted to the idea that she had been the topic of discussion by Dani and Ed. She wasn't really upset with either one of them;

it was Julia she had been hurt by and didn't want to deal with or be reminded right now. She was angry that, once again, she was expected to make the first attempt to make things right. In Julia's mind, she was always the victim, no matter the argument.

Charles parked in his parents' driveway. Their house looked similar to Charles and Darla's, but on a much grander scale. There was an impressively large fountain in the yard, surrounded by an English manicured garden. Sam gave Dani's hand a reassuring squeeze before they got out of the car, to assure her that Ed's call was let go without further anger.

It was Angela who answered the door. Sam could see the open, very formal, sitting room on one side, that flowed into a formal dining room, which opened into an expansive kitchen. The marble floors glistened throughout the massive space. It was like walking into a Florentine mansion. Sam thought it must be a nightmare trying to keep it all clean.

Dani introduced Sam to Angela. Angela, clad in a white server's jacket, nodded and told them that Mr and MrsTyler were waiting in the living room. Dani guessed that Angela was present just to formally serve the dessert and to impress and, hopefully, intimidate Sam with their stature in the community.

Charles led the way. Mr Tyler was sitting in a very ornate and uncomfortable looking chair across from his wife. Charles spoke first. "Sam, this is my mother, Lottie Tyler."

Before he could introduce her to his father, Lottie leaned back in her chair, straightening her posture. She corrected her son. "I'm Loretta Tyler."

Sam nodded to her. Her message was clearly received.

Next, Charles turned to his father. "And this is my father, Walter.

Dani's mother remained seated, like the queen in her court. Mr Tyler stood up when Sam reached her hand out to shake his. "Hello, Mr Tyler. It is nice to meet you."

He was a large handsome man. He locked eyes with her and took her hand. With a sneer on his face, he clamped onto her hand like a vice and shook it, much too strongly. He increased his crushing grip, causing Sam's ring to bite into her finger. Sam refused to flinch. Keeping a menacing face, he finally released her hand with a slightly dismissive flick of his wrist. He pulled his broad shoulders back, taking his full height before silently reclaiming his uncomfortable looking chair.

Without discussion, Loretta announced that dessert would be served in the dining room. Like sheep, they followed. Loretta, nor Walter, had even attempted to look into the baby carrier to see their grandson. Darla placed him in the chair next to her and sat down. Everyone else took their seats. Angela hurriedly placed the dessert dishes before them and was ready with the choice of coffee or tea. Sam half expected that Angela would have been summoned with a bell. Sam reached for her napkin and discreetly wrapped it around her throbbing finger.

The parents remained silent. They had yet to speak. Dani was first to try and cut the silence in the room. "This is Sam's first visit to Atlanta. We gave her a tour of the city today."

Only the sound of cicadas could be heard out on the patio.

Sam tried next. "Atlanta is beautiful. I'm not used to seeing everything so green and lush. You don't see much of that in Tucson." She could have been talking to a wall. Their placid faces reflected that they were in a hurry to get this visit finished, quickly and in silence.

The baby began to fuss in his carrier. Darla leaned over to check on him. Loretta's observation was instantly commented on. "He has you trained, I see. He doesn't need to be picked up each time he makes a sound."

Darla hesitated only a second, glancing at her husband, who remained quiet, then she picked CJ up. She gently rocked him against her chest, and he settled down immediately. Darla stated, to no one in particular, "He is a very good baby and not demanding. He just needs a little comforting."

Loretta set her jaw and rolled her eyes in disgust. Charles quickly changed the subject to distract his mother from further comment toward his wife. He addressed Sam. "It must be interesting traveling around the country for book signings and meeting people. Do you enjoy it?"

"That's not my favorite part of the process. Meeting people all day in a strange town is not always enjoyable. I would prefer to just be in my home office writing."

Charles looked relieved that conversation was finally taking place. "I'm sure. I'm curious. Earlier in our discussion, I meant to ask you something.. Since I work with websites, I see all kinds of prejudicious comments. Do you get many on your website?"

Loretta snapped at her son. "Seriously, Charles, she's a white woman. What does she know about prejudice?"

Having planned to limit her interaction with her parents, this was the last straw. Dani jumped out of her chair. "Mother!"

Sam calmly took her arm and gently pulled her back down.

Sam addressed Dani's mother in her calm and controlled manner. Her voice eased out like a well-greased sliding door. "Lottie." She purposely chose 'Lottie' over 'Mrs Tyler' or 'Loretta'. "Unlike your beautiful community here, I grew up in a small, poor, black community. My father was a refinery worker and my mother a stay-at-home mom. Our family of five were one of four Jewish families in town. My best friend, CeCe, lived in the duplex attached to ours. Directly across the street was the First Black Baptist Church where CeCe's dad was the reverend. Reverend

Johnson would take down the crucifix from the alter on Friday nights, so that the Jewish families could have our Sabbath service in his church. It was a tight, close community. Anytime a neighborhood kid scraped a knee, a mom would come out of her house and take care of it, whoever's kid it was. If you were a kid getting into mischief, you could count on a lecture and or a good swatting on your butt, from whoever's mom was closest by.

"One night, CeCe was at our house for a sleepover. We were awakened by my little brother, because he thought our house was on fire. It was the reflection in our front window from torches held by six white-hooded Klansmen. We believe they were from the town next door where no Jews or Blacks were allowed. They had spray painted Reverend Johnson's church with racist language, and they had burnt a swastika on our lawn. My father and Reverend Johnson stood side by side at our front doors, with bats in their hands, to prevent those animals from entering our homes. CeCe and I must have been seven at the time. That was the night our childhoods ceased to be carefree. That was the night we learned that the world is a very scary place."

Sam nodded at Charles. "Yes, Charles, I have also experienced prejudices being a lesbian, outwardly as well as insidiously. My mother used to say, 'Beware of the silent ones that hate, they can be even more dangerous'." Sam kept her napkin-wrapped finger in her lap. "On more than one occasion, when I have reached out to shake a man's hand, I have received, instead, a high testosterone show of strength in the form of a painful, crushing vice grip. It's usually accompanied with a knowing smirk, as a reminder to me to remember my place in a man's world." Sam discreetly glanced at Walter to see his reaction. He quickly lowered his eyes and fidgeted with his dessert fork. Sam continued to speak in her soothing voice. "Unfortunately, Dani and I have already felt the bite of scrutiny, judgment and prejudice. We have just begun, I'm sure. Many more judgmental comments about our age differences will follow. Prejudice comes in all shapes, forms and ugliness, it seems. People seem comfortable with overstepping their boundaries."

Sam took a sip of her coffee with her left hand. Loretta bristled. From what Sam had seen, bristling was what she did best. There was complete silence in the room. The ticking clock over the fireplace mantle suddenly seemed to echo all around the room.

Sam had had enough. "Charles, it's been a very busy day." She smiled at him. "I wonder if you could take us back to the house now?" Their whole visit had taken less than an hour; Sam's dessert remained on her plate.

Dani did not wait for a reply. Still raging inside, she got out of her chair and headed to the foyer. Charles picked up the baby carrier, and Sam and Darla followed. No goodbyes were exchanged. The silence was broken only by Dani slamming the front door.

Charles secured the baby in the back seat, while Dani paced furiously beside the car.

He turned to Sam. He looked like he was going to cry. "I have never been so…"

Sam reached out to gently touch his tortured face. "No. No, Charles it's okay."

Dani saw that Sam was still clutching her napkin. She took the napkin from Sam's hand. There were traces of dried blood and a nasty, dark-blue bruise between her swollen ring finger and pinkie. Charles had seen it too. He and his sister suddenly made the connection to Sam's earlier comment about handshakes.

In a rage, Dani turned toward the house, and, once again, Sam reached for her arm. "Honey, please don't." Tears of anger poured down Dani's face. Sam took her into her arms and held her while Dani sobbed.

Charles's statement to Darla was muffled slightly, due to his clenched jaw. "We won't be coming back here. I don't want them around you or our son."

The following day, as much as Sam tried to continue the pleasurable atmosphere they had shared before the visit to their parents' house, somberness covered them like the oppressive humidity outside that Sam was not used to. Dani and Charles were angry and embarrassed by their parent's disgraceful behavior. They couldn't relax. Finally, Darla suggested that the two of them should take a walk and talk it out. Sam and Darla played with the baby and cooked a special curry chicken for their dinner, while they were away. They were leaving in the morning, and Sam wanted to end the visit on a happy note.

When the siblings returned, they looked a little more settled and joined the girls in the kitchen. Dani kissed Sam on the cheek and said, "Something smells wonderful."

Charles removed the lid from one of the pots on the stove to take a look. Darla lovingly slapped his hand away. "Stop that! You'll let the steam out of the saffron rice."

He picked up the kicking baby from the playpen and rubbed his head into his tummy, making CJ giggle.

He then sat down on the counter barstool, with the baby in his lap. "We must have walked ten miles. I'm really out of shape." He let out a dramatic sigh. "I'll be glad when the humidity changes, so I can get back on the golf course."

Sam looked up from the contents in the skillet she was stirring. "You play? Then you will love Tucson. We have some beautiful and challenging courses. My daughter's boyfriend, Matt, is the golf pro at one of the resorts in town. You can play almost year-round. Summers can be brutal, unless you get an early tee time."

Charles face lit up with a smile. "Cool, you play then?"

Sam had not thought about Laura in a few days, and sadness momentarily crossed her face. "I haven't played in a couple years since my partner died." She forced a smile and continued. "But I do go out to the driving range, especially when I get writer's block. There are few things better than the sound of the thwack of a driver hitting a ball off the tee. There is nothing like driving a ball to release tension." Sam glanced at Dani and saw a slight smirk on her face. She instantly knew that Dani was thinking of her favorite tension releaser.

Charles broke the side-thought distraction. "Maybe I can convince you to play again, when we visit Tucson?"

Sam knew it was time to start enjoying golf again. She nodded with conviction. "I think I just might be ready."

Charles set the plates on the table. "I made some of my best business deals on a golf course. Learning the game in college was one of the best decisions I made."

Sam's face lit up. "I played collegiately as well. Girls' team UC Berkeley. I guess I better get out to the range more often and practice before your visit."

Dani asked her brother, "When do you think that might be?"

Sam turned the flame down on the curry to let it simmer and smiled encouragingly at Charles. "March is beautiful in Tucson."

Charles put his sleeping son into the playpen. CJ put two fingers into his mouth and contently continued to sleep. "I have a few projects scheduled. Maybe we can shoot for May."

Dani poured herself and Sam a cup of coffee. She sat down at the counter. Darla joined her and said, "I was online last night. I'm excited about seeing Tucson."

Sam took a sip of her coffee and addressed Darla's comment. "I must warn you; summers can be hard if you aren't used to the heat."

"That is one of the things I'm looking forward to."

Charles clarified his wife's statement. "Darla sufferers from asthma. The dry heat will be good for her. I don't think the heat will be an issue for me, either."

Dinner turned out to be a hit, all-round. They cleaned up the kitchen and relaxed in the family room with cake and coffee, while Darla nursed the baby in her rocking chair. The rest of the evening was relaxed, and the tension of last night's dinner was, thankfully, gone. Dani and Charles laughed about memories from their childhood. Darla lovingly spoke of her grandmother.

It was Charles who wanted to know more about Sam's life. "It fascinates me that you grew up in a black community. Tell us more about that."

As Sam talked about those experiences, she found herself at ease. The generational differences did not make her uncomfortable, as she had been when Dani and her kids had first met. Sam really liked Charles and was glad that he and Dani were going to get a chance to be closer.

Later, cuddled in bed, Sam kissed Dani and said, "I feel like *us* with them."

Chapter 8

Addie had not expected to see Dani when she picked her mother up at the airport. She had not discussed or enquired about their relationship since Dani's last visit. No one in the family had.

On the drive to her mother's house, she asked, "How was your visit in Atlanta?"

It was Dani that answered. "My nephew is absolutely adorable. We stayed with my brother and his wife, Darla. It was lovely getting to know him again. Darla is a sweetheart."

Addie, being anything but subtle, continued her questioning. "How did the visit with your parents go?"

Dani was quick to respond, with anger. "It went as expected; actually, above and beyond what was expected. They were rude and completely awful."

Sam was in the front passenger seat of the car. Addie squeezed her mother's hand and looked at her with deep concern. "Mom, are you all right?"

Sam rolled her eyes. "Addie, really! I'm capable of hearing harsh words and surviving. I survived your Aunt Julia, didn't I?" She knew Addie had no filter and, if not cut off, would ask what had been said by Dani's parents. She wasn't going there and quickly changed the conversation. "How's work going? "

Thankfully, her message was heard. Addie chattered on about work and the kids, until they reached the house. Her daughter didn't stay long and didn't bringing up the subject of the Atlanta visit again, although Sam knew she really wanted to.

Sam and Dani unpacked. No sooner than Sam started a load of laundry from their trip, the phone rang. It was Connie. "Addie went back to the office and called me from there. So… how was mommy dearest?"

Sam discreetly took the call in her office, while Dani called to check in at the hospital. Sam lowered her voice. "What did my inquisitive daughter have to tell you?"

Connie laughed. "All that she could get out of Dani and you, which it seems, wasn't much."

Sam let out a long sigh before continuing. "Mommy dearest is a piece of work, all right. She assumed I was a privileged white woman who couldn't possibly understand prejudice."

This information made Connie laugh. Then she said, "So, you cut her down above the knees, I hope?"

"We were sitting at the time, while I was trying not to focus on the pain in my hand from daddy dearest's punitive, crushing handshake. Needless to say, it did not go well."

Connie's voice softened. "Oh honey, I'm so sorry. I still hope you didn't take it lying down?"

"No. I didn't. It wasn't pleasant. I felt really bad for Dani and her brother, Charles. They were so embarrassed and humiliated by their parents."

"So, I hear Dani came back with you?"

Sam's mood lightened up immediately. "Yeah, I'm really excited. She is interviewing tomorrow for a position here in Tucson. Hopefully she gets the position, and we can stop commuting back and forth. The kids don't know yet, so please don't say anything until we know for sure."

"I'll keep my fingers crossed. I'm just happy you aren't moving up to Walnut Creek. I couldn't deal with that."

In the morning, Sam made them breakfast, and they sat down to eat. "Are you nervous about the interview this morning?"

"No, I survived our Atlanta trip. I can do anything. If not this job, I will eventually find something here. I just don't want the process to drag out. I'd like to know about this position right away, before I'm due back to the hospital. I'm still going to have to clear schedules and surgeries and give notice."

"I just want it to be something that's going to make you happy. Your work is so important to you."

Dani chewed and swallowed a piece of her toast. "Wherever I practice, is fine. As long as I can cut into someone's head, I'm happy."

Sam's words came out of her disgusted face. "Well, *bon appetite!*"

Dani laughed and reached for Sam's car keys on the counter. She sat down on Sam's lap. "How about a kiss for luck?" The kiss turned into Sam's hand reaching into Dani's blouse. "You keep doing that, and I'll forget all about the interview."

Dani returned a couple of hours later to report that she felt the interview had gone well. Unfortunately, they wouldn't know if she would get the position, before having to get back to Walnut Creek. There was another candidate to be interviewed tomorrow.

Sam was more impatient than Dani. She was unsettled and paced the rest of the morning. Dani patted the couch and Sam sat down. She rubbed Sam's hand with her thumb and looked into her eyes. "The past year has been stressful for both of us. Being apart, the meeting of our families, culminating with the horror of my parents' behavior. We have yet to talk about that. Did you want to?"

Sam felt badly for Dani. "Honey, it is what it is. Someday, maybe you and your parents can work things out between you."

Dani stopped rubbing Sam's hand and, with wide eyes, replied, "Listen to you. I can't even mention Ed or your sister without you losing your shit."

Sheepishly, Sam replied, "Okay you're right. I'm sorry about that. I wasn't angry with you or Ed. I'm just not ready to deal with Julia."

"Okay, I won't press you about it. On your own time then. I'm just saying that Ed and I care a lot. Let's promise to not shut each other out when family crap happens. God knows it's been a lot."

Sam nodded. "I promise. I really think the worst is behind us now."

Sarcastically, Dani said, "The perpetual optimist speaks while she paced all morning. Why don't you go to the driving range and work off some..." Dani's eyebrows raised, as did her inflection on the last word of her sentence. "*Tension?*"

Sam giggled at the tension reference and lightened up. "Good idea. Got to practice for Charles. Why don't you come with me?"

"I didn't know you played, you mysterious woman. I don't know the first thing about golf, but I can watch."

The trip to the range was a short one, and Dani followed behind Sam with a bucket of balls. She sat down on the grass next to Sam's spot, to watch. Sam took a five iron from her golf bag. Holding it at both ends of the club and over her head, she leaned side to side to stretch. Next, she slowly rotated her hips. Dani smiled as she watched her. "I can see, from that movement, that I'm already liking golf."

Sam looked at her over the top of her sunglasses and wiggled her eyebrows. "Baby, you ain't seen nothing yet."

Dani threw her head back and laughed. "God, I love when you talk dirty to me."

Sam chuckled and took a few practice swings. She placed the ball on the rubber mat. She took her stance and hit the ball. She hit a few more balls and then changed clubs to her driver.

Sam looked around; they were alone. She winked at Dani and said, "Take a deep breath; I'm about to make you come, right here and now."

That made Dani double up with laughter. Sam lined up her drive and, with a perfect swing, hit the ball. That distinctive 'ping' sound was as familiar to her as the scrape and squeak of shoes to a basketball player on a gym floor. Her club was still above her head, as she watched it jet straight ahead and land over two hundred yards away. She turned to Dani with a grin on her face. "I don't know about you, but that creamed my pants."

"Am I to assume that means it was a great shot?"

Sam pulled her head back in mock shock and said, "Girl, you are one tough audience!"

"I don't know. It doesn't look that hard."

Sam reached out her hand. Dani took it and let herself be pulled up from the grass. She handed the club to Dani and placed a ball on the mat. Sam opened her arm toward the ball, as if in invitation. Dani copied Sam's prior stretching movements and rotated her hips, with a smirk and a wink for good measure. She swung and missed and quickly swung again, this time even harder, almost falling over.

A large grin crossed Sam's face. "Not such a smart ass now, are we? Slow down and keep your eye on the ball."

Dani tried once again and missed. "How about a lesson?" Dani place her free hand on her hip and raised one sexy eyebrow. "From very personal experience, God knows you can teach me new skills."

"I'll think up some new ones for tonight. Now, however..." Sam took the club from her and handed it back to her, in order for her to see her grip. "Little finger in between the opposite index and middle finger." Sam watched and then patiently said, "No, your pinkie in between your index and middle finger. That's it. Now take an easy swing and watch the ball, not the club, while you rotate your top half, keeping your hips still."

Dani wrinkled her brow. "That's a lot to remember." She did most of what she was told and missed the ball again.

Sam adjusted her stance for her and gently encouraged her. "Now, don't grip the club so hard."

This time, Dani topped the ball, and it advanced four feet in front of her.

She turned toward Sam and pouted.

Sam smiled and said, "That's okay. Damn, you have the sexiest pout. It makes me want to take that lip between mine and suck on it."

Dani handed the club to her. "What do you say we pick up some delicious Mexican food and go home.

Then I can pout for you, and you can do what you said, which will definitely cream my pants, too."

"Hopefully, you won't have your pants on by then."

Like each time they were together, it passed too quickly and, once again, Dani was on a plane back to California. Sam returned from the airport and wandered aimlessly around the house. She went into the office and started working. She was just starting to concentrate, when the doorbell rang. It was Clancy. She had picked up Garrett from pre-school and stopped by on the way home. Sam got her hugs and kisses from both of them. Garrett announced that he needed his afterschool snack, and they went into the kitchen. He headed straight to the cookie jar, and Sam poured him a glass of milk. He contently sat at the counter, eating. Clancy took a cookie for herself. She looked around. "Addie said Dani's here."

"I just got back a little while ago from taking her to the airport" Sam made a funny face that made Garrett giggle and said, "What else did your Aunt Addie have to say?" Garrett shrugged his shoulders and made a silly face back at his grandmother.

Clancy took a sip of her son's milk. "She said your visit with her parents went badly. I'm sorry. I haven't really talked to you about Dani, and I just want you to know that I'm really okay with your relationship with her."

Sam's heart melted. "Thank you, sweetheart. That means more to me than anyone else's feelings about us."

Clancy said matter-of-factly, "I miss mom a lot, but I will always have you, and that's what matters. I just needed you to know."

Sam knew how hard it was for Clancy to show her emotions and that her comment came from her heart. "You always will, and I need you to know that, as well."

Clancy reached into the cookie jar, handed one to Sam and munched away on another.

Garrett piped in. "Me, too."

She handed him another. "That's the last one before dinner. So, are the two of you going to continue commuting back and forth?"

"Dani had an interview this morning, for a job here in town. If she gets it, how do you think your sister will handle it?"

Clancy gestured with a dismissive swipe of her hand. "You know Addie; she always comes around. She just needs something to worry about. Once she knows you're happy, she'll be fine."

Garrett's adorable little face crunched up with concern. "Why is Auntie Addie worried?"

Clancy wiped the chocolate of his cheek. "Because that's what your Aunt Addie does best." She turned to Sam. "By the way, Susan called to check up on you, too. It seems your niece loves the idea of you and Dani. I personally think she just loves it because it gets under your sister's skin."

Garrett was definitely working on his listening skills. "Whose skin got stuff under it?"

This was the third time in a week that Julia's name had come up in conversation. Twice with Dani, and again, now.

Sam ruffled Garrett's hair. "Softa's sister, little man, but it's okay, she has very tough skin.

The following Monday, Dani called to announced that she had gotten the job in Tucson, and she had given notice at the hospital. They were both relieved and excited about finally moving forward with their life together. Dani wanted to clear her surgery schedule and take the last weekend at the apartment to pack. This would happen in mid-April, and Sam planned to fly up to help her pack her home office and personal items. Dani would drive a small U-Haul truck down to Tucson, with Sam following in Dani's little sports car.

Sam made the announcement to her family and Connie at their family dinner the following weekend, after Dani's call. As far as Sam could tell, everyone seemed happy for her. Connie totally approved of Dani and was thrilled for her best friend.

Clancy already had a heads-up from her discussion with Sam, but she had kept it to herself, allowing Sam to make the official announcement. It had given Clancy time to mull over her thoughts about Addie's possible response. Since they were children, Clancy had been the one to calm her sister's volatile reactions to any kind of change. Addie did not handle change well. Clancy was relieved Addie hadn't commented at dinner and waited to talk to her until after dinner, in the playroom, away from the others.

Addie was obviously in a hurry to discuss the news with her sister. "Do you think Mom has thought this through? I mean, you know how independent Mom is, and she is used to her privacy." Addie shrugged her shoulders, questioningly. "Dani just upped and quit her job? I don't know, I just think this is way too fast, don't you?"

Clancy patiently listened to her sister's concerns and gently shook her head as she responded. "Addie, I think you should trust her decision. It's Mom's life, and I'm confident she knows what she's doing. Listen, I'm glad you brought this up, privately, with me first."

In her dramatic way, Addie's eyebrows shot up. "Right! You saw how crazy Mom got when she told us about Dani and her relationship. She was so unlike herself. I swear, I thought she was ready to attack me."

Clancy suppressed a smile at her sister's one-sided view and interpretation of that night. "We both care about Mom. She's getting *older,* but she is not *old.* Sometimes I think you treat her like she is." Addie started to protest, and Clancy stopped her. "Hear me out. When my mom died, I think part of your mom never recovered. I think this new relationship is going to be the best thing for her. She lights up when she is around Dani, like she did with mom. We haven't seen her like this for way too long. It's going to keep her younger for longer, and we should be totally supportive."

Clancy waited a few seconds, giving Addie a chance to mull over what she had said. Finally, Addie spoke. "I have been so worried about her since Mom died. You're right; she hasn't been herself since. I think that's what has been making me hover over her the way I do." This was the point where the tears were released and flowed down her face. "People are going to judge; they are going to get dirty looks. People are going to make snap comments. They are going to get hurt."

Clancy, remembering Addie's remarks when Mom had first told them about Dani, struggled to suppress a smile at the irony of Addie's statement. Addie's habit had always been to make comments without thinking.

Addie continued with her list of concerns. "I have been worried about you, too. You always keep so much bottled up, that I was concerned that this new development was eating you up inside."

Clancy wrapped her arms around her and laughed. "God, you are so intense." She gently pushed Addie back, looking into her concerned face. "When Mom told us about Dani, my first response was hurt, but you heard what she said that night. She will never stop loving Mom. I knew, then, it was all going to be okay, even before we met Dani. You know I love you, but you have got to stop worrying. You are driving everyone crazy! You need to talk to me when you are upset and not shoot your mouth off to Mom." Clancy shook her head in puzzlement and asked. "How does Josh do it?"

Addie's faced instantly tightened with frustration. "Don't even! He is so totally on my shit list this week. Since I went back working full time, for months now he comes home and collapses on the couch. After my long day, I have to get Macy from school, rush home and start dinner. Jesus, you think he could do a load of laundry or maybe start dinner or even give Macy her bath?" She continued sincerely, as if to pat herself on the back. "I waited patiently so as not to nag. I am so done with this shit!"

Clancy nodded. "So, is it safe to say King Josh has been dethroned?"

Addie threw her arms up dramatically. "Hell to the yea!"

Sam peeked around the door. "Wondered where you guys disappeared. Did I just hear King Josh has been dethroned?"

Clancy smiled. "Yep, Addie is months behind me. Matt has been dethroned for a while. She doesn't know it yet, because she waited way too long. Now, she will have to constantly be at him to get him off his ass and help around the house. I'm shocked she didn't start before Macy was born."

Chapter 9

Time crept by, once again. Mid-April finally came, and Sam was preparing to leave for Walnut Creek to help Dani move. Addie had volunteered to water Sam's plants and bring in the mail. Usually, Connie enjoyed doing it for Sam when she was away on business. However, that weekend, Connie would be out of town, visiting her son and grandkids.

Knowing that Addie was busy, Sam called to remind her.

"Mom, I totally don't want to be pushy, but..."

Sam smiled to herself; pushy was just another word for Addie.

"Maybe you should see Aunt Julia while you're there," Addie finished.

Julia had been on her mind for the last few days leading up to the trip to the Bay Area. She had been surprised, in Atlanta, when she had learned that Dani and Ed continued to keep in touch, and she wondered if maybe it was time to bury the hatchet. Of course, Julia *could* take the first step, just as well. "I'll think about it."

Addie couldn't stop there. "Because you know, Susan said..."

Sam interrupted her and calmly, but firmly, said, "Addie, I said I'll think about it."

Addie relented on giving further advice. "Right. Okay, so… don't worry about the plants and the mail. Have a safe trip. Call me when you get there."

The flight to San Jose had been delayed and then diverted to Salt Lake. By the time Sam arrived, she was tired, hungry and irritable. Dani had no problem picking up on Sam's mood. She kissed her and suggested getting something to eat. They found a quiet Indian restaurant near the apartment.

Sam had been stretching and looking uncomfortable since Dani had picked her up at the airport. She reached in her purse and took out a bottle of aspirin, handing it to Sam. "Your hip?"

She took the bottle and removed two pills. "At least they could have brought us back into the terminal so we could have walked around, instead of keeping us on the damn plane ninety minutes, waiting to take off. You want to explain to me why we then had to fly up to Salt Lake, only to wait, again, another hour?"

Dani silently handed her the glass of water on the table. Sam swallowed the medication. Dani took her hand. "Look at me." Sam did so and tried to release her frustration by focusing on Dani's beautiful face. "You're here now. We don't have to do this commuting any more. We'll get to the apartment, and I will massage your hip, back and anything else you want me to."

Sam finally smiled. "Anything? Promise?"

Sam was rewarded with Dani's heart-melting smile. "Promise."

Suddenly, Sam felt her tension and anger start to dissipate. The food helped as well. She looked up from her Chana Masala. "So, does Ed know I'm here?"

Dani smiled and said, "You don't have to tip toe around. Yes, he knows you are here."

Sam took a moment and swallowed a forkful of food. "Then I assume Julia knows as well."

"Since you are the one bringing up the subject, we have been invited to their house for dinner tomorrow."

Cautiously, she inquired, "Who? Who invited us, Ed or Julia?"

"Jesus, Sam. Ed has informed her that I'm moving to Tucson, and she feels it's time to talk things out with you while you're here. Before you ask anything more, I did not accept on your behalf. I told Ed we would get back to him."

Dani was trying so hard to appear to be nonchalant, it made a smile creep across Sam's face.

Giving Sam space to decide about committing to the dinner invitation, Dani cleared her throat and changed the subject. "I have to be out of the apartment tomorrow, so I made reservations at a hotel for tomorrow night. They have space to park the U-Haul."

"Why would you do that, when we can stay the night at my loving sister's house? Their guest room isn't far from the master bedroom. One good sex scream from the woman I love would really send her vomiting into the bathroom."

Dani sighed and rolled her eyes. She tossed her cloth napkin at Sam, shaking her head. "You sometimes can be so intense. Now I see where Addie gets it."

While they were eating, two guys sat down at a table next to the window. A memory flashed into Sam's mind, and she smiled.

It did not go unnoticed by Dani. "Penny for your thoughts."

Sam wiped the corner of her mouth with her napkin. "I just had a Michael moment. When those gay guys came in, I could almost hear Michael's voice. We had our own gaydar game. When we saw a gay couple, we would look at each other and say at the same time, 'the boys are bent as forks.' Then it just became 'forks', when people were around. We usually blurted it out at the same time. It might sound disrespectful to you, but for us it was assurance we were not alone in a straight world. You would have loved him. His sense of humor was contagious."

Dani laughed. "I love that you are comfortable sharing Michael and Laura with me. You make me feel trusted with your memories, good and bad."

The next day, they finished packing the U-Haul and cleaning the apartment. Dani already had her few furniture items picked up for donation. She only had her desk, books, bike, clothing and a couple of personal items to put in the small rental truck. Sam opened the kitchen cabinets. They, too, had been emptied. "Did you pack up dishes, pots and pans?"

Dani looked over her shoulder at Sam. "I only had a frying pan, and it went with the donation truck. But I saved my favorite travel coffee container." She took it off the counter and held it up to show her.

Sam laughed. "You extravagant woman, you. Addie had three times more stuff than you in her college dorm room."

"All that is left is the bathroom. I think that will just take one box. I left towels out so we can shower before going to your sister's. We can take the rental truck over to the reserved hotel space and just take the car."

It was almost five when they knocked at the door. Ed answered and gave them both a hug. They went into the kitchen, where Julia was cleaning off the kitchen table. It was an awkward hello. Sam went to the cabinet where they kept their dinner plates and glasses. She started to set the table to give herself something to do, to keep her busy.

Julia smiled at Dani. "So, are you all packed up?" They started speaking, and Ed took Sam's elbow and led her out to the patio.

"Are you angry with me?"

Sam always felt comfortable with his directness. "No, Ed. I'm not angry with you. I know this is a difficult situation, for both you and Dani. I don't want to do anything that is going to hurt your friendship with her." She wanted to make it perfectly clear where the problem was. "It is Julia's choice if she wants to make it uncomfortable."

"Well, that's the point, isn't it? Julia has no problem with Dani and me. The problem is you and Julia. The two of you are making it a difficult situation."

Sam leaned forward in her chair, clasping her hands in her lap to keep herself calm. "Well then, Ed, what do you want me to do? I can do as I always have done with her my whole life. I can tell her everything is okay, so she doesn't have to own up to her hurtful comments and actions. If that's what you want, then I'm sorry, I can't do that any more. I won't do that any more."

Sam's calm voice had carried through the open kitchen window.

Dani followed Julia out to the patio.

Julia looked like she was about to cry. With a choked voice, she said, "I am no longer a child, and I did apologize to you. You refused to listen. You wrote me off as if I was nobody to you. I have a right to express how I feel."

Sam gestured to a chair, and through a tightened jaw, she said, "So, tell me, I'm listening. How do you feel?"

Ed started to get up. Sam gestured with a finger for him to sit down and pointed to Dani as well. "You, too, Dani, this affects all of us."

Like docile children, Dani and Ed sat down.

Julia took a deep breath and began. "First of all, I know I hurt you with my comments about Laura and you…" She looked down.

Refusing to let her off the hook, Sam finished the sentence for her. "Picturing us sleeping together."

Embarrassed, she hissed, "Yes!" She looked up and continued. "Jesus, see that's it right there. I'm not putting a judgment on the way you live. I have always just had an uncomfortable time with the subject of homosexuality. I don't have to apologize for my feelings. I know you loved Laura, and I loved her too, you know I did."

Sam was trying to keep an open mind. She asked, "Have I ever spoken to you, or family, or your friends, about my sex life?"

"No, of course not, but, Sam, you write about those things in your books. Family and friends can read about it, don't you see?"

"Have family or friends talked about my sex life with you because of my books?"

Julia became outraged. "Samantha, I just told you I can't think about it without feeling uncomfortable; how could I ever talk to them about you in that way?"

"Then you have no idea how they feel, or if they have even read or are interested in any of my books. You are embarrassed because that is how you feel. Julia, I can't change that for you. You do have every right to your feelings, but so do I. I didn't feel I had the right to my feelings growing up, because of people who feel like you."

Julia was outraged. "Are you calling me prejudiced?"

Sam blinked and reluctantly nodded her head. "I guess I am." The shock of Sam's answer rendered Julia silent for a minute. Sam then said, "Sometimes people's feelings turn to judgments, and then it becomes a slippery slope. When judgments turn to prejudices, they create invisible boundaries that isolate or shun people, or worse. Are there any other feelings you want to express to me?"

Julia's forehead wrinkled in concern. "I hate the thought that you feel I'm a prejudiced or judgmental person."

Sam signed deeply. "Julia, your opinion and outrage about Dani and my relationship was more of the same. You questioned my ability to place boundaries for myself, when you have none when it comes to judging others. You are my sister, and I love you, but I cannot live within the boundaries you place on me. That's not your right, or anyone else's.

Julia listened intently and then replied, honestly, "I will really think about what you have said. I have missed you, and I'm glad we talked about this, I really am." She turned to Dani and said, "I'm sorry if I have hurt you as well."

Dani took her hand. "The only hurt I feel is for you and Sam. I know you are a kind and caring woman, you couldn't be anything less if Ed loves you."

Throughout the evening, the tension between sisters improved but remained an unsettling issue for both of them. Sam wondered if they would ever feel close again, after learning how Julia had felt most of their adult lives.

The trip home to Tucson was long and uneventful. They were exhausted and dropped into bed upon arrival. The truck could wait until morning.

It was after ten a.m. when they heard voices in the living room. Addie and Josh had let themselves in. Sam wrapped her robe around herself. She ached from the move, and muscles she had forgotten she had, were sore.

Josh explained. "Hi, Mom, hope we didn't wake you. I'm off today, and Addie wanted me to empty the truck for you guys."

Addie had wandered off into the kitchen and garden to make sure she had not killed her mother's plants while she was gone.

Josh said in a whisper, "Actually, you didn't answer Addie's text last night, and she wanted us to check on you."

Sam rolled her eyes. "Of course she did."

Addie entered the room. "I have to head off to work. Welcome home. Talk to you later." She kissed her husband and mother and waved to Dani, who was now standing in the doorway. "Later."

Dani waved back as Addie took her leave. Josh chuckled. "Don't take offense, but you two look like death warmed over. Give me the keys, and I'll unpack the truck."

Sam patted him on the back. "Thanks." She pointed to the keys on the counter. She put up a pot of coffee and went into their bedroom to shower. She stood there, letting the heat of the water pound on her muscles.

Dani opened the shower door and joined her. "If it's any conciliation, I need you to know; I can't believe how sore I am."

Within the next few days, the home office was rearranged to accommodate Dani's desk, and there was ample closet space in the master bedroom for her clothes. Josh hung a bike rack in the garage for Dani's bike, and Sam had readjusted her parking space to make room for a second car. Sam wasn't sure how she would feel about the house space being shared again, with unfamiliar things that did not belong to Laura.

Dani watched Sam pensively staring out the bedroom window. She quietly wrapped her arms around Sam's waist and leaned against her back. Lovingly, she asked, "Is it hard for you to see Laura's things replaced?"

Sam turned and kissed her. A smile slowly crept across her face. "How is it that you can always read my mind?"

Dani smiled. "I can mostly read the questions in your mind, not so much the answers all the time."

Sam ran her finger across Dani's beautiful mouth. "When your smile is directed at me, somehow it always lingers in my mind. I love you very much, and thank you for always lingering in my heart, too. Laura will always be there, as well, but please believe me when I say there is no longer conflict there."

Dani kissed her tenderly and said, "I wouldn't be here if I thought there was. I just want you to know I understand."

It didn't take long for their day-to-day schedules and routines to settle comfortably into their lives. Dani had adjusted quickly to the new practice and hospital staff. When Sam wasn't traveling, it was best when they were home together. Dani found the new medical practice and surgery rewarding and challenging. However, unlike in her past life, she always looked forward to coming home to Sam at the end of the day.

Dani found Macy and Sam in the backyard garden. Macy was focused on gently sprinkling seeds into a colorful flowerpot, with her little fingers. Sam looked up and smiled at Dani. "Now what do we do, Macy?"

Next, she carefully sprinkled more potting soil over the seeds, as if she was decorating a cupcake with jimmies. With vast experience in her voice, she said, "Softa, you know. We have to water them and put them in the sun."

Sam nodded. "Very good. Then we will wash our hands and start dinner."

Macy wiped her hands on her jeans and looked up at Dani. "You want to cook with us?"

Dani nodded. "I would love to."

Macy took Dani's hand and lead her back to the house, jabbering continuously, as Sam followed. Macy quickly lost interest in culinary skills and headed off to the playroom. Dani munched on a carrot, watching Sam prepare dinner. "Addie and Josh getting a date night?"

"Yep. Looks like a sleep over for Macy, too." She kissed Dani. "How was your day?"

"Good. Got a text from Charles. I can't believe it's been so long since we've seen them. CJ is almost a year old. He said to send him hotel contacts near the house; they're ready to come out to look around the area.

Sam shook her head. "No. Tell him we have a perfectly good guest room. Addie still has a portable crib for CJ. Tell them we insist. When are they coming?"

Dani smiled broadly. "I'll text him. I was sure you would insist. He said if our schedules were free to visit, he would book flights for next week."

"Cool. Tell him to also bring his clubs. How are things going with them and your parents?"

Dani looked a little concerned. "He was a little vague on that subject, but said we had a lot to talk about. Do I have time to shower the hospital off before dinner?"

"Sure."

Dani left the room. Sam could see that she was worried. It sounded like Charles was still struggling with his parents' interference. She turned the heat down to a slow simmer and went to check on Macy.

Later that evening, after a Disney movie and two stories, Macy fell asleep in Dani's lap. Dani carried her to the playroom bed and tucked her in with a kiss to her forehead. She returned to the family room and curled up on the couch next to Sam. "You know, Macy and Garett have melted my heart. I'm looking forward to having CJ in our lives too."

Sam pulled her closer. "Well, I'm glad. Clancy and Matt have a date night this weekend. Did you ever want kids of your own?"

Dani weighed her answer before speaking. "I had never thought about it until a year or so after David and I were married." She paused momentarily. She continued. "It was a brief consideration, thinking maybe that would give me the connection I never felt with him or family. When I realized that, I knew that would only complicate our lives even more. I would probably end up resenting the time away from work by adding a baby to the mix. When David and I decided to divorce, it was the first time he told me he never really wanted children. You know, it released me from feeling badly about having those same feelings. It's just sad to me that we had never even discussed it, or for that matter, anything else that could have been part of our future." She looked into Sam's eyes and smiled. "You have given me everything I have always wanted, to feel completely a part of someone's life; that, and a family."

Sam ran her thumb over the silky smoothness of Dani's cheek. "Looks like our family is growing. I really feel close to Charles and Darla, and I'm so happy that they will be here too."

Dani hesitated and then spoke cautiously. "I have wanted this for so long, sometimes I think I've forced too much on you, too quickly. Moving in, and now, CJ and his family, too. I know I make decisions and move quickly. You are the thinker, worrier and analyzer."

Sam chuckled. "You are certainly right about both of our personalities, but you don't give me much credit. It works both ways. You wouldn't be here right now if I didn't want you in my life."

Dani released the excess air from her lungs, realizing she had been holding it there through Sam's response. She shifted her position on the couch to look up at Sam. "Well then, I have some news for you to worry about."

Sam's eyebrows raised in question. "Okay… which is?"

"It looks like our first test of '*us*' is about to happen. We are invited to a get-to-know staff dinner this Friday night. I know it's already Wednesday. I didn't want to give you too much time to worry over it."

Sam jokingly pushed Dani's shoulder. "I think you have me confused with Addie."

Friday came quickly, and Sam was proud of herself for not overthinking the dinner. This would be the first time stepping out of her comfort zone with Dani, away from family.

Sam texted her from the car, that she had arrived at the restaurant. It was seven p.m. Dani had changed and showered at the hospital and had arrived five minutes earlier then Sam. She watched as Sam stepped out of the car and handed the keys to the valet attendant. She smiled as she watched him take a double look at her stunning partner exiting the car and making her way to the entrance, where Dani greeted her. She kissed Sam and said, "You amaze me that you are oblivious to how you turn heads."

Sam rolled her eyes. "Oh please."

Sam was always in jeans or shorts. She had only dressed up because tonight's dinner was semi-formal, and she didn't want to embarrass Dani. She was wearing a silk, blue wrap-around dress that hugged her body and flowed over her hips and long legs like a waterfall. A modest slit on one side reached up to her knee. Her silver necklace nestled just above her cleavage. Matching silver earrings caught the entry, overhead canopy lights and twinkled against her spiked, white hair. She didn't wear makeup, thinking it pretentious.

The moment was seared into Dani's brain, like the first night she had met Sam in Chicago and how gorgeous she had looked to her. "I may be biased, but my mind is home in bed with you right now."

Sam stood back to give Dani the once-over. "Well, look at you. Even though it isn't that outfit you wore at your presentation in Chicago, that got me hot; I was wet from wanting you that afternoon, by the way. Tonight, you look even sexier."

Dani laughed. "You are just used to seeing me in scrubs." She spun around to show Sam the new dress she had bought to surprise her with. It was also floor length for the occasion. It was turquoise blue with spaghetti straps. The bodice was covered with very fine lace. The low cut of the dress showed off her ample breasts. The material gracefully draped over her curves, ending at her strapped turquoise heels, giving her a few more inches when standing next to Sam.

A voice from the entrance to the restaurant that addressed Dani, interrupted Sam's next comment, that would have been inappropriate in front of the approaching man. "There you are. I thought maybe you hadn't been able to get away from the hospital."

The man glanced at Sam, and Dani took her hand. "Marcus, this is my partner, Sam."

He looked momentarily surprised for just a second and quickly extended his hand. "Nice to finally meet you, Sam. Thank you for being the reason that Dani came to join the practice."

Dani continued the introduction. "Sam, this is Dr Marcus Ortega, the gentleman that hired me."

He released Sam's hand and said, "Oh, please, just Marcus. I'm Marcus."

Sam smiled and nodded. "Very nice to meet you, Marcus." Sam guessed Dr Ortega to be in his mid-fifties. The slight graying on the sides of his black hair framed his handsome face. He had a warm smile and the dimple on his cheek looked like it was winking at her. He was slight of build, with just the beginning of a roll around his waist.

They followed him into the restaurant and saw that he had reserved two seats at his table for them. They were introduced to his wife as 'Dani and her partner'.

It didn't go unnoticed that his wife, Claris, stifled a nervous giggle at some unreadable thought. The moment passed quickly. "Marcus told me you were bringing your partner; I'm so glad to finally meet you both."

At one point, after dinner, a nurse Dani worked with at the hospital, awkwardly stated how lovely it was to see a mixed couple of age and color. The statement was made in a group of others, that only added to everyone's discomfort. She might as well have stated the bad cliché, that some of her best friends were black, or perhaps, next, she was going to say that some of her other friends were elderly. Sam's hope was to have all the evening's initial shocks over with, so that Dani could be comfortable around her colleagues.

Later in the evening, Dani was using the restroom and heard a conversation outside her stall. "Can you believe Dr Masters is with a much older woman? Although she is stunning, she could be her mother."

Dani recognized the voice of her nurse practitioner, Jean.

The second woman laughed and referenced color. "Not really, unless she was adopted." This response was made by Carol, her snooty office manager.

Dani could feel her anger growing, and she took a cleansing breathe before joining the women at the wash basin. She looked directly at them, watching their faces turn red with the realization that they had been heard by the subject of their gossip. With a placid face, Dani said, "Samantha has two daughters my age. One biological and the other not. They are both Caucasian."

They were stunned into silence, as Dani took a towel from the decorative basket on the counter to dry her hands. Carol's hand was trembling, and she looked like she might cry. Jean sheepishly looked at her and said, in weak defense, "Please forgive me. I didn't mean to offend you, I was just making an observation."

Dani nodded and added, "And a judgement."

Jean's dry mouth made her swallowing, difficult.

No further words came from either one, and they both left the ladies' room. Dani waited a few seconds to let her silent anger dissipate. She fixed her makeup and went back to their table, where Sam was having a conversation with Marcus's wife. Sam glanced up at Dani, as she took her seat. She instantly knew something had happened to upset her. Sam tried keeping her eyes on Claris, as she continued to talk. Dani and

Sam's eyes connected briefly, and Sam saw a forced, unconvincing smile cross Dani's face.

Dancing was planned to commence in the adjacent ballroom after dinner. There was no way they would subject themselves to further scrutiny by getting on the dance floor. Marcus returned from a dance with his wife, and he held out his hand to Dani. She took his hand and joined him for a dance. Sam, at this point, had tuned out most of Claris's nervous, non-stop talking and watched Dani and Marcus, who were engaged in what appeared to be a serious discussion.

Soon after the dance, Dani smiled and announced that it had been a lovely evening, but a long day.

Because they had arrived in their separate cars, the way home gave Dani time to struggle with the idea of telling Sam what had taken place in the ladies' room. Their first night out as a couple had only reinforced what they were in store for, going forward. She knew she had to tell Sam. This had to be dealt with as a couple. The memories of Julia's comments and the night of introducing Sam to her parents came back in full force, and she stewed in hurt and anger.

Sam reached home a few minutes ahead of Dani. She was in the bedroom shedding her clothes, when Dani silently entered their bedroom to undress as well. Sam gave Dani some needed space but knew Dani would tell her what had happened. It would take place when Dani was ready and on her own time. Sam tied the belt around her robe and said, "I'm going to make some coffee. It's late; I'll make the decaf. Interested?"

Dani nodded, and Sam went into the kitchen. A few minutes later, Dani joined her on the couch where a mug of hot coffee waited for her on the end table. Dani took a sip of her coffee and leaned back against the cushions. Wasting no time with further second-guessing Sam's response, she said, "So this is what happened…" With a lot less anger, she told Sam, in detail, what had taken place in the bathroom at the restaurant.

Much to Dani's surprise, Sam laughed and said, "God, I only wish I could have seen their faces."

Dani finally relaxed enough to smile. "You have definitely rubbed off on me."

Sam's feigned innocence. She pointed to herself and said, "Me? You are the direct one, remember?" Soon they were both laughing. "So tell me, what was your serious discussion on the dance floor with Marcus?"

Dani's face instantly returned to harsh focus. "I told him what happened in the ladies' room and why I might not be myself in the office for a while, until I calm down. I assured him I will remain professional with staff, but if he hears other such comments, I must have his assurance he will not put up with it. He had no problem promising me he would not put up with that behavior."

Sam nodded thoughtfully. "Honey, we know we are not in control of other people's opinions or gossip.

People will only open their minds because they want to know us and, unfortunately, many will just be ingenuously curious."

"Of course, but that doesn't mean that when judgments and prejudices are directed at us, we remain silent." She hesitated momentarily and then confessed, "I wasn't sure I was going to tell you what happened tonight. I didn't want you to be upset or worried. Then I realized we are in this relationship together, and we never keep things from each other."

Sam took her hand and kissed it. "Good. I want you to know, that the moment we were introduced tonight, I could see the writing was on the wall, but I feel much better about being *'us'*. It was our first test run, and we are going to be okay."

Chapter 10

Sam didn't want to overwhelm CJ and Darla with her rambunctious family, the first night they were at the house. It wasn't until the next day that Connie and the family came for dinner to meet them. They took to each other right away. Connie had to fight Macy to hold CJ. Macy was enamored with him and acted like his little mommy. CJ took to the attention right away and instantly endeared himself to everyone. Even Garett would pat his head as he exited a room. CJ was walking now and followed the kids wherever they went, if Macy didn't pick him up first. Josh and Charles hit it off well, as they discussed their work in web design. Addie, Clancy, and Darla were off in another area, talking and laughing.

Dani put her arms around Sam in the kitchen and looked out over her shoulder at all the interaction. She reached up, kissed her neck and whispered into Sam's ear. "Look at everyone. We are a family."

Sam sighed contently. "We are, aren't we?"

Connie entered the kitchen and put her coffee cup in the dishwasher. "Darla and I have been talking, so I have a good idea of the kind of house she is looking for. I'm going to line up some showings on Thursday. I guess Charles and Matt are playing golf in the morning. Sounds like you and Charles are being planned for Friday, Sam."

Dani teasingly said, "They are playing on Friday while I'm at work, so I can't watch them compete. They are both very competitive."

Connie chuckled and said, "My money is on her. She's a force to be reconned with. She always whipped Martin's ass."

Sam rolled her eyes. "Not true. I had to buy lunch as often as he did."

Macy interrupted their conversation with a sad face. "Softa, CJ won't let me put him in the bed."

Sam lifted her and placed her on the counter next to them. "Sweetheart, CJ isn't a doll; he's a real little boy who wants to play. He doesn't want to go to bed yet, and you can't always carry him around, but you can show him things to play with."

"I love him, and I won't drop him, I promise."

Sam kissed her pouty mouth. "I know you do. He loves you too, but you have to let him get used to all of us, okay?"

Darla had entered the kitchen and had heard the exchange between Sam and her granddaughter. She took Macy's hand, who was still sitting on the counter. "It's almost time for him to go to sleep. When it's time, would you like to help me get him in his pj's?"

Macy's eyes lit up, as did her smile. "Yes. I can help you!"

Darla lifted her off the counter and took her small hand. "Let's go see what he's gotten into, shall we? You know babies get into everything."

Macy sternly nodded her head in agreement, like an experienced mother. "They poop a lot, too."

Dani and Charles went out to the garden with their drinks, while the others continued to interact comfortably. Macy was able to play mommy a little longer then helped Darla get CJ down for the night. Soon after everyone headed for home.

Dani and Sam curled up together on the couch, while Darla and Charles sat together on the loveseat across from them.

Charles cleared his throat and spoke. "Darla and I want to thank you for welcoming us the way you have." He stopped, and before Sam could respond, he continued. "I was just telling Dani that our parents still don't know that we are moving." He sounded almost like he was proud of himself. "We have little contact."

It had been months since that night had happened and all its unpleasantness. Sam was shocked and wondered if Dani had been shocked at the news as well.

Sam quietly stated, "I'm so sorry to hear that." She momentarily felt that she, in some way, was the cause for that separation. She decided not to accept that guilt and remained silent.

Charles explained. "You see, they always expect us to come to them, never them to us. I have no idea if they are embarrassed by their behavior, or more likely, choosing to ignore and pretend the whole night's events didn't happen." He was visibly uncomfortable. He quickly glanced at Dani and then continued. "I believe Dani thinks that my part should be to confront them with the news. By avoidance, I am not standing up to them, again."

Dani held her palms up in protest. "Hold on, I never said that or anything else. I listened without comment. Don't put words in my mouth or interpret my unspoken thoughts."

Dani turned to Darla. "What are your thoughts, if I'm not out of line and you don't mind me asking?"

Darla didn't look the least bit uncomfortable with the question. "Charles has not asked me for my opinion. He and your parents have always had their relationship which has never included me, which is fine, but CJ is in the mix now, and I don't want him influenced by them. So, whatever Charles needs to do, he should do. I just don't want CJ exposed to them on any level."

She had honestly spoken as if Charles had not been in the room. It sounded to Sam that Darla had stepped up while Charles still had problems doing so.

She then turned toward her husband. "I realize this is news to you, Charles, and it's not an ultimatum, just a fact. I'm sorry if my feelings make the situation more difficult for you, but you have never asked me."

Sam and Dani exchanged looks of approval, reassessing their opinions of Darla.

It did not go unnoticed by Charles. He leaned forward with his hands on his thighs. He let out the air he was holding in his lungs. He smiled weakly and jokingly said, "I feel I should go with Dani's unspoken thoughts. I have to explain to them why we are moving away and honor Darla's feelings and support her." He grunted. "Growing some balls and growing up is fucking hard, isn't it?" He looked up at Sam. "Do you have an opinion?"

Reluctant to get involved, Sam clasped her hands in her lap and said, "No, I do not."

Dani took a deep breath and addressed her brother. "I hope you shared with Darla the other matter you discussed with me?"

Feeling somewhat vindicated, he said, "Yes, we did talk about it." He addressed Sam. "I asked Dani, that if something ever happened to Darla and myself, would she be willing to take custody of CJ. We did agree that we do not want him raised by my parents. Dani said that, although you are not in a legal marriage, it would involve your life as well. She would have to first discuss that with you before giving us an answer."

Sam was grateful that Dani had responded to him by including her. "We will get back to you after we have had that talk. You might want to consider Macy as an alternative; she has fallen head over heels with him."

Finally, the strained discussion of family was broken, and they all laughed.

That night in bed, Dani and Sam had that discussion. They decided they would tell them that Dani would take custody of CJ in the event of such a tragedy. Dani insisted that Charles should take care of the legal paperwork, so it would not come down to her having a battle in court with her parents. Sam asked her if she had had any contact with her parents since that last night in her parents' house. She let out a huff, responding only with a "No". She added it wasn't something she intended to do with her parents, who were not anything like Julia, who at least had an open mind.

That made Sam laugh and say, "We are all so fucked up."

"Well, at least we are happy in our dysfunction." Dani reached under Sam's night shirt and caressed her breast. "Can we have some private *us* time now?"

Sam rolled on top of her and stroked between Dani's smooth, silky thighs. "I thought you'd never ask."

On Friday, Charles and Sam played golf. Sam paid for lunch, but it was only by one stroke. She was confident that once she was back on her game he would be paying for lunches more often. The more they got to know each other, Sam's fondness grew for Charles.

They sat in the clubhouse eating, when Charles brought up the discussion of CJ. "I want to thank you for agreeing to support Dani's responsibility for CJ, in the event there is a need. I see how you are with your *own* grandchildren, and my mind is put at ease, knowing he would be a part of your and Dani's lives." He took a sip of his soda before continuing. "Thank you, also, for opening your home to us and giving Dani the family she has always wanted. Yours is a loving family."

Sam chewed and swallowed a bite of her sandwich. "You and Darla are a welcome part of our extended family. I hope you both feel comfortable with that."

"We are. Since Darla's grandmother died, she has felt a terrible loss for family. I realize I have played a huge part in her isolation because of my own family dynamic. I'm sure Dani has explained my relationship with my mother." He openly admitted, "I have always been a momma's boy, even though I always seem to fall short of her approval. I have never had the courage to stand up to her. I want CJ to have a good and healthy relationship with you, like Darla had with her grandmother; like how you are with your grandchildren."

Sam felt a little uneasy with his statement. It was the second time in the conversation that she felt that he was assuming her relationship with CJ would be a substitution role for his mother. "Charles, do you mean a healthy relationship with *a* grandmother or *his* grandmother?"

He looked puzzled and stared questioningly at her.

They stared at each other in silence for a prolonged minute. Finally, she spoke again. "Please. Please don't misunderstand what I'm about to say." She softened her voice and continued. "I don't want to become CJ's substitute grandmother. I am not Dani's mother, and I don't want you to see me as yours. We are now an extended, and hopefully happy, family, which is wonderful, but I do not wish to take on that role." Sam wasn't sure if his face was looking confused or disappointed. "Let me explain in a more personal way. When Dani and I got together, I was the one in the relationship that struggled to see us as a couple. I was busy seeing us as the world would view us. So far, we haven't been that far off the mark, unfortunately. We are viewed differently and judgmentally, both in social situations and with certain family members. Your sister is also much stronger than I am, with the issue. I'm adjusting to the reactions of others. It's been easier for me to view myself without roles or titles. I need to see myself as an individual. Does any of this make sense to you?"

Charles nodded, his eyes registering her comment. "Yes, I think I understand what you are saying. I have seen myself only as my mother's son, until I married Darla, and ever since, I've struggled with my new role as a husband and, now again, as a father."

Sam smiled broadly, relieved that he had understood and was not offended or hurt. "I hate to tell you, but it gets even more complicated as things change in our lives. We see ourselves in terms of our relationships. When our parents die, no matter how old we are, we are orphaned in our mind, and that makes us see ourselves in our world differently. When loved ones die, we are no longer a sister, a wife, a mother, etcetera. Our definition of self is altered in terms of who we might be with each change. Since falling in love with your sister, I have learned that it doesn't necessarily take a death to alter the definition as we see ourselves."

Charles was now fully engaged in the concept. "Isn't that also true in terms of how you view yourself in society? Or your career choices? You are subject to definition as well."

"I believe you are absolutely right. When you are introduced to someone, the first question usually is, 'What do you do?' If you're a professional, the person might jump to the conclusion that you must be smart. If you say you are a janitor, you might be looked at differently, even though you might have a vast education in linguists. Only after getting to know that person better, does that snap judgment and first impression change… or not, depending on if they have an open mind." She chuckled. "First-hand experience has taught me that. When I am asked what I do, and I reply that I'm a writer, the reaction is usually interest in me as a person. That may or may not change dramatically, with the second question, 'What do you write about?' When I tell them 'Lesbian fiction', that usually tells me if their first impression changed, instantly."

Charles smiled. "The human race needs a lot of work." He pushed his empty lunch plate aside. "So do I."

"What do you mean? We all do."

He sighed defeatedly. "I guess I'm back to my relationship with my mother."

"Do those feelings include your dad as well?"

Matter-of-factly and with no emotion in his voice, he said, "No. I've never been very close to him. He basically pays the bills and has my mother run the family. He has very little interest in how she does that. If Dani and I look to be successful to his colleagues and friends, then that's all that matters to him. Dani is the shining star, and I've basically squeaked by."

Sam was now more comfortable discussing personal issues with him, so she asked, "Is that maybe why your mother's opinion and expectation of you is so important?"

"I have been struggling with understanding my fear of confrontation with her. I have recently learned that Dani has never felt part of any relationship until meeting you. That includes family ties. I, on the other hand, am so desperately tied to a relationship with my mother, that I have allowed myself to be controlled, so that I don't disappoint her."

Sam felt badly for him and could relate to her own closeted childhood, for the same reason. Not wanting to disappoint. "Is telling her that maybe a way to open a discussion with your mother?"

He swallowed hard, keeping himself in control of his emotions. "It's time to put on my big boy pants, and maybe that's how to start a conversation with her."

Sam knew how scared he was, but she wanted him to know it should be sooner than later, before he lost his nerve. She reflected on her own experience of years of secrecy. "Now that we are family, please know Darla and CJ can stay with us, while you take care of that."

Realizing Sam meant right away, he knew she was right. He shouldn't wait any longer, especially now that they were moving. If not now, he would find another excuse not to take care of his issue with his mother. "Yes. I think it's time." For fear of showing how nervous he was about returning to Atlanta, he changed the subject quickly. "Darla thinks Connie has found the house she wants." He laughed. "I think this time, I will have no opinion about which house, which is perfectly fine with me."

Sam smiled. Wanting this to happen, as much for Darla as for him, she said, "She will be in good hands with Connie, while you are away in Atlanta."

While Charles was in Atlanta, he put their house on the market. He didn't want his mother to see a 'for sale' sign on the lawn before speaking with her, so right after, he took his mother to lunch. Dani and Sam knew that he and Darla checked in with each other daily, but they did not ask her how things went with his mother. They were both just getting to know Dani's brother and wife and the dynamics of their marriage. They did not want to assume that they would want to share everything with them. He was due back in Tucson the next day to check out the house that Darla had decided on for their family.

Sam was busy with edits to her newest book, and Dani was busy relieving Marcus's workload by taking on new patients at the office. The office environment had changed after the welcome dinner. Carol, their office manager, was no longer at the office. She wasn't sure if Marcus had asked her to leave; Sam hadn't asked him. The new office manager was organized, efficient and easy to work with. Marcus and Dani worked well together, and they enjoyed each other's sense of humor and company.

Dani relayed that a dinner invitation had been extended to them. Sam wasn't thrilled at the prospect of listening to Marcus's wife talk their ears off, but she knew Dani's feelings about Marcus. He wanted them over for a casual BBQ and to get to know Sam better. Dani didn't seem to be concerned.

Claris met them at the front door with a big smile and welcomed them into the foyer. Before leading them into the living area, she turned to address Sam. "I have an apology to make to you." Sam's confused face made Claris chuckle. She explained. "I have to apologize for talking your ear off the first time we met. It's a nervous habit of mine in large social situations, and your presence exacerbated my behavior, I'm afraid."

Sam was now very confused, as Claris could see by Sam's face.

Claris chuckled and gestured toward the kitchen. "Please come in, and I'll explain." They followed her into the kitchen, and she gestured for them to take a seat at the small breakfast table.

"Marcus will be joining us shortly. He is picking up our daughter, who is very eager to meet both of you. Katrina lives in the dorm at the University here. She is a huge fan of yours, Sam. I knew who you were the minute I met you and was caught off guard. I've seen your photo multiple times on your books. I think Katrina has every book you've written. I couldn't wait to text her that night, to tell her I had met you. I was giddy and nervous, so I must have come off as a lunatic. You look just like your photo on your book covers."

Sam nodded, not really sure how to respond.

Claris smiled and continued. "I looked up when Marcus introduced us, and there you were. I should have told you that night, but I wasn't sure if that discussion would make you uncomfortable at the table with the others. I didn't want to add to your discomfort, so instead, I'm afraid, I rambled on like an idiot. Marcus later told me about what had happened to you, Dani, in the ladies' room that night." She shook her head. "I have known Marcus's colleagues for a long time, and it is amazing how you think you know people, until they show their true selves."

Dani patted Claris's shoulder. "It is not your place to apologize to us, but thank you for your concern over our feelings. Sam and I are learning that judgments cause a domino effect of consequences and can put up invisible boundaries." Sam smiled inwardly, admonishing herself for her first impression of Claris. She realized that she, too, had jumped to judgment.

Their discussion was interrupted by voices coming from the entry. Marcus and Katrina entered the kitchen. Marcus introduced them to their daughter.

She reached out to shake Sam's hand. "Thanks for letting me crash the BBQ." She continued to pump Sam's hand until she realized she needed to stop and then turned to shake Dani's hand. "Nice to meet you, as well, Dr Masters."

Dani smiled and insisted she call her Dani.

Katrina placed her backpack on the counter and turned again toward Sam. She looked at Sam with enamored puppy eyes. "I have been so excited to me meet you ever since Mom told me about Dad's welcome dinner." Dani hid a smirk behind her hand, as Katrina looked like she wanted to hug Sam. "I've read every one of your books; I love the vintage stories about growing up in the sixties."

All Sam could do was smile and nod.

Marcus and Claris exchanged open smiles over their daughter's excitement. Marcus cleared his throat. "Sweetheart, they aren't going anywhere. I'm sure you have lots of questions for Sam, later." He hugged Dani and shook Sam's hand. "So glad you guys were able to make it tonight. I'm going to fire up the BBQ and let you ladies talk." He kissed his wife's forehead and went out the patio door.

Claris provided everyone with a beverage, and they nibbled on snacks at the table. Marcus soon returned and joined them. Sam was feeling much more comfortable with Claris's explanations about the welcome dinner and that she could speak freely in front of Katrina, who asked question after question about her books, while Dani and Claris got better acquainted.

They fixed their hamburgers and sat on the patio, eating. Dani decided she wanted to know something and went for it. "Marcus, I told myself I wouldn't ask you, but did you fire Carol, or did she quit?"

He didn't hesitate with his response. "I had a discussion with her about the respect and professional behavior that I expect from our office staff. It was her choice to give two weeks' notice." He took a sip from his bottle of beer. "I don't know if your question was in regard to the comments on our web page."

Dani looked puzzled and shook her head. "I haven't looked at it; what was said?"

Marcus cleared his throat. "It didn't take her long. She didn't sign it, of course, but it basically said that she could not recommend our office to people with good Christian standards." He laughed. "That's a pretty ironic statement, isn't it?"

Katrina asked what they were talking about, and her mother filled her in with the detail of what had taken place. She was outraged. "Dad! You should have fired her on the spot."

Marcus calmly explained. "Everyone is entitled to their beliefs and politics. All we can do, when it is shoved into our faces, is to point out that we think differently. In this case, I had an obligation to state what my standards are and what was expected of her in the office. It was her choice to leave."

Katrina was visibly indignant and enraged. "Rosa and I wouldn't stand for anti-gay comments made about us. How dare they make any comments about age and race!" She turned to Sam. "Don't you agree that Dad should have marched over to them and said that they shouldn't show up on Monday?"

Sam rather enjoyed Katrina's animated outrage and could see, in her mind, Addie reacting similarly. She took a deep breath and let it out slowly. "I'm afraid I have to agree with your father. You, and I'm assuming, your girlfriend, Rosa, have yet to feel the anger and judgments that are out here in the world against you being gay. You are very lucky to have been raised by parents who are open and supportive of you. The reality is, you are going to meet people like Carol, and it will frustrate you to no end. Their view of the world cannot be changed by your anger, it can only make more division and reinforce their sense of misplaced righteousness." Sam could see the frustration on

Katrina's face. "All you can do is respect yourself and let them know you expect respect in return. Education can only be passed on to people who are willing to listen and learn. Hopefully, you will meet more people of that kind."

Katrina looked deflated. "People suck!"

The rest of the evening was comfortable, and Sam and Dani felt very relaxed. Sam could understand why Dani enjoyed working with Marcus. Claris, too, was very engaging and much more comfortable.

After dinner, Katrina handed Sam a copy of her latest book and asked her if she would sign it.

On the way home, Dani and Sam were pleased to know that the Ortega family could be added to their small, but hopefully growing, list of friends and family.

The following day, Charles returned to Tucson. Nothing had changed on the issues with his parents. He sat at dinner, sharing his disappointing experience. Not only was his mother blaming Darla for taking him away from his family, but now he was being accused of betraying his mother by siding with Dani against them. He didn't hold back relating how his mother had said Dani had been written off when she got involved with Sam. She was no longer in their lives to embarrass them with her divorce and now, this shameful relationship with Sam. They had washed their hands of her. Lottie had said that she only hoped that Charles would come to his senses and be the man of his family and put his foot down with

Darla and put her in her place. She had said that CJ is their grandson, and they have a right to him and his future.

The whole time he relayed that discussion, Darla remained composed and detached. She had been getting daily reports from him while he was in Atlanta, and it wasn't something she hadn't already experienced, since marrying Charles.

Dani could almost read these thoughts, watching Darla's face. Darla looked sad and quietly sighed in her resignation. Dani felt so badly for her sister-in-law. Wanting Charles to emphatically declare to Darla his loyalty, she asked him, "What did you say to them when they made those comments about Darla?"

Charles shrugged. "What could I say? She just says the same thing over and over. Nothing new."

A flash of hurt then turned into mild indignation. However, Darla spoke calmly. "At any point during your discussions with her, did you make it clear that you are not going to keep trying to change her? Perhaps you haven't yet been able to acknowledge, yourself, that she is not going to change. Charles, her expectations of you will never be met. You are a successful man, and until you recognize your life is not to convince her of that, you're right; nothing is going to change. Frankly, I'm done giving her my husband and will be damned if I even consider CJ as my next sacrifice." Her whole body trembled slightly as she stood up. Her lip quivered as she added, "If you need counseling, get it. I'm done taking their abuse and watching you continue to allow it for the three of us." She left the room.

Charles's humiliation and defeat was palatable. His shoulders dropped, and he stared at his hands in his lap. Dani and Sam didn't want to add to his embarrassment. They got up and busied themselves in the kitchen. Finally, he got up to join Darla in the guestroom. There was muffled, angry conversation heard from the room.

CJ woke, crying, from his nap. Darla went into the playroom where his crib was and picked him up. She sat in the rocking chair, speaking softly to him.

Sam suggested to Dani that they take a walk and give them some privacy. Dani peeked around the doorway of the playroom to let Darla know they were going out for a walk and offered to take CJ with them, so they could continue to talk.

Their house was in a lovely neighborhood with a park nearby. They headed in that direction. CJ was looking around, contently, from his stroller. A neighbor, three doors down, was watering her potted plants and glanced up at them with a smile. "Good evening." Sam recognized her from a previous meeting with her and her grandchild, when Sam had taken Macy and Garrett to the playground. "My, what a cutie." She squatted down to CJ's level and cooed at him, while holding his chubby little hand. She stood up and addressed Dani. "Your little guy is adorable."

"Thank you; he's my nephew. My brother and sister-in-law are visiting us from out of state."

She looked at Sam, confused. "Oh." she said. "I thought you lived alone."

"No longer. This is my partner, Dani."

There was silence, while the announcement sunk in. Then another, "Oh." She seemed to find her voice again. "Well, welcome, Dani. It's nice to meet you."

Dani replied, "Thank you. And your name is…?"

"Marsha."

"Nice to meet you, as well, Marsha."

Even before Darla and Charles moved into their new house, the news about Sam and Dani had been spread around the neighborhood. Two women actually appeared at their door with baked goods, welcoming Dani, and obviously wishing for an invite into the house, for more detailed information about their union. Sam had lived there for eight years and only met her next-door neighbor once, while getting her mail out of the mailbox. She had never received a welcoming gift, let alone a visit. It was difficult to know if the curiosity was in good will or made with more gossip in mind. It was exhausting to constantly have to think in those terms about the people around you. She and Dani talked about it and instead of questioning motives, they decided to just take each new encounter without preconceived ideas. Their conclusion had been, that otherwise they, too, would be making snap judgments, like Sam had done with Claris.

Chapter 11

Darla and Charles' house was a ten-minute drive from theirs. She and Connie had chosen the perfect house for them. It fit their personalities perfectly. It was large enough for their growing family, while remaining comfortably casual. Connie had made sure the area was family and pet friendly, since Darla wanted CJ to grow up with a large yard for a dog. Darla had had a dog at her grandmother's house as a child. Within the first week of settling in, they met their next-door neighbor who also had a small child and was thrilled to have them as new neighbors. Darla was outgoing and carefree and seemed to glow with her new life and freedom away from her in-laws.

She asked Clancy and Addie for advice on where to shop to decorate the house. The three of them went together, making a day of it, leaving the kids with the men. Darla endeared herself even more to Connie, with a beautiful ceramic bowl Connie had admired on one of their excursions, as a thank you gift for finding them the house.

Sundays became family dinner night at Sam and Dani's house, when Sam wasn't traveling. Charles loved to grill, and Connie made sure to find a house that included an outdoor kitchen for him. Darla had planned the first BBQ, hoping that it, too, would become a family tradition at their house.

Sam was out of town at a book signing when Dani got the call at the office. "Dani, it's Ed. I tried to reach Sam, but she didn't answer her cell."

Dani could hear the strain in his voice. "She is at a book promo. What's wrong? Are you okay?"

"It's Julia. She…" His voice quivered. "She overdosed and is on a vent."

Dani reached for the office chair and shakingly sat down. "Ed, did she…"

She didn't have to finish her sentence. He replied, "I don't know if it was an accident or not. Before they put her on a ventilator, she asked for Samantha."

Dani's hand was slightly shaking, as she gripped the phone. "Sam is in Colorado. She is probably on her way to the Denver airport; she's coming home tonight." She glanced at her watch. "I'll get in touch with her right away; maybe she can change flights. Do you need me to come? You know I will."

He sounded so weary. "No. No, thanks. It's okay. Susan is here with me now."

Dani could not reach Sam on her cell. Just as she exited the shuttle and was entering the terminal, Sam had not heard her phone in the busy airport, but she did hear the announcement, calling her to pick up a paging phone for a message.

Although she was able to change her flight, it was hours later when she finally arrived. She drove the rental car directly to the hospital, where Susan and Ed met her. It was after visiting hours, but Ed was able to convince the night staff to let Sam in to see her. Sam's heart ached seeing her sister looking so small and vulnerable, laying there, hooked up to tubes and monitors and unable to communicate. Ed explained that they would know more after seventy-two hours of observation. Her stomach had been pumped. However, she had to be put on a ventilator because she had fallen, and the meds she had taken aspirated into her lungs. She was in an induced coma. Heart and brain damage were also risks for concern now. It was serious.

They got a few hours' of sleep and returned to the hospital the following morning. The memories of all the time Sam had spent in similar situations with Michael, Laura, her brother and her parents, left her body heavy with physical and emotional exhaustion. She sat next to Julia's bed, hour after hour, staring and hoping this time for a different result. She walked the halls when she could sit no longer and drank bad vending machine coffee, only to return to the room to do it over again.

Finally, two mornings later, Ed came out of the hospital room and announced she had been taken off the ventilator and was breathing on her own. She hadn't yet opened her eyes, nor did they yet know the extent of any damage.

The waiting was long and intensely frustrating. Dani had spent any free time during the day on the phone with Sam and Ed, receiving unchanging reports. She was swamped, herself, at the hospital and hadn't been home much, only to sleep and eat meals that Sam's girls and Darla had left for her.

Two more days passed, and Julia opened her eyes and gestured for water. Ed helped her to a sitting position, while Sam poured water from the pitcher on her tray and handed him the glass. He instructed her to drink slowly, and Sam took a sigh of relief when she understood him, nodded and sipped at the water slowly. Julia glanced over Ed's shoulder and saw Sam. Tears spilled from her eyes, and she motioned for her with a brief movement of her hand. Susan had called for the nurse, and she entered and warned Julia that it might hurt her to speak, now that the tube was out. Julia was still gripping Sam's hand and looked desperate to talk.

Sam leaned over her and kissed her forehead. "Shush," she said. "We have time to talk later. Rest now."

Julia nodded, closed her eyes and fell back to sleep from the effort. Julia had been very lucky and was expected to make a full recovery.

She was released a day later and was settled comfortably in her bed at home. Ed had left to take Susan to the airport to return home to her family.

Sam entered the bedroom with Julia's lunch tray and placed it across her lap. Julia pushed the plate away. "I'm not hungry."

Sam sat down next to her on the bed and picked up the fork and handed it to her. "You have to eat a little, you've lost weight."

Julia took the fork from her but just held it over the plate and focused, instead, on Sam's face. "Sam, I didn't try and kill myself. I laid in that hospital bed and all I could think was, 'Sam and Ed have to know!' I would never do that. I won't deny that I've been depressed and absent-minded lately." She explained further. "I sort my day and night pills for the week and didn't realize I had put multiple sleeping pills in one container. I was distracted and took them all at once, in error. Please believe me."

Sam said, "I have no reason not to. If you said that is what happened, then that's what happened. But why have you been depressed?"

Julia put the fork down on the tray and shrugged her shoulders unconvincingly. "I don't know, really. Since Ed has retired, my routine has changed. Our life together is different, and we get on each other's nerves much more often." Her voice caught in her throat momentarily and she continued. "And... part of it is what has happened between us. I just hate it. We are our only family left. I want it all to go back the way it was between us. It plays over and over in my head, like a bad movie."

Sam nodded and replied, "We are so different, but we have one thing in common. We both do not do well with change. I have struggled with that all my life. Yet, through all the deaths, hardships and kids growing up, we survived, haven't we?"

Julia smiled weakly. "Yes, I guess we have."

"Julia, you told me that we are sisters and always will be. You're right. We have a bond, and it's been tested. Now, it's a matter of how we move forward from here. Our relationship has changed, but that doesn't mean we can't move on. When I saw you in the hospital, I was terrified that I was going to lose you. I didn't think about my anger and hurt for one moment. Letting things go is very difficult for both of us, but it seems so trivial when crisis hits."

Julia squeezed Sam's hand. "I really want to move on and forget what happened between us."

Sam shook her head. "What was said, was said. We can't forget it. We have to learn something from it, to make us want this change."

Sam stayed on a few days longer, before returning home. They talked about their childhood experiences together and separately, outside their parents' house. They explored their feelings about their parents. It was the first time Sam shared her feelings about what it was like growing up gay and in secrecy. She told her about her open marriage to Michael and why. Julia saw her sister in a very new light, with a better understanding. Sam was surprised to hear all the insecurities Julia had felt growing up; how their mother's approval was the most important driving factor in Julia's life. It was as if they had been raised in separate homes. Sam could not help making the comparison to Charles's relationship with his mother as well.

It was a wonderful two days of deeper communication, laughter and healing for both of them. Julia wanted to know all about the changes Sam was going through in her new life with Dani. She was surprised about the addition of Dani's family moving to Tucson, and wanted to hear all about them. Ed watched as it all unfolded before him, and it was a huge relief to see them together again. Julia was excited and promised that, once she was stronger, it was time for her and Ed to come to Tucson for a visit.

The difficult days of Julia's hospitalization had taken its toll on her, but Sam returned home feeling refreshed and much less burdened, having cleared the way to move forward with her sister. There was so much to tell Dani about, but all she wanted now, was to be in her arms.

She had, for the most part, ignored all the emails and work on her desk and spent Dani's day off sharing all that happened with her sister. Dani was thrilled and relieved both for Julia's recovery and for the sisters' reconnection.

Dani caught Sam up on all the news at home. The whole family had a BBQ at Darla and Charles's house. The backyard had a pool, and the kids had had a great time. Dani jokingly told Sam that she would now have to share her best friend, Connie, with her sister-in-law. They had become close, and Dani was under the impression that Connie reminded Darla of her grandmother. Given Connie's strong personality, Sam was not quite able to see that relationship in her mind. She laughed and told her she couldn't wait to see this for herself.

Dani told her she couldn't get over the change she saw in Darla. She was telling Charles what was on her mind, with confidence. Sam laughed again, saying she now understood Connie and Darla's budding relationship. Connie had definitely rubbed off on Darla.

Dani continued her report. Darla wanted a security fence built for the pool. Charles and Josh were planning to install it before the next BBQ, which was to be expected to be the next tradition added to the calendar, with Sunday dinners remaining at their home. Life was moving on here, too, it seemed to Sam. The change was a welcomed one.

Chapter 12

Sam and Dani's first fight, not counting their tumultuous reunion at Julia and Ed's house, happened three weeks later. Dani had worked a double shift at the hospital, and when she got home, she found Clancy applying ice to Sam's bandaged ankle. There was also a bruise on her temple.

Clancy read Dani's concerned look, as she had walked into the room, and said, "She's fine. Her ankle doesn't appear to be broken. She fell in the office, and hit her head on the corner of the desk."

Dani and Sam's eyes met. "Did you get x-rays?"

Sam's response was curt. "There is no need. I'm fine."

Clancy, picking up on the instant tension, sheepishly said, "She wouldn't let me take her to get an x-ray."

Dani was pissed for other reasons. "I guess there was no need to call me, either?"

"Dani, why would I call you when I knew you were busy at the hospital? I sure wasn't about to call Addie and be rushed off in an ambulance. Besides, Clancy had just come by to pick up Garrett's backpack a few minutes after it happened."

Dani could see that Clancy had stayed, evidenced by the dinner tray left on the coffee table. "How long ago did this happen?"

Sam raised her shoulders with an annoyed look on her face. "Jesus, Dani, why the inquisition?"

Dani refused to back down. "How long?"

Clancy, trying to head off more building confrontation, answered honestly, for fear her mother wouldn't. "It happened around three. I got here about four-thirty."

Sam gave her daughter a look that said, 'Thanks, traitor.'

"Oh, so Clancy didn't get here a few minutes after it happened. When were you planning on calling me?" Sarcastically, Dani added, "Or maybe you couldn't get to your phone." She knew that Sam always had it on her, or on her desk, when working. Dani looked at her watch; it was after seven.

Clancy was already on Sam's shit list for betraying her about the timeframe of the accident, and she decided to leave the two of them to work it out. "Well, now that you're here, I better get home."

Dani thanked her for staying and walked her to the front door. They hugged, and Clancy made a hurried exit.

Sam's foot was elevated on the coffee table. Dani sat down on the coffee table and unwrapped the bandage to examine Sam's ankle. Still very pissed, she asked if Sam had tried to put any weight on it.

Sam's response was short and brusque. "I can't."

Dani then gave her attention to the bruise on Sam's head.

Sam made a fatal error by saying, "I believe you were the one that pointed out that the girls were very overprotective."

Dani suddenly dropped her hand from Sam's bruised face. She reared back and gave Sam a look that could have sent a tiger in retreat, with its tail between its legs. "Are you fucking serious right now? You actually said that to me?" She stood up and glared at her. "Well, since I'm being over protective, I'm taking a shower and going to bed. If you need help getting up… well, I'm sure you can handle that, too, without calling me. Good luck with that." Dani went into the bedroom and slammed the door shut.

Sam, later, hobbled and hopped to the bathroom in pain, and with much effort, made her way back to the couch, where she stayed the rest of the night.

Having finally fallen asleep around four in the morning, Dani found Sam asleep where she had left her the night before. She refilled a bag of ice and left it in an igloo cooler within Sam's reach.

She purposely left work early to get home, having not once called Sam during the day.

Connie was in the easy chair talking to Sam when Dani got home. She put the bag of fast-food down and went into the kitchen to get plates. She served Connie first and handed Sam a plate without looking at her.

Dani knew that Connie had arrived mid-morning, because she had called her the night before to ask her to come to the house to take care of Sam.

Connie took a bite of her taco and wiped her mouth with a napkin. "It's not broken. I put her in the car and took her to get an x-ray. There is no fracture to her stubborn, hard head, either."

Dani swallowed a mouthful of food and said, "Thank you."

Words still had not been exchanged between Dani and Sam, until Connie left, a few minutes later.

Dani gathered up the paper and napkins from the fast-food and put it into the bag. She started to head for the kitchen.

Sam quietly said, "I'm sorry."

Dani turned toward her and put the bag back down. "Samantha, what could you have been thinking? Don't ever do that to me again. First, you don't call me and then you accuse me of being overprotective. May I remind you, we are on the same 'we' page in this relationship?"

Sam looked like an admonished child. "Of course we are."

Dani sat down next to her. "Then please explain to me what was happening to make you act this way."

Sam knew she had no choice but to come clean. She closed her eyes for a minute. When they slowly opened them, she took Dani's hand. "I was scared. You know I get defensive when I'm scared. I'm sorry." She painfully readjusted her foot on the pillow, now under her ankle. She couldn't look at Dani's face as she continued. "This is the second time I've had a dizzy spell and fell."

Tears instantly welled up in Dani's eyes in concern. She patiently waited for Sam to look at her and continue.

"The first time was in Colorado, when I was at the book signing. Actually, it was in the hotel room. When I came to, I realized I had fallen halfway on the bed and really didn't get hurt, except for my wrist."

Dani was now alarmed. "You mean you passed out?"

Sam nodded. "Yeah, like yesterday. It just suddenly happened, both times. I didn't want to worry you and I…"

Dani knew what Sam was thinking and interrupted her. "Sam, this does not mean you had a stroke. We are going to run some tests. I'll set them up in the morning. For God's sake, don't ever keep things from me again. Swear, Sam, swear you won't!"

Sam squeezed her hand and said, "I swear."

Dani scheduled a battery of tests for Sam at the hospital. It turned out that her blood pressure was the issue, and she was put on medication. Dani sat on the couch next to her, going over all the test results, as well as the medical history questionnaires that Sam had filled out.

"So, it looks like mostly heart issues in your family." Dani was sure Sam had been concerned about a stroke, that had taken both her parents in their mid-seventies. "Honey, you know that in your parents' generation, they didn't have all the preventative knowledge and technology we have today."

Sam nodded. "I admit, that scared me. After the first time it happened in Colorado, I just thought it was because I hadn't eaten all day. But this time, my thought process was much different. I did think it was a stroke, but the few hours before Clancy dropped by, most of my thoughts were angry."

Dani's brow wrinkled in question.

Sam continued. "I thought, 'Shit, don't let a stroke take me now'. I want so much more time with you."

Dani's face softened and she said, "Baby, we have so much to look forward to."

Sam smiled weakly. "I know you don't like me talking about my age, but I need you to see through my eyes for just a few minutes. The reality is that Julia and I are the last family of our generation. When I saw her so sick at the hospital, my mortality became much more present in my mind. I was so afraid she would die without us being able to make things right between us. Family took on new meaning. I don't mean to sound so dramatic, but I do see the world differently, just by the fact that I'm at this stage of my life."

She could see that Dani was mulling over what she had said. "I understand. I'm so glad that you and Julia are speaking again. Ed told me you guys talk now, once a week. Honey, you are in great physical condition for your age."

Sam cleared her throat before speaking. "Your parents are my age and time…"

Dani could see, instantly, where this was headed. She interrupted Sam's sentence. "Sam, you can't possibly be suggesting that Charles and I go back to being kicked in the teeth by our parents?"

"I just don't want you to have any regrets. That's all. But that isn't the only thing I've been thinking about since falling. I don't have a medical directive." She laughed. "If I left that decision up to Addie, I would be on life support until *she* died of old age."

That finally brought a smile to Dani's face. "It is left up to the designated family member to decide. I'm not family and would have no authority to stop her."

Sam leaned over and kissed her. "Then perhaps it's time to change that."

Dani looked quizzically at her.

Sam took a small jewelry box from her pocket and handed it to her. "Dani, will you marry me?"

Dani was momentarily paralyzed, before her shaking hand took the box from Sam. Her head was moving like a bobble head, and she exclaimed, "Yes! Yes! Of course I will marry you!"

A broad smile crossed Sam's face. "Well… aren't you going to open it?"

"I don't care if it's a cigar wrapper." She opened the box and removed two wide gold bands. Across each was written, *Crossing Invisible Boundaries*. Then the tears of joy came. "Shit, you don't walk well with those crutches, and I can't carry your glorious body to the bedroom. So, either we make love here on the couch, or you better start hobbling to the bed."

They began, the next day, discussing how and when they wanted to get married, before sharing the news with family. They agreed that they just wanted a small wedding of family and a few friends and wanted to keep it simple. They didn't want or need wedding gifts so, instead, they would ask the guests to make donations to their favorite charities. Sam started an invitation list and, once again, Dani's parents were mentioned. Dani was quick to point out that, even if they were included, they wouldn't even respond to the invitation.

"Isn't that their decision? Look, it may just be a way to open the door to communication, at least. You guys are at a stalemate."

"Sam, you heard what Charles said. They have written me out of their lives. You can't get much clearer than that."

"Well, you might want to discuss it with Charles, when we tell them about the wedding." Sam snorted with a rising laugh. "Wouldn't it be great to watch Darla command the whole situation. My God, that woman has grown some cojones."

An evil grin crossed Dani's face. "I must admit, that would be fun. Then there would be Addie. She would have bodyguards surrounding you throughout the ceremony."

That made Sam snort laugh, again. "Ah, the joys of family."

Dani refocused. "Okay, back to the list. I would like Marcus and Claris, and Katrina and her girlfriend, Rosa, there." She hesitated a moment, tilting her head, uncertainly. "I would love for you to meet David, if that wouldn't be too awkward for you? I know he will be happy for us."

Sam was curious. "Have you kept in touch with him?"

"He texted me a few months back to see how I was doing and wanted me to know he is seeing someone. Unaware that I no longer keep in touch with my parents, he didn't want me to hear the news from them."

"That was sweet of him." Then she chuckled. "Something tells me you are as curious about his girlfriend. Of course, invite him. I would love to meet him."

They decided they wanted the wedding at home in the back garden, early in May, before it got too hot. That would give them three months to prepare.

The announcement was made at the following Sunday family dinner. Without exception, everyone seemed very excited. It had been over a year, now, that Dani and Sam had been living together in the house. In that time, family had become even more important, and they all looked forward to being together on family nights, at their house and at Darla and Charles's house.

The strained interaction between Charles and Darla only occurred when the subject of his parents was brought up. Dani saw her brother and Darla glance at each other uncomfortably, when the announcement was made that it would be a small ceremony with family and a few friends. Dani found an opportunity, later in the evening, to get Charles alone and feel him out about his thoughts of inviting their parents to the wedding. "So, have you had any communication with Mom and Dad?"

Charles looked around and saw Darla and Connie talking across the room. He lowered his voice and answered, "I send her pictures, occasionally, of CJ." In an almost apologetic voice, he continued. "Look, Mom is miserable. She feels alone; you know how Dad can be so distant. She's really feeling it more, now that David's parents have moved to the east coast to be closer to him. Mom feels completely abandoned."

This was all news to Dani. "Is Darla aware of all this?"

He hung his head, guiltily. "No. She doesn't know I keep in touch." He looked up at his sister, and as if to vindicate himself, he added, "It would just cause friction, so why tell her?"

Dani was disappointed in him. She tried to keep her annoyance to a minimum. "Maybe because she's your wife."

He didn't respond.

"Charles, your marriage is not my business. I've come to respect and love Darla, that's all I'm saying."

Later in the evening, when they were alone, Dani told Sam about the conversation she had with her brother. "If I was Darla and found out he was keeping in touch with Mom after he stated their relationship was done, I would be devastated."

"Honey, I get that, but I think he is trying to find a middle ground for himself. He is really torn, and I kind of feel badly for him."

"I understand that, but he is wrong to not include Darla in his feelings. He's being deceitful in telling Darla one thing and then going behind her back, to Mom." Before Sam could inquire, she said, "And no, I didn't state that opinion."

Sam chuckled at the ability the two of them had, to usually read each other's minds.

Dani smiled back at her. "We do that a lot, don't we?" It was a rhetorical question, so she didn't wait for Sam's response. "I just feel all this is going to go badly for them. He has a good woman, and I hope he doesn't fuck it all up. I'll send my parents an invitation to the wedding, because I know they won't come. Now that I know Charles keeps in touch, I'll be dying to ask Charles what their comment will be."

Sam was amused and took Dani's face between her hands and said, "You have a thin line between masochism and revenge, when it comes to your parents."

Everyone wanted to help with the wedding. The girls and Connie had their own little question-and-answer session about Sam and Dani's preferences and set about coordinating tasks. Darla wanted to be the one to help shop for dresses separately with Sam and Dani. She wanted the dresses to complement each other since the women wouldn't see each other's choices until the wedding.

Dani and Sam really didn't care what was being planned. "Surprise us," they said. They set an amount for the wedding and told them to keep receipts, so Sam and Dani could split the bill. They were just thrilled that everyone was excited. They chose their invitations and the date for the ceremony; the rest was up to everyone else in the family.

Julia and Ed were the first to respond to their RSVP. Sam insisted they stay at the house. Susan, Scott and their daughter, Katie, would be staying with Clancy and Matt. Next, a 'yes' came back from the Ortega family, including Rosa. David and his girlfriend were juggling schedules so that they could attend.

Addie thought the wedding should be catered. Sam and Dani were fine with that. Garrett and Macy were excited that they got to be part of the ceremony. Garrett would be the ring bearer, and Macy, hand in hand with CJ, would be sprinkling rose petals. Macy was beside herself with excitement and talked about her dress and shoes, until Addie and Josh thought they would go crazy.

The out-of-towners arrived two days before the wedding, except for David and his girlfriend, who would be arriving the day of the wedding. The house was total chaos when everyone congregated nightly, for dinner.

The first night, Sam cooked with Julia, and they both decided it would be a lot easier and less stressful to have pizza delivered the following evening.

The night before the wedding, pizza boxes and drinks covered the kitchen counters, island and dining room. Connie and Darla went over their final check list, and they checked with the girls to see if all was ready to go.

Sam felt jealous that Dani was getting away for a couple hours, to check on patients. She kissed her at the door and said, over all the noise and laughter in the house, "You wanted family; baby, you got it!"

Dani was just getting into the car, when Charles approached her, looking very nervous.

"Hey, can we talk for a minute?" She nodded, and he climbed into the passenger seat. He was actually wringing his sweaty hands. "I just got a text from Mom. They just checked into the local Hilton."

Dani's jaw dropped. When she caught her breath, she said, "Are you fucking with me right now?"

All he could do was place his large hand over his mouth and shake his head.

"Charles Tyler, what did you do?"

Both hands went up in defense of her onslaught. "I swear, I didn't know they were coming. All I know is that Mom got your invitation, and all she said to me was that it was an abomination. What are we going to do?"

Dani grabbed his shirt and pulled him toward her. "*We*! What are *you* going to do?" She didn't take a breath before she said, "I'll tell you what *you* are going to do. You are going to get your ass over to the hotel and tell them, that if they ruin my wedding, I will personally call the cops and have them removed."

Charles put his face into his open hands. He looked up at his sister and nodded slowly, letting that sink in. "Right."

"I'm going back into the house to tell Sam. I think you might want to warn Darla." She slugged his shoulder as hard as she could and headed back into the house.

She spotted Sam at the back of the room, talking to her niece, Susan. Sam smiled as Dani went to her and put her hand on her arm. "Forget something, babe?"

Dani smiled at Susan and said, "I need to steal her away for a minute." She led her into the bedroom and shut the door. She turned toward Sam, with rage written across her face. "I'm going to kill Charles!"

Sam tilted her head in question.

"My parents are at the Hilton, a mile away. He swears he didn't know they were coming."

Sam looked shocked, but not upset.

Dani proceeded to convey the conversation she had had minutes before, in the car, while Charles took Darla into the backyard to give her the news.

Sam led Dani to the sitting area of their bedroom. "It's okay. Honey, it's going to be all right. I need you to try and calm down. I really don't want you driving to the hospital when you're this upset. Do you think you can have Marcus check on your patients?"

Dani took a cleansing breath and texted Marcus. She looked like she was going to cry. "I'm so angry right now. Everyone is so happy and excited about tomorrow, and this happens."

She punched the seat cushion in frustration. Marcus's text came through immediately. She signed in relief. "He's such a good guy. He's still at the hospital. He'll check on them." She leaned back into the chair.

Sam rubbed her thumb over Dani's soft arm. "Let's look at this calmly. You really don't think your parents would make a scene in front of strangers? Your mother is way too proper to step over that line, and your father is Mister Urbane, himself."

"As you have witnessed firsthand, you know what they are capable of."

"Honey, they'll be on our turf this time. I'm more concerned about what is happening between Darla and Charles, right now."

It didn't take long to find out. A few minutes later, there was a knock at the bedroom door. Darla stepped in and took a seat on the bed, without the same panic that Dani had displayed, although she looked upset.

Calmly, and seemingly in control of the situation, she announced, "There has been a change in plans. Dani, you and I are staying at Connie's tonight, so that you can get dressed there in the morning, for the wedding. She is picking up your dress and CJ's tux at our house, now, and coming back for me. Addie's taking CJ home with her. I want to make sure he is safe."

Sam was alarmed. "What do you mean, safe?"

Darla's jaw was set in anger for a brief moment, before she spoke. "Charles is so gullible when it comes to your mother. I can see her talking him into bringing them back to the house tonight. CJ and I will not be there."

Dani was still hung up on the word *safe*. "Why wouldn't CJ be safe?"

"The two of you have only seen the tip of the iceberg when it comes to how they treat me. CJ was still an infant when she started threatening me that they had no problem filing for custody of my son, if he wasn't being properly raised."

Dani jumped to her feet, no longer able to contain her anger. "And Charles! What did my brother have to say to that?"

"She said this to me in private, and when I told him what she had said, his reply was that I should ignore her, that it was just more nonsense from her." Now Darla's anger began to surface. "That's why I insisted you get custody of CJ instead of them." She shook her head, vehemently. "I don't trust them as far as I can throw them. At this point, I can't even trust that Charles won't be conned into letting them take him back to Atlanta on the next flight."

Sam sat on the bed next to Darla's, now quivering, body and pulled her into her arms. "That is not going to happen. Do you hear me? I can assure you that every member of this family will have their eyes on CJ, starting now, until they leave."

Dani sat down on the other side of Darla and put her arm around her, as well. She added, "And as far as Charles is concerned, I can tell you, right now, his ass is about to get seriously kicked and his head put on straight."

Darla's shoulders dropped, releasing some of her tension. "Thank you, because right now, I need Charles far away from me!" She stiffened up again and indignantly said, "Can you believe he did not tell me he was still speaking to your mother? He has been, since we left Atlanta. God knows what kind of influence she has had over him. What is wrong with him, to keep this from me? His defense, when I asked him, was that he needed to be there for your mother, because she has been thinking about leaving your father. She found out that he has been having an affair, now, for over a year."

Dani had not been expecting that bit of news and it showed, by her surprised and wide-eyed face.

"Charles's confidences with your mother, have always taken priority over our marriage."

Sam thought that she and Dani would have to discuss the news about her father, later, but for now, Sam patted Darla's back, reassuringly, "I'm glad you'll be with Connie tonight. Has Addie and Josh left with CJ, yet?"

"He was getting fussy; it's past his bedtime. So, she was packing him up to go. I told her my concern about not going back to the house. Addie was the one to insist."

Sam chuckled. "Now that Addie knows your concern, she will have Josh barricading the front door and texting everyone to watch CJ like a hawk tomorrow."

They were interrupted by an almost simultaneous text on Dani's and Darla's phone, from Charles. Dani read it out loud. There was a thumbs up emoji. 'It's okay, everything is okay for tomorrow. Not to worry. They are here because they want to show their support to Dani and tell her in person that they are sorry how their meeting went with Sam, and of course, they want some time with CJ. Mom wants to see the house, so I will pick them up in the morning and give them a little time with him, since I know Darla will be busy with getting Dani dressed. I'm about to head back to Sam and Dani's now.'

They exchanged uneasy glances and returned to their company. Darla was relieved to see that Connie was back from picking up Dani's dress. She wanted to leave immediately, before Charles returned. She put on her best smile, and she and Connie said their goodbyes and left the house.

Clancy whispered in Darla's ear, at the front door, and headed toward Sam and Dani, to also let them know that Addie and Josh had left with CJ. Quietly, she asked, "Is Darla okay? She was so upset. Is she really afraid they might try and take CJ? Would they really try to do that?"

Dani reassured her. "She is going to be fine. She just needs a little space and time to recoup. Connie will see that she gets it. We won't let that happen to CJ. We made it clear to her that none of us will take our eyes off of him."

Clancy was shocked it could even be a possibility.

Dani turned to Sam and said, "I'll be taking Charles back into our bedroom, as soon as he arrives. Honey, I'm sorry I'm leaving you to entertain our company. Please make my apologies."

"Of course," Sam said. Knowing how Dani's volume could rise when angered, she added, "You may want to turn on some quiet music."

Dani understood her subtle, but clear, message and nodded.

The Hilton was close, and Connie's and Charles's cars must have passed on the street. Charles had barely closed the door behind him, when Dani took his arm, lead him to the bedroom and closed the door.

It was about an hour later that Susan and Scott left, with Clancy and Matt. Only Julia and Ed remained. Dani and Charles were still in the bedroom.

Finally they emerged, and Charles kissed Sam's cheek after searching for an indication of how she was feeling. She smiled meekly and patted his back. Charles said goodnight to everyone and left.

Julia looked at her watch. "It's almost nine. I'm going to say goodnight, too. We have a long day tomorrow. You two need your beauty sleep for the big day." She and Ed headed to the guestroom.

While Dani started packing an overnight bag, she filled Sam in with a synopsis of her discussion with Charles. "I got the same defense Darla did. He felt bad for Mom and that someone had to be there for her support. I told him that Darla was the one that needed his support, and once again, he let her down. He was annoyed that Darla could possibly believe that Mom would try to take CJ and that she was totally overreacting. I reminded him of all the shit she has put up with from our parents, as well as himself. All he could say was that he was trying to be there for both Mom and Darla. He said that sharing his conversations with both of them about each other, only added to the overall tension between them, and so he kept his correspondence with Mom to himself. He knew how I felt, so he decided to keep it from me, as well."

Sam kissed her. "I'm sorry about all this. You look exhausted. We can talk more about it after the wedding and everyone goes home."

Dani looked miserable and like she was wanting to cry. "Sam, I just want to enjoy our day without all this drama."

Sam reassured her as best as she could. "We will, and it will be beautiful. Get some sleep tonight. I'll miss you in bed."

Dani smiled. "You will have your *wife* in bed with you tomorrow night. I'm sorry I can't get away for a honeymoon. We will as soon as we can."

"I'm not concerned. It will be fun to plan and look forward to."

Chapter 13

The morning of the wedding, Sam was instructed to stay out of the garden. The kids had hung a sheet over the entrance from the patio door to the garden, so she wouldn't sneak a peek. She could hear voices in the backyard from her office, where she tried to work to keep busy and keep her mind off Dani's parents.

Julia had made breakfast and brought Sam coffee and a bagel. She sat down in the office easy chair and placed her coffee on the small side table. Sam didn't really mind, since, with all that was going on, she couldn't concentrate anyway.

"Are you excited for today, or is there something more going on, Sam?"

Sam took a sip of her coffee. She looked up at her sister, as she leaned back into her office chair. "I told you a little bit about my introduction to Dani's parents."

"You just told me it was very unpleasant and everyone was uncomfortable."

"Dani has since ceased contact with them, and Charles has been corresponding with his mother behind Dani's and Darla's back." She leaned forward for another sip of coffee. She turned to Julia with a concerned face. "They arrived last night and are at a hotel nearby."

"Oh my. So that was what the behind-closed-doors was all about last night?"

"I'm worried about Dani. It could get volatile if her mother even looks at her cross-eyed. To make it worse, Darla didn't go home last night and isn't speaking to Charles."

Julia's eyebrows rose. "Well, this could become rather interesting."

Sam sighed. "Add Connie and Addie's take-no-prisoner attitude; it can get ugly. At this point, I'm ready to pick up Dani and drive off to Las Vegas to elope."

"Oh Samantha, I'm so sorry. Does Dani know how you feel?"

"No. I'm trying to keep it light. Tensions are high enough. I don't want to make it worse for her."

Ed stood at the doorway. "I was in the living room and couldn't help but overhear. So, the shit hit the fan last night?"

Sam nodded.

"I'm so sorry, Sam. Knowing Dani, she's pretty worried about you right now. Mind if I text her and take her to breakfast?"

Sam looked relieved. "Ed, that would be great, if you don't mind."

"Of course." He took his phone from his pocket. They all went back into the living room, and her response came back before they could all sit down. Ed read it to himself and said, "If you give me Connie's address, I'll put it in the GPS."

The wedding was at two. Ed returned around twelve to report that he had allowed Dani the space to rant and rave, away from Darla, to eliminate the risk of upsetting her even more. He wasn't too sure how the customers in Starbucks had felt about it, but Dani got it off her chest, before he returned her to Connie's house. "Her mother sounds like a piece of work. Her brother is on her shit list and she, as I expected, is worried about you. I told her the same thing I'm going to tell you. This is your day, and let the chips fall with the rest of them. You will pick them up after we all go home." Ed kissed Sam's forehead. "It will all be okay if you two keep that attitude right now."

Julia and Addie fussed over Sam, getting her dressed. Sam brushed Julia's hand away from her face.

"Just a tad of eye shadow and mascara to bring out your eyes. Sam, it is not going to kill you," Julia said in frustration.

Surprisingly, Addie refrained from getting on the band wagon with her aunt, knowing how nervous her mother already was. Sam was grateful, and to keep from being more upset, she just gave in to her sister's insistence. Addie handed her a small bouquet that matched the flowers that had been placed in her spiked hair. The colors brightened her floor-length, light-blue dress. The dress perfectly brushed the floor when she walked, allowing the slightest view of Sam's shoe's, that matched the colorful, flowing scarf that belted her waist.

Julia opened a little jewelry box, with a warm smile. "You have to have something old." She removed a dainty silver bracelet. "It's mom's." She put it around Sam's wrist and kissed her cheek.

Addie, too, had prepared something. She handed her mother a pair of silver earrings. "And something new."

Sam swallowed the emotion that was building, but it had not gone unnoticed by her sister. "Don't cry. I just put on your eye makeup."

Sam held it together and said, "Thank you, both. I'm so lucky to have you guys in my life."

Dani had been hurriedly rushed into the guestroom, where Darla and Connie put on her finishing touches. Darla had put her hair in cornrows the night before. They now circled her head and were dotted with the same flowers that had been chosen for Sam's hair. Dani's choice for her dress was Sam's favorite color, which brought out her green eyes. It was a mint-green, full-length dress with a bodice that crossed and tapered down to her hips. She always wore heels when she was in public with Sam. They had been dyed to match the color of her dress. A silver, delicately laced heart nestled between her breasts. Matching earrings dangled against her slender neck.

People were arriving, and Clancy was with the kids, while Josh and Matt were escorting the guests to their seats. In front of the chairs was a chuppah, with intertwined flowers covering the structure. They had both agreed that they did not want a mixed religious ceremony. Josh had gone online and was certified to officiating at the wedding. He was asked to please keep it simple.

Sam was escorted out of the bedroom with Addie and Clancy by her side, and they walked her down the path that was created between the neatly placed folding chairs in the garden. They stood next to their mother. Sam told her daughters how beautiful the garden looked. She kept her eyes straight ahead but noticed, with a sideways peek, Dani's parents and a couple that Sam assumed was David and his girlfriend. Darla was not seated with them. She and Connie sat together on the opposite side of the pathway with Ed and Julia. The Ortega family was present, along with the new office manager, now Dani's newest friend.

Sam stood under the chuppah and watched as Dani appeared through the patio door and walked with Charles toward her. All the worry and tension dissipated, as Sam's heart fluttered at the sight of her. She saw that broad, sweeping smile on Dani's face, and she knew Dani was feeling the same way. They took each other's hand and stood side by side. Dani quietly said, just above the softly playing music, "You look absolutely stunning."

Sam rolled her eyes and whispered back, "Julia put this stupid shit on my eyes. You, you are amazingly sexy."

Dani suppressed a giggle at Sam's reference to the eye shadow and mascara.

Their locked gaze was interrupted by 'oohs' and 'aahs' throughout the gathering. Macy and CJ made their way down the path, holding hands and sprinkling flower pedals. Macy finally got to wear her frilly, pink dress and shiny, patent leather shoes that everyone had been hearing about for weeks. Her little face was beaming. CJ's adorable tux and little bow tie matched Garrett's, who followed with their wedding bands hooked to a velvet pillow. Darla led the children back to their chairs, returning with the rings and handing them to Charles.

The music stopped. Josh cleared his throat and began the ceremony. Because Sam was a very private person, they had written their own vows and chose to exchange them privately to each other. They had already been placed in a decorated lacquer box that sat on their bedroom dresser. They repeated and answered the traditional questions that Josh asked. Charles fumbled for a second, to retrieve the rings from his pocket. They placed the rings on each other's fingers and were pronounced wife and wife. It was over, and now the real stress was just beginning.

Their guests formed a reception line to congratulate them, one by one, and they were both acutely aware of where Dani's parents were in the line. They appeared in front of them, with David and his girlfriend beside them. Her parents remained silent, while David wrapped his arms around Dani and told her how happy he was for both of them. Sam shook his hand, as he introduced them both to his girlfriend, Nari. She was an attractive, Asian woman, slightly shorter than David. Her shiny, thick, black hair was tied behind her head in a large bun. Her head dipped ever so slightly, and with a voice, smooth and almost musical, in a British accent, she said, "Thank you for inviting me to share your special day. David has been looking forward to being here, almost as much as me."

Lottie's jaw was clenched.

Sam was enchanted by Nari's grace and beauty.

Dani took Nari's hand and patted it. "We are so glad you both were able to make it. I look forward to catching up."

Her parents didn't even attempt smiles and said nothing, as they followed David and Nari into the house, without speaking a word to the newlyweds.

After everyone had else congratulated them, they went inside to the fill their plates at the buffet and find seats in the garden and house. Dani was able to avoid her parents with all the interaction going on, but kept a close eye on their whereabouts in the room. They seemed to be sticking like glue to David.

Addie couldn't resist, her curiosity getting the best of her. She pulled Clancy with her to Dani's parents.

Clancy held her breathe and gave her sister a stern warning look. Addie purposely ignored it. "Hello, we are Sam's daughters. I'm Addie, and this is Clancy. Hope you are enjoying the food. Are you having a nice time?"

Lottie gave them both the once-over, from head to toe. A fake smile was plastered to her face. Walter just stared at the girls. Lottie's response was, "Yes. I take it that those children at the ceremony are yours?"

"Right. Macy is mine and Garrett is Clancy's." She smiled broadly. "CJ is all of ours. He fits in the family seamlessly. The three children adore each other."

Clancy held her breath, praying Addie wouldn't continue down this dangerous road. Lottie bristled and made no attempt to hide it. Addie had ruffled the woman's feathers sufficiently, and she was quite proud of herself. Clancy didn't intend for this to escalate any further and said, "Well, if you need anything at all, don't hesitate to ask. So nice to finally meet you." She pulled at her sister's arm, leading her to greet other guests.

Addie chuckled to herself.

Walter followed his wife into the kitchen where CJ was in his highchair, eating. Darla had changed Garett and CJ out of their tuxes and into play clothes. Macy, of course, had insisted on staying in her new dress. Connie and Darla sat at the counter, watching the children eat.

Lottie addressed her daughter-in-law in a forced pleasant voice, for show in Connie's presence. "He has grown so much since last we saw him. He looks like Charles." Darla glanced up at her and said nothing.

Connie held out her hand to Lottie. "I'm Connie."

Lottie shook it limply.

Next, she cautiously held out her hand to Walter, remembering Sam's description of her handshake with his introduction. He shook her hand. Connie was just as bad as Addie, and couldn't resist saying, "Well, you have a firm handshake, don't you?"

Her statement hit its mark. He knew exactly what she was referring to. His eyes bore holes into Connie's face, and he dropped her hand. Darla looked down to conceal her smirk. Connie continued to address them both. "How long will you be staying?" Her question was not particularly friendly.

Lottie straightened her shoulders and looked past Connie, to Darla, who had yet to utter a word. "We were hoping to spend some time with CJ."

Connie faked a sad face. "Oh, well that's too bad, Darla and I are taking him up to my cabin in the morning."

This was news to Darla, but she kept a poker face.

Lottie was now pissed. "We came all this way to spend some time with CJ."

Finally, Darla spoke, "Unannounced."

Lottie was not about to engage with her daughter-in-law. She turned and marched out of the kitchen to find Charles. Darla received a menacing look from

Walter, and then he followed his wife, like an overgrown bear cub.

Charles was talking to David and Nari, and Lottie interrupted them mid-sentence. "Charles, I need to speak to you."

Charles nodded at his mother and turned back to finish his and David's conversation.

Shy of stomping her foot, she barked, "Charles. Now!"

Nari's eyebrows jumped in surprise, and she looked at David, who suddenly had the need to clear his throat instead of attempting to complete his sentence for a second time. Charles submissively followed his parents out to the front porch. Dani had been talking to Marcus and watched her mother fuming, with Charles in tow. She excused herself and joined them on the porch.

Lottie had already started talking. "Darla is going to take CJ to some cabin in the morning! She didn't come home last night and is willfully keeping him from us. What is going on, Charles? Have you no control over your wife? I told you this move of yours was a very bad idea, from the beginning. We have come all this way to have time with him."

Charles looked confused about the cabin comment and before he could get that clarified, Dani spoke. "Charles said that you had come to apologize to Sam and me, in person."

Lottie's eyes got as big as saucers, and she glared at her son. "Apologize! I have nothing to apologize for."

Dani's head instantly turned toward Charles. She gave him a furious look and turned back to her mother. "Then why the hell did you suddenly arrive last night?"

"We will talk later, Dani. Right now, I want Charles to go inside and inform his wife that we will be spending tomorrow with Charles Junior."

Dani would no longer be put off. "Sam and I will be at your hotel this evening for an apology. If we do not get one, you will not see me again, any more than Darla wants you to see CJ." She turned and walked back in the house, leaving Charles to get out of his own webbed mess of lies.

Sam could see, through the window, that a heated discussion had taken place and that Dani was heading back into the house, angry. She knew the shit had finally hit the fan. She was going to let Dani calm down on her own, not wanting to make things worse. She was getting to know David and Nari, and she didn't follow her. She glanced, one more time, through the window to the porch and watched her in-laws climb into their rental car and leave. Charles was pacing on the porch.

Darla and Charles had not seen each other since last night. She had avoided her husband throughout the wedding. Tensions were high between them. Sam knew this would be the next volatile encounter.

David could see the concern on Sam's face. He had watched as her attention had been occasionally directed to the porch. "Wherever Lottie goes, fires tend to flare. Actually, I'm surprised they are here. My mother has kept me abreast of all that has gone on. It's been hard for my mother to be supportive to Lottie. She says Lottie continues to be obsessed with controlling her children's lives. In fact, that is one of the reasons my parents moved closer to me; they needed to be out of it all. Lottie does not want to hear my mother's opinion about you and Dani, or of Darla. Charles is a great guy, but he has always had issues with his mother, since we were kids. I'm afraid, from what I've seen today, that things have not changed with that situation. I feel badly for Darla." He hesitated, considering if he should continue and then decided to do so. "Sam, Lottie is desperate. She has lost her daughter, my parents, and she is having problems in her own marriage. She is not going to stop at any cost, to keep her son in line."

Sam listened intently. "David, thank you for trusting me with this information. Since you have, may I ask you if you think she has an agenda in mind?"

David smiled. "She never does anything without an agenda. I may be way off base, but I think the only thing she has to control Charles with is his son, and Charles is weak when it comes to his mother's agendas."

Sam was beginning to fear that Darla was not overreacting, and that Lottie may be trying to take CJ from her.

The Ortega's came over to Sam, with Dani, to say their goodbyes. She and Dani saw them to the door. Sam could see that Dani was still upset and needed to talk. Sam was relieved that the family could relax, now that

Dani's parents had left, but she was concerned about what David had shared with her. "Honey, where is Charles?"

Dani had a disgusted look on her face. "Darla refused to leave with him, and he stormed out of the house."

The news actually made Sam calm down a little more.

"He lied again, Sam. They did not come to apologize to us."

"Why did they come?"

"I didn't get an answer to that. My mother was furious, because Darla and Connie are taking CJ to her cabin in the morning, and she wanted the day with him."

"Did Charles know about this?"

"Apparently, Darla didn't know either, until Connie squashed my parents plans, right in their faces. I told them we will come to the hotel tonight for an apology and explanation as to why they came at all, or they will not see me again."

Sam was becoming more exhausted by the minute. "I told you we should have eloped."

Dani was determined. "I deserve an explanation. No more lies from Charles and surprises from my parents."

Finally, the wedding part of the day was over, and only Julia and Ed remained. The four of them sat in the living room, talking about the wedding and all the events of the day.

Ed put his stockinged feet on the coffee table. "Are you sure you two need to go over to the hotel tonight? Maybe you've had enough stress for one day."

Dani stated, forcefully, "We are meeting Charles there at eight. I want them to apologize to Sam, and I want the truth from all three of them."

Sam couldn't have cared less if she ever got an apology from them but did want to hear their explanation for their appearance. She hoped she was wrong about CJ being the real event and that Charles wasn't being used by his mother to that end.

Chapter 14

Dani and Sam waited in the hotel lobby for Charles. He arrived, looking very nervous, with good reason. The three of them went upstairs and knocked on the Tyler's hotel room door. Walter answered, avoiding Sam's eyes and waved them in. Lottie was sitting at the small room desk, like the chairwoman of the board. Dani and Sam sat down on the bed, and Charles and his father in the two side chairs. Sam, wanting to keep this as civil as possible, gently nudged Dani and glanced down at her defiantly, crossed arms against her chest. Dani put her hands in her lap and waited for her mother to speak.

Lottie looked up and directed her comment to Sam. "This is all very unpleasant, and since this is really between Dani and us, you need not be here."

The hair on Dani's neck raised like the hackled feathers of a bird. "She is the reason why we are here! You came to our wedding after your horrendous behavior toward her in your home. Why are you here unannounced?"

Lottie slapped the desk with her open hand. "That is the second time today I have heard the word 'unannounced.' I am your mother and do not need announcement of my presence."

Dani refused to back down. "Okay, let's try this again. Why did you feel your presence was needed at my wedding?"

Lotte looked at her husband for support. He spoke. "Your mother and I are separating. It was an opportunity for us to see our children and grandson all together, since you and Charles refused to come to us. We wanted to tell you in person."

Lottie added, "And once again, Charles's wife had to ruin our last time together by running off with CJ. We came all this way, and she refuses to change her plans so that we can have him for a few hours."

Dani waited for her brother to respond, and when he didn't, she turned to him and said, "And... why do you think that is, Charles? Could it possibly be because you have been lying to Darla, as well as to me?" She really didn't want to hear his lame excuse again, so she let her statement remain rhetorical. Instead, she addressed her parents. "I'm sorry to hear you are separating. Our family is small, and it would be lovely if attitudes could change, so we could act like a family. Without an apology to my wife, as far as I'm concerned, that isn't going to happen."

Lottie was visibly offended by the word 'wife', as she rolled her eyes. Sam just bit her tongue, not wanting to escalate the situation. She started to stand.

Dani pulled her back down onto the bed. "Mother, what is your decision?"

It was Lottie's turn to cross her arms across her chest. "It is very apparent, my dear daughter, that you already made that decision to break up this family today, at your so-called wedding."

All Sam could do was shake her head and grab Dani's arm to hold her back from getting into her mother's face. It was clear to her that Charles and CJ were Lottie's last, desperate hope at controlling what was left of her family.

The final confirmation came, just as Sam and Dani reached for the doorknob. "By the way, this ridiculous marriage you chose, does not change the fact that you are not going to be named CJ's guardian, under any circumstances."

Charles was visibly embarrassed. "Mom, I said I would revisit that." He couldn't look at Dani.

Dani stared at him, slightly trembling. "One more thing you haven't yet shared with your wife or me?"

He finally looked up at his sister, pleadingly, "Dani, Sam, I swear this has nothing to do with your marriage. I promised nothing."

Dani opened the door and they exited. Sam turned to Dani in the downstairs lobby and said, "I think Darla is in for the fight of her life. I don't want to alarm you, but I would not be surprised if she is trying to convince Charles to move back to Atlanta with CJ. Charles is the only one working. Money is control and power, and Darla has none. Your mother knows that."

Dani nodded. "I think we need to go talk to Darla. She is the only one left in the dark, and it's not fair."

"God, Dani. I really hate interfering in their marriage. I don't want to start crossing that line by taking sides in their marriage."

Dani had already done so. "I know, but the cards are stacked against her. Charles has no backbone, and Darla has to be prepared."

Reluctantly, Sam nodded. They drove to Connie's house. On the way, Sam texted her sister to let them know they were okay and would be getting home late. Connie peeked through her front door blinds and let them in. "What's up?"

Sam asked, "Are you guys really going to the cabin tomorrow?"

Connie shook her head. "No, but they don't need to know that."

They found Darla seated on Connie's couch. Before Dani started to tell them what had happened at the hotel, Sam asked, "Darla, if I may ask, after Dani's parents left the wedding, what did Charles say to you?"

"He was furious with me that I hadn't told him I was taking CJ and going with Connie to her cabin. I wasn't about to tell him that I was taken off guard as well, by Connie saying that." She turned to Connie and smiled. "She came to the rescue." She continued telling them what had happened next. "I told Charles he had a lot of nerve admonishing me about keeping secrets from him. I said he had been doing that to me for months; it all came firing back in his face with his parents showing up last night."

Dani was thinking how to approach the subject of CJ, without frightening her. "I need to ask you a question, too."

Darla nodded for her to go ahead.

Dani, as gently as possible, asked, "Were you aware that Charles was rethinking the choice of me being CJ's guardian if needed?"

She was instantly shocked and shouted, "No! He told you that?"

Connie took Darla's arm. "Shh. You'll wake CJ."

Dani shook her head sadly. "We found out this evening from my mother. We had another encounter with my parents at their hotel room. Charles was there and was very embarrassed that she threw that into our faces, when she refused to apologize to Sam. He lied to us with his text last night. Mom had no intention of apologizing to us for anything she did."

Darla stood up and began to pace, with a clenched fist.

Sam watched Connie fume and try to stifle her outrage. She just couldn't do it. "What the fuck! Darla is right; that woman is trying to break up her family."

Darla made the final connection, with the news about the guardianship. She instantly stopped pacing. "How can he be so stupid? She is planning something, and it's all about my son. I am not being paranoid, after all."

Sam reached her hand out, and Darla took it and sat down on the couch with them. "Unfortunately, I'm afraid you might be right, but this time, the stakes are higher. She's desperate and afraid of being alone. Has Charles said anything to you about wanting to move back to Atlanta?"

She shook her head vigorously. "No. Do you think that is what she's up to? He is not going to take my son with him!"

Dani was done weighing her comments. "I think you need to get a job, Darla. Without money, he could get custody." She heard how strong her statement had sounded and softened it the best she could by adding, "I'm sorry to be so alarming, but I'm trying to figure out her next move."

Sam knew that Dani meant well and tried to calm down everyone's emotions. "I know all of this is overwhelming right now. I think the best place to start, is for you and Charles to bury the hatchet and start talking to each other. Not through us, but with each other."

Darla closed her eyes for a moment to regain some control of her fears. When she opened them again, she said, "I will talk to him when I know they are on a plane for Atlanta, without CJ. If Charles chooses to go with them, then I will deal with that separately."

Finally, all their out-of-town guests had left for home. Dani had taken two days off after the wedding, and she and Sam decided to check into a hotel, to be away from all the drama and questions about CJ, Charles and Darla, from concerned family.

They were finally alone and turned to each other in bed, after a long-awaited romantic night and morning. Sam laid on her side, reached across the pillow and brushed Dani's hair from her face. "Can we stay like this for at least another week? Just us having sex, peace and quiet and then more sex?"

Dani pulled her face to her, and they lingered over a deep kiss. "Ahh. Wouldn't that be heaven? We do get one more day, though. We can just get room service and stay in bed."

Dani's phone beeped. She looked at Sam apologetically. "It could be the hospital." She frowned. Sam slipped her hand between Dani's thighs, as Dani rolled on her side and reached for her phone on the nightstand. Dani giggled, while Sam kissed her between her shoulders and moved her fingers higher up between her legs. Dani glanced at the text. "It's Charles. He said he's sorry to bother us, but could I call him, please."

Sam removed her hand and rolled on her back, frustrated. Dani kept the phone in her hand. "I'm sorry, honey. I don't think he would call us if it wasn't important."

Sam nodded her head.

Dani called him, and Sam got into the shower. A few minutes later, Dani joined her. "Darla isn't answering his texts. I told him she wouldn't, until he told her our parents left." Dani soaped up her hands and slid them over Sam's breasts. "Now, where were we?"

Sam instantly responded with a smile and replaced her hands between Dani's legs. "I believe I was here. At least I know you can't hear the phone from the bathroom. Maybe we should just stay here in the shower."

Dani laughed. "I am quite aware that you write about sex all day for your job, but I believe you think about sex every minute of the day."

Sam looked at her with a mocked, thoughtful face and said, "That's not true. Every other minute and any spare time left over, I think about food."

Dani slapped Sam's butt. "That's just to keep your energy up for more sex."

Chapter 15

Charles and Dani's parents had left, and Darla returned home. Darla asked him outright if he was thinking of returning to Atlanta and informed him emphatically that, if he was, he was not taking CJ with him. She was assured that he would not do that. His promise lead them into her next concern. How was she ever going to trust him again? He had lied and kept things from her. She didn't want apologies, she wanted changes. She demanded those changes, starting immediately. He promised that he would not keep things from her again and assured her that she and CJ would always come first.

Darla was not yet satisfied. "Charles, I will not stop you from being in contact with your parents, if that's what you want. But I will not allow them to ever be with CJ alone; I must be present. I frankly don't care if you think I am overreacting or not. Your mother may have you wrapped around her finger, but I will not be. I'm finished keeping my mouth shut in their presence. So, if you think tensions are high now, don't plan any family get-togethers with them in Atlanta; our son and I will not be going back there. If you want them to visit with him, it will be here, and I will be present the whole time."

He looked a little uncertain, and she read his mind. "If you can't tell them that those are the conditions, I will pick up the phone and tell them right this minute."

Charles had never seen Darla so determined, nor did he believe that she would speak to his parents like that, since she rarely spoke to them at all, even under their attack. He was not yet strong enough to tell his mother that there would be conditions for seeing her grandson. He would have to text it, because he was no match in a conversation with his mother's wrath.

"Darla, I promised I would not keep anything from you again, and I won't, starting now. When I said goodbye to Mom, she said she was expecting a visit from CJ and me in the very near future."

Darla waited for him to continue.

He stared at her.

She continued. "And you said... what?"

He just looked at her sheepishly and finally he said, "I said I would have to look at my schedule."

Darla picked up his cell phone from the table. Charles was sure she wouldn't go through with it.

She pulled up his contacts and punched in his mother's number. He held his breath, sure that she would hang up.

Darla was done playing games with him.

He could hear his mother's voice. "Hi, dear."

"This is Darla. Charles and I have come to an agreement, that if you wish to visit with CJ, it will be here in Tucson only, and I will be present throughout your visit."

First, the momentary silence was shock, and then Lottie's voice could be heard across the room. "How dare you! Don't you ever tell me when and how I will see my grandson. I will see him on my terms, when I want to see him! Have I made myself perfectly clear?"

Darla face was calm and serene. "Lottie, you can stand on your head and spit nickels, but he is my son and those are the conditions. I am done with your demands, and I am done with your disrespect. I kept my thoughts to myself and remained silent and was dismissed by you and Walter, since Charles and I married. That was my fault, but I felt it made things easier for Charles that way. The game has changed, since CJ is my first priority. If you choose to see Charles Junior again, it will be within my conditions, and if you ever disrespect me in front of my son, then my offer will be terminated immediately."

Lottie's voice trembled with anger. "Put Charles on the phone, this instant!" was shouted out across the room.

Darla punched the speaker option on her husband's phone, and said, "You are on speaker — go ahead."

Lottie was so angry, her words were spoken through clenched jaws. "Get off the phone this second, and give me my son."

Darla moved closer to Charles and said, "Your mother wishes to speak to you. Since we are no longer keeping secrets, I'm sure you don't mind if I hold the phone for us."

His bluff had been more than called, and her challenge to him was here and now. It had been the first time that he heard that her past silence had been to make things easier for him. He felt ashamed. He suddenly *felt* Dani's words, rather than just *heard* them. He needed to respect his wife, but how could he, when he couldn't even respect himself? "Mother, I'm here."

"What in God's name is going on? Did you hear what she said to me? Have you lost all control over that woman? Are you not the head of your family? Charles, I'm so disappointed with you."

He felt intimidated and very uncomfortable, whenever his mother was disappointed with him. He was paralyzed into silence.

She was so desperate, that her next tactic was to cry. "Your father left yesterday. He packed up and moved in with that whore. I'm alone, Charles, I'm all alone, now. Come home and stay with me, until I feel stronger to handle all this stress. I can't get through this on my own."

His mother and wife both waited for his decision. Finally, he spoke. "I can't do that, Mom. Darla and I have some issues of our own to work out. You will be fine. I'll touch base with you next week." He reached for the phone and ended the call. He was visible shaken, and Darla ached for him, but was not sorry for her actions.

He remained standing, and she took his hand and lead them both to the couch. She squeezed his hand. "I know this is difficult for you." She spoke softly and caringly. "Honey, you are overwhelmed right now. It's been months that you have been under this stress with your mother, as well as with Dani's and my disapproval. You have to take a deep breath and let it go. We have got to heal and then start working together on our marriage and family. I think perhaps it's time to get some counseling."

He patted her hand, leaned over and kissed her cheek. "I'm so sorry I disappointed you." His biggest sin and fear was unveiled to her. "I want to be a good husband and father."

"Darling, you are. You are amazing with CJ. You just have to stand up to your mother. I know that's so scary for you, but that is what you have to do, not only for CJ and me, but most importantly, for yourself. You are a wonderful man, and she has to understand she is not allowed to treat you in her controlling way. I can't find that strength for you, but if we are to survive her, then you have to find it for yourself."

It was barely a week and a half later, when Charles was, once again, tested by his mother. He finished with her call and began to pace. *Jesus, what am I going to do?* Dani was still angry with him; he wasn't near ready to break the news to Darla. *I can't handle this any more.*

He sat down in his office chair and buried his face in his hands. He hadn't been able to sleep, eat or concentrate on work since Darla had given his mother her visitation ultimatum, concerning CJ. The pressure and rage from his mother had been relentless since that call. Now this. He just wanted to disappear; run and hide from everyone. Darla had mentioned counseling, but he couldn't imagine talking to a stranger about his weaknesses and fears. He had trouble enough talking to Darla about his shame.

He stared at his phone, and his finger scrolled down to Sam in his contacts. He hesitated, and realized he had just punched her number as her phone rang and he heard, "Hello."

He was about to disconnect, when she said, again, "Hello. Charles, are you there, or did you just butt call me?"

He swallowed to moisten his dry throat. "No. I was... hey, what are you doing?"

Sam heard the uncertainty in his voice. "I'm in the office, working. I could use a break. What's up?"

He attempted an even voice. "We haven't played golf in a while." He let the statement hang there.

Something wasn't right. Sam was now reassessing the purpose of his call. "I was going to put up a pot of coffee; interested?"

He sighed into the phone. "Yeah, I'll be right over." He hung up.

Sam sat a few minutes before going into the kitchen. *This has to be a new Lottie development.* Darla had shared with Connie her conversation with her mother-in-law, and of course, Connie had updated her and Dani. It had become the old game of telephone, and she was no longer sure of how those messages had been altered in the retelling.

When Charles entered the kitchen, she handed him a fresh mug of coffee. They sat down together at the kitchen table. He poured half and half and three heaping teaspoons of sugar into his coffee. Sam tried to lighten his mood by saying, "You and your sister should be diabetic; she drinks it that way, too, when she is stressed." She quickly became direct. "You look like shit. You've lost weight and have rings under your eyes. I'm guessing you are stressed about something."

He nodded. "Yeah. It's my mother." He wrapped his large hands around the mug and leaned back into his chair. "I don't know if you are aware that my father has filed for divorce and moved in with the woman he has been seeing for over a year. My mother is a mess. It seems that everyone at the country club, and his office staff, have known for some time that he was having this affair. Mom is humiliated and angry and has stopped talking to everyone. Since David's parents left, they have distanced themselves and pushed Mom out of their lives. She feels totally alone."

Sam had already known about both situations and said, "I'm sorry she is going through this." She patted his shoulder. "Charles, I hope things work out for her. I'm sure this has been very stressful for you, being in the middle of the drama between your mother and Darla."

He rolled his eyes. "You have no idea. It's escalading. I'm at my breaking point, Sam, I mean, I'm really there now. She has been pressuring me to come home and help her through this. Last week, I told her that it isn't possible right now. She called this morning to tell me that she will put the house up for sale and move here to Tucson. She said that if I don't come to her, she has no choice but to come to me."

Sam was shocked that she actually threatened to do that, and it instantly registered on her face.

He read her right away and said, "Right? What am I going to do now? When she gets something in her mind, she's like a locomotive at top speed, and she can't be stopped. I have to tell Darla. Sam, Darla is going to say it's my inability to stand up to her, and she's right. Darla is going to leave me." He instantly wilted from letting out his fear and looked like he might cry.

Sam said, as comfortingly as she could, "Okay. Try and calm down. We'll talk this through. Do you remember what we talked about at the golf course, about roles we peg ourselves into?"

He looked at her, confused as to where she was going with this. Uncertainly, he nodded.

Sam continued. "Take yourself out of the son and husband role for just a minute. Let those feelings be replaced with not taking sides or accepting responsibility for Darla or your mother. Because your burden is too much, you can make them responsible, without putting you in the middle. They have to deal with each other directly. Can you tell Darla what is happening and inform her and your mother that the pressure is too much for you, and it is now their problem to work out?"

Charles blinked rapidly, letting the idea sink into his head.

Sam continued. "I know that sounds simple, but it won't be. You also have to tell yourself that you are not a failure and a disappointment to your mother. She has programmed that into you your whole life. That is how she controls you. Each time issues and drama between your mom and Darla come up, to make this work, you have to step away and remind them both, that it is their responsibility now."

He was nodding, but still doubting himself. "Dani has made it very clear that I need to step up and support Darla. In my heart, I know I should, but…" He let his thought dangle in midair.

"Charles, since you have moved here, I'm sure you have seen Darla's empowering confidence and determination. She has made a conscience decision to no longer be disrespected by your mother. Now that CJ is in your lives, this issue becomes even more important to her. Trust me, she can more than hold her own against your mother. She is not the same woman that remained silent in Atlanta. She has become a grizzly when it comes to her cub, Charles Junior. Survivor skills and amazing strength come with motherhood." She chuckled. "Even the ability to stop locomotives."

His mind immediately returned to Darla's last conversation with his mother. His shoulders finally relaxed, with all that had been said. "Maybe, maybe this can work. I'm going to ask you a favor. Please be the one to tell Dani my mother's plans. I don't think I can handle one more crisis today."

"I will do that." She patted his hand. "Charles, removing yourself from being the go-between for your mother and Darla, is just a Band-Aid to release some of your stress and the pressure for now. It is not a long-term solution. You might want to get some counseling. There is no shame in that. It can be a first step in understanding how to make a lasting solution."

Charles couldn't add that thought to his already paralyzing stress. He replied, "I will think about it."

Dani got home, and when Sam told her the news Charles had shared with her, Dani went off like fireworks. Dani reached for her phone, and Sam retrieved it first. "You need to listen to the whole conversation we had, before you call him in anger."

Dani looked enraged. "I was going to call my mother!"

Sam frowned and looked at her over her reading glasses. "I know you wouldn't do that. It's between your brother and your mother. Honey, I don't want to alarm you, but I'm really worried about his mental state right now." Sam told her all the details of his fears and described how he looked physically.

Dani listened. She ached for her brother, but she was still angry. "Why can't he stand up to that woman and put her in her place? He infuriates me!"

"Because he is not you, Dani," Sam reminded her. "Your mother has told him, all his life, that he is a disappointment and a failure and needs to man up. He continues to seek approval from her. He doesn't have your strength, and you should understand that more lectures and stress from you isn't going to help him right now. Shit, you are the analytical one here. That seems pretty black and white to me."

Dani could see her genuine concern and backed down. "You really are worried about him, aren't you?"

Dani's rhetorical question didn't need conformation. Sam just nodded.

Darla did not take the news about her mother-in-law's threat to move to Tucson, well. Charles was able to calm her down after the initial burst of anger, by telling her that he was no longer playing the middleman. She and his mother were now going to have to deal with each other and not through him. Darla expressed that she was skeptical that that strategy would last long. She reminded him of how his mother could easily get under his skin and have him do her bidding, when he felt pressure from her. She held up two fingers and stated, "If she goes through with selling her house, I'm going to tell you two things that will happen." Her second finger went down. "One. I will not hold back how I feel when she interferes or treats me disrespectfully. When she comes at you with her complaints about me, I trust you will keep your word and remind her it's between me and her." Her second finger reappeared. "And two, if you or she go behind my back, I will take CJ and leave. Have I made myself perfectly clear?"

Charles was shaken by her second statement. "You would actually leave me?"

"In a New York second. You obviously refuse to see how high the stakes are here. These are my rules, now. Charles, when we discussed how we want to raise CJ, we agreed that he would have rules, not as a cage, but as a structure. I am giving you and your mother the structure to move forward, if she is sincere and deals with me and no longer puts demands on you. I am done if she doesn't back off me, with or without your support. This is not a threat, it's how this is going to play out if you can't do what you are telling me." She turned to leave the room. She stopped and turned around, again, to face him. "Charles, if she is really thinking of moving here, she is not staying with us. She can stay in a hotel, until she finds a place to live." She watched him swallow down what she surmised was a rising plea on his mother's behalf. Only after he remained silent, did she go into the kitchen to make dinner.

Chapter 16

He texted his mother the new ground rules about dealing directly with Darla and not through him. It was answered swiftly, with a profound, 'Just who runs your house, Charles?'

He texted back that he wanted to give her fair warning before she made her final decision to move to Tucson and added that he was the one who set the new rules. He wanted everything out in the open before she arrived. He added that if she still wanted to move here, to let him know when the time came closer and he would find her a place to stay, until she found a home. Texting his mother was so much less stressful than talking on the phone or face-to-face. His heart sank, when his phone instantly rang. He had hoped she would mull over his text and maybe, just maybe, decide to change her mind about selling her house. He had barely answered, when his ear was assaulted with, "Has that woman totally pussy whipped you? You tell her, *I will* be staying at my son's house as long as it takes to find a place to live."

Charles head was pounding, and his mouth had gone dry. How did he ever think he could do this? "Mom, this has to be the way things will be, if we are to make this new change work." He knew he had to come across strongly. He found his father's authoritative voice, that ended conversations when his dad had finally had it. "I will not be stressed by both you and Darla's hostilities. Enough is enough! Would you prefer to go back to the way things were when we were not speaking? If not, then this is how it will be." He wasn't sure why his mother didn't shoot back a threatening response. She backed down as she did with his father's anger, and for now, that was all he needed.

They continued to communicate weekly, and a few months went by before he got the dreaded news. She had called his bluff. Her house had sold and her relocation was looming a little too closely now, for his comfort. He let Darla know and told her he would update her with information as he learned it. That was the only information they had exchanged about his mother since their discussion about rules. He kept Sam abreast, and she was there for support and to remind him of his capabilities to handle the situation. Since Dani's discussion with Sam, she had stopped lecturing and giving advice to her brother, and she tried to be more supportive as well.

Charles picked his mother up at the airport and helped her settle into the hotel he had arranged for her. Darla was genuine in showing Charles that she would give Lottie a chance. She had prepared dinner, and Charles brought his mother to the house. The meeting began awkwardly but remained civil. Not really knowing CJ since he was an infant, he cried when Lottie picked him up at the front door, pulling away and reaching for his mother. Darla stepped back and did not take him from Lottie's arms. She explained. "It will take a little time for him to get to know and trust you."

Charles wondered if his wife's statement was also made about herself. CJ continued to wiggle, and Lottie put him down, and he wandered off to play with his toy truck.

During dinner, Lottie said that she had taken only two suitcases and a carry-on; everything else had been sent ahead and put into a Tucson storage unit.

Darla handed her mother-in-law the bowl of mashed potatoes and asked, "Will you be looking for an apartment or house?"

It was difficult for Lottie to have to acknowledge Darla's presence, but now she was forced into engaging in conversation with her. She decided not to be short with Darla in Charles's presence and simply replied, "I don't know, yet. I have to first see what options there are here."

Darla had seriously listened to Dani and Sam about the importance of being financially independent, in case she ever needed to fight for CJ against Lottie in a courtroom. She casually said, "I am studying for my realtor license, and I have become pretty familiar with what is available here. If I can help, let me know."

That information came as a total surprise to Charles. He kept a poker face, realizing that Darla was setting a new set of rules herself. She was just as capable of announcing, not discussing, her demands, as he was.

"Darla continued. "Once I get my license, it will give me much more flexibility, choosing my work hours. Once CJ is in school, I might go back into the medical field. We'll see."

Lottie really didn't care about Darla and her plans, and dismissing her daughter-in-law, she turned to her son with a more important inquiry. "How is it going with your company, Charles?"

Charles swallowed a mouthful of his roast chicken. "Fine. Being able to work remotely made the move much easier. I like being home more and having time with Darla and CJ." It seemed that he and his wife were now sending each other messages across the table.

Lottie couldn't help herself and lapsed into her true, meddlesome ways. "In my day, mothers stayed home and raised their children. If more of that was being done, it would solve a lot of problems in our society." Satisfied with her vocal slap to Darla's face, she tapped her napkin at the corner of her mouth.

Darla realized she should not start off on the wrong foot and needed to choose her battles wisely, however, she wanted to reinforce her determination to keep her mother-in-law on track with the new terms of their relationship. Charles had not responded to his mother's comment, so Darla said, calmly, "Society and economics have changed dramatically, and there are many more women raising children on their own, now.

A lot of other changes have taken place in society since your day."

Charles was now convinced Darla would indeed leave with CJ, if he couldn't control the situation with his mother.

Lottie huffed and said, "Many changes for the worse, unfortunately; that *is* something we can agree on. Like gay marriages, for example."

Charles wanted to stop what he saw turning ugly. With a diversional tactic, he quickly changed the subject. "Mom, have you settled all the legal issues with father? Have you been in contact with him at all? He has not reached out to me, and as far as I know, not to Dani either."

Lottie shook her head, wearily. "All I can tell you is, this divorce is a nightmare. Your father is the one that cheated, and yet, he is making my life miserable every step of the way through this divorce process. I'm not surprised you haven't heard from him. He is too busy screwing his half-his-age whore to think about his children." She turned, momentarily glared at Darla and sarcastically said, "Our present society's morals now consider that to be the norm as well, it seems. Marriages being destroyed by older spouses preying on the young. Now we have two examples of that in this family."

Darla refused to be baited in defending Dani and Sam's marriage. She stood and said, "I will check on CJ. It's much too quiet in his room. I better see what he's gotten into. Then I will get us coffee, and we can have our dessert, before Charles takes you back to your hotel."

Once again, Charles received his wife's message; it was time for his mother to leave. Darla couldn't get out of the room fast enough.

A few weeks passed with similar tension, when Lottie was at their house. Charles tried to keep his mother away from Darla as much as possible. So far, she and his wife did not share with him their interactions with each other. He was waiting for that second shoe to drop at any time. The stress was building again, and he wished that his mother would stop calling him two or three times a day, just to pick something up for her or to talk non-stop about the monster his father had become.

Charles had spent the morning grocery shopping with his mother and had taken her to lunch. He was returning her to the hotel after hearing yet another tirade about Walter. "I have meetings in the morning, so I will pick you up around noon tomorrow, to see about you leasing a car. Mother, I think it's time. It will give you more freedom to get around on your own. Have you thought about the type of car you would like?"

She sighed, to display her stressful predicament. She said, "I never had to do these things before. Your father always took care of major purchases. Thank God I have you, Charles, to help me get through all this. You know, they see a single woman walk in, and they will take advantage of me by selling me an overpriced car."

"Well, Mom, I won't let that happen."

She patted his leg. "Thank you, son." She hesitated briefly and then said, "There is something else I will need your help with, Charles." Her voice became singsong and needy. "Charles, dear, your sister knows I'm here now and has yet to call me. I've moved here to be close to the only family I have left now. Could you please speak to her on my behalf?"

Charles was already exhausted by the morning, turning into afternoon, with her and just wanted to go home and shut down his brain. "Mom, even at her wedding, you never apologized to her for the disastrous meeting with Sam in Atlanta. I can't do that for you."

Lottie's staged needy voice disappeared instantly. "Well, for god's sake, that was over two years ago! She needs to get over it. You did."

"I have to tell you, it took me a very long time to forgive you and Dad's behavior that night. Sam is a wonderful person, and Dani loves her very much. She will never forgive you without your apology to both of them."

Lottie was frustrated and fumed silently at his response. The quiet that followed was welcomed by him, and remained so, as he drove up to the hotel. He leaned over and kissed her cheek. "I will see you tomorrow, then."

Lottie's car purchase gave her less reason to ask Charles to run errands with her, cutting down the time she could spend with him. She had no intention of spending any time with Darla, and she was getting bored with exploring Tucson. It was early May and already getting too hot for her to be out much. She spent most of her days sitting at the pool, reading. She had driven by Dani's house a few times in the evening but couldn't muster up the courage to knock at the door. She had always been easily intimidated by her daughter's strong personality. She had even considered showing up at her office, lessening the chance of Dani's crusty rejection of her in a public setting.

She had never spoken directly to Sam, but she decided to take her chances with her instead. It was midday, and Sam was working in her office when the doorbell rang. She peeked through the glass section framing the double doors. She was a little taken aback to see Lottie standing on the porch alone. She opened the door and instead of saying hello, she said, "Dani is still at the hospital."

Lottie cleared her throat and announced, "Actually, I came to speak to you. May I come in?"

Sam stepped aside to allow Lottie to enter. "I am working in the office. Make yourself comfortable, and I'll be right back. I need to shut down my laptop."

When she returned, she found Lottie standing in front of the sliding door, looking out to the garden. Sam took a seat in the living room and waited.

Lottie turned, looked at her and took a seat, with a placid demeanor. "Something is cooking; it smells delicious."

Sam's voice was nonchalant as well. "Thank you." She was not going to make small talk or exchange recipes with her. She was not about to prompt her to explain why she had come to the house. She waited patiently.

Lottie nervously straightened the collar on her blouse. Not sure of how to continue, she said, without feeling or genuine convincing, "You have a lovely home."

Sam was good at the waiting game. Once again, she only offered, "Thank you."

It was clear to Lottie that Sam wasn't going to start the conversation. "Well, I was hoping you could help me. I've moved to Tucson to be closer to my children, now that Walter and I are divorcing. Dani knows I'm in town and, as of yet, she has not contacted me. I was wondering if you could encourage her to do so?"

Sam was amused but stifled a grin. "I see. Mrs Tyler, Dani and I have a marriage in which we respect each other's choices in whom we wish to communicate with. If Dani has not contacted you, the only thing I can suggest is that you reach out to her."

Lottie fought to remain calm and tried again. "Being a mother yourself, you know how independent and stubborn children can be."

Sam was no longer amused. "I am not Dani's mother. I'm her wife."

Lottie flinched slightly at the word 'wife' and cleared her dry mouth. "I wonder if I can trouble you for some water?"

"Of course."

Lottie followed her into the kitchen and sat down at the kitchen table. Sam realized Lottie was in no hurry to leave. She was curious what she would try next. "Would you prefer ice tea? I have some in the refrigerator."

She forced a smile. "That would be very nice, thank you."

Sam poured them both a glass and placed fresh cookies she had made that morning on a plate, with napkins. Lottie looked a little startled as they both heard the garage door open.

A few seconds later, Dani's voice was heard. "Stuffed cabbage! Dinner smells heavenly, you made my favorite." She appeared and stared at her mother munching on a cookie. "Well, isn't this cozy." She kissed Sam and said, "I got away early." She reached for a cookie and sat down with them. As usual, Dani came right to the point. "Please tell me that the reason you are here is to apologize to Sam, or I'm afraid I'll have to ask you to leave."

Lottie's reaction was instant; her shoulders went back, and she barked, "Daniella! I am your mother; show some respect."

Dani glared at her mother. "Respect? You have some nerve. If you want respect, then you need to show my wife some respect." She turned to Sam and asked, "Did she, or did she not apologize to you?"

Sam looked at Dani's face and could see her anger was building. She rolled her eyes. Pleadingly, she said, "Could you both please calm down?"

Lottie spoke next. "I just arrived a few minutes ago. I haven't had a chance to discuss that night."

Dani laughed. "Mom, in my entire life, I have never, ever heard you apologize for anything you have done. So I am so glad I came home early and have this opportunity to witness a first."

Lottie's jaw was set, and she said nothing as she stared angrily at her daughter.

Dani shook her head in disgust. "Obviously, you cannot teach an old dog new tricks."

The front door opened and this time, Connie's voice was heard. "God, it smells like Jewish soul food. Am I right? What's cooking?" She walked into the kitchen and stopped short when she saw the three of them together at the table. Her head wobbled back and forth, slightly. "Oh my, indeed, what *is* cooking here?"

Sam smiled and said, "Dani was about to give a dissertation on the inability to teach senior canines new tricks."

Connie continued into the kitchen and kissed Dani on the forehead. "Well done, sweetheart, you just insulted three of the four women in this room."

A broad smile crossed Lottie's face at Connie's humor.

Connie pulled back in surprise. "So that's where Dani gets her sexy smile."

Dani pushed a plate into Connie's gut and placed one in front of her mother. Still angry, she said, "You needn't panic, Mom, Constance is not coming on to you; she's straight." She turned to gather the silverware.

"Connie smirked. "I don't know, my dear. If my friend of over forty years makes love the way she can cook, I could be persuaded to reconsider switching.

Dani was always amused by her humor. She raised one sexy eyebrow and cooed at Connie. "Wouldn't you just love to know. You have no idea, woman."

Sam was relieved that Connie was able to cut the hostility and continued the banter. "Well, do the two of you need cold showers first, or can we eat?"

Lottie's face did not show that she had been shocked or offended, but she was more startled that her daughter was placing a setting for her at the table.

While Sam and Dani plated the food for their dinner, Connie asked Lottie, "So, have you found a place to live, yet? Living in that hotel has to be getting old."

Lottie hadn't realized how much everyone knew about her activities, since she had arrived. "I'm working with a gentleman from Long Realtors. His name is Greg Norton."

Connie snorted. "He's no gentleman. He's a sleazebag." Having made her opinion known, she continued. "I don't know if you have considered a retirement community. There are some really nice ones, and you can make friends easily. Also, there are nice townhouses with little or no yard maintenance. You wouldn't have to bother Charles so much."

Lottie was now annoyed. "Has my son expressed to you that I have been a bother to him?"

Connie shook her head, unconcerned by Lottie's accusing voice. "No. He said he and Sam were playing golf on Saturday. Darla is practicing showing a few of my listings to clients. He would need to check on you and wondered if I could watch CJ until Darla was back. I'm guessing he is having to juggle his time more since you arrived."

Lottie had no idea of how close her children had become in Sam's circle of family and friends.

Connie addressed Dani. "If you're not working Saturday, I'm taking CJ to the zoo, if you want to come."

Before Dani could respond, Lottie announced, almost as a challenge. "I would like to come."

Connie showed no expression and immediately picked up her phone. She motioned to Lottie with her finger to wait a moment. She punched in a number. "Hi. Your mother-in-law wants to come with CJ and me to the zoo on Saturday. Any problem with that?" There was a brief mumble heard on the other end. Connie chuckled and said, "Copy that." She hung up, and Lottie immediately wanted to know what Darla had said. "She said it's okay."

Everyone in the room, including Lottie, knew that it had not been Darla's full response.

They all began to eat. Lottie attempted to be a part of the conversation and was starting to understand, with Sam's help, who was who, as the names and relationships of the family members popped up. She remembered Clancy's and Addie's names from Addie's brief, annoying meeting with her at the wedding.

Dinner ended, and the kitchen was cleaned up. Connie explained that she hadn't planned on staying for dinner but was glad she did, since Sam had made her favorite tzimmes side dish. She turned to Lottie before leaving and told her the time she would pick her up on Saturday. It didn't go unnoticed by Lottie, that Connie didn't need to ask where she was staying.

Soon after Connie left, Dani was determined not to let her mother off the hook. "I'm very happy that you seemed to enjoy the evening, Mother. Perhaps you are more comfortable, now, in giving both of us your long, overdue apology."

Lottie rolled her eyes and looked to Sam for help before she said, "Dani, you are like a Pitbull. I am getting pretty tired of my children setting down rules for me."

Dani crossed her arms. "We all make choices, Mother. You chose to move here. Sometimes choices turn into dilemmas. So, how are you going to handle this one?"

Lottie swallowed her pride, for the first time in front of her daughter. She looked up, made eye contact with both women and said, "Sam, I apologize for my rude behavior to you when you came to my home."

Sam nodded and said, "Thank you, Mrs Tyler." Relived that was over with, she instantly stood up. "Would anyone like a cup of coffee?"

Lottie smiled at Sam, grateful to her for making it simple, and said, "I believe we are now officially beyond that point. Please call me Lottie."

Sam continued into the kitchen and said, "What do you take in your coffee, Lottie?"

Chapter 17

The following Saturday evening, Connie gave Sam a call. "That woman is an enigma to me. At one point, CJ took her hand at the zoo, and I thought she would cry with happiness. The next moment, she would make some cutting remarks that could take one of those elephants down." Although she couldn't see Sam's smile, she knew what she was thinking. "Yeah, yeah, I hear your mind talking. I might be abrasive, but at least I'm consistent. This woman is all over the place. She can turn on a dime."

Sam had always respected Connie's judgment. "So, do you think she still has some kind of an agenda?"

"I'm not sure. In her better moments, I get the feeling that she is really very vulnerable and then becomes embarrassed by showing it, afraid that it looks too much like weakness. She is always on guard."

Sam nodded silently into the phone. "I think you're right. She puffs up her chest aggressively, because she's very insecure. The other night when she showed up at the door, she was seeking my help. She wanted me to convince Dani to make the first move, like she had to win some contest with her daughter."

Connie chuckled. "Well, that old dog was sure barking up the wrong tree."

Sam smiled. "I kind of feel sorry for her mother. I think she really wants family as much as Dani has needed it all her life. Lottie didn't know how to go about it, and now that she is older, maybe she just wants to make up for lost time. I hope Dani is wrong, and that maybe her mom is capable of learning new tricks. In her case, new skills and attitude."

"Well, if you are right, she has a long way to get there."

When Dani got home, they curled up on the couch after dinner. Sam told her about the discussion she and Connie had earlier in the day.

Dani looked thoughtful for a moment. "I remember you asking me to try and put myself in your shoes to understand how you were feeling at this stage of your life. You thought you might actually lose Julia, and with her, the last connection to your generational family. Maybe you're right about my mother, she really might be scared and is trying to make up for all those years of fucking up our family."

Sam laughed. "Every family is fucked up. It's just a matter of to what degree of fuckdom."

Dani kissed Sam and said, "Your hypothesis about my mother is kind. But please remember who we are talking about. I think you are being very sweet to welcome my mother to be part of our family. After all, we are talking about my mother, so please don't delude yourself in thinking there is going to be any kind of fairy-tale ending."

Sam gave her a sexy smile and started to unbutton Dani's blouse. "A girl can dream; it was fairy-tale for us."

For Charles's sake, Darla had extended an invitation to Lottie for their family BBQ night. Since Sam and Connie had their discussion about Lottie, Connie felt she was going to give Lottie the benefit of the doubt. Darla, on the other hand, told her she was not yet convinced that her mother-in-law was to be trusted.

Everyone was there and, as usual, everything was chaotic. Kids running around, in and out of the pool; adults talking over each other; Connie complaining, a little too loudly, about a client of hers. Dani was in the kitchen with Darla. The guys had the TV on, yelling at the basketball game. Clancy was talking to her sister, in the pool.

Sam was sitting in a deck chair, keeping an eye on the kids splashing and playing. "Garrett, watch CJ behind you on the step. Don't knock him over."

He yelled back to Sam, "Okay. I won't, Softa."

Lottie moved a deck chair over and sat down beside her. "Why do your grandchildren call you Softa?"

"It's Hebrew for grandmother."

"I take it you were raised Jewish. How did your parents handle your sexuality?"

Sam, although surprised at the question, turned to her with a smile. She saw where Dani got her directness. "Like yourself, they would not have handled it well. I didn't come out until they both passed. Being of the same generation, I'm sure you can appreciate what the consequences would have been, in those years."

Without hesitation, she continued her inquiry. "When did you choose that lifestyle?"

As if she were teaching a sex class, Sam explained. "Gay people do not choose to be gay." Trying to keep the sarcasm out of her voice, she continued. "Being gay is not a learned skill or choice. When you realize you are gay, then you can choose whether you wish to come out or not."

"Then how do you explain Dani's going from straight to gay?"

Sam was puzzled by her obvious challenge. She pointed to herself. "How do I explain it? Perhaps you should ask *her* that question."

Lottie plowed ahead. "All she said, when she told us, was that she had had fallen in love with a woman. If you are gay at birth, then why did she marry David?"

Sam knew that Lottie was not a stupid person, but she wasn't sure if she had not listened to what she had said two seconds ago, or just wanted to prove some point. "Lottie, I was married to Addie's father. My reasons for marrying a man was, again, a situation dictated by the fifties and sixties, and by me not yet having the strength or courage it would have taken to come out to my family.

"Dani is a strong, confident woman. When she realized we had an attraction to each other, she understood that she was gay. She fell in love with me, not a lifestyle or a label." Sam hesitated momentarily, but decided that since their discussion had moved on to this level, she would continue. "I want you to know that David and Dani already knew their marriage was a mistake, way before Dani and I first met. They stayed together because they did not want to hurt their parents. They basically lived as good friends and roommates. Our children love us. They tend to do what they think would please us, even, at times, to their own detriment."

Sam hoped Lottie could see how that transferred to Charles as well. "I tell you this, not because it is my business to tell you, but because I know how fond you and your husband are of David. They remain good friends, and I enjoyed meeting him at the wedding."

Lottie was listening and seemed to be analyzing what had been said. It was hard to read her reaction, or if she was open to any of their discussion.

She finally spoke. "Sometimes, we as parents, hear our children but don't really listen."

Sam's moment of hope was dashed when, unfortunately, Lottie couldn't leave the statement to stand on its own and added, "Dani is so intense and confrontational. It makes it difficult to deal with her."

The irony of her own statement was obviously overlooked by Lottie. Sam decided she would cut her losses, and she remained silent.

Later in the afternoon, Clancy and Addie were organizing a craft with the kids at the kitchen table, while Darla and Connie were setting out condiments to be brought outside to the picnic area. Dani was talking to her brother on the loveseat, adjacent to the kids. CJ became frustrated, threw the glue stick on the ground and pushed his sheet of paper off the table. He stamped his foot and crossed his arms with a big pout on his cute little face.

Charles had been nervous all day about his mother interacting with the whole family and the silence between her and Darla, and he was on edge. He jumped out of his seat, pointed to the glue stick and paper and in a harsh voice, he demanded CJ pick them up. The little boy froze at the unfamiliar harshness of his father's voice. Charles ramped up his fury. "Right now, young man! That is unacceptable behavior. You *disappoint* me!"

Addie and Clancy had never seen Charles act that way, but they did not interfere.

CJ started to cry. Darla came over and knelt down beside her son. She looked up at her husband, who was also shocked at his unusual knee-jerk anger. She looked questionably at him. Hoping to calm Charles down, she said, quietly, "Charles, he's only three, honey." She put her arm around CJ.

Lottie was there in an instant. "Charles is right!" She snarled at Darla. "At least one of his parents know how to discipline. You obviously give in to my grandson at every turn. You baby him. How do expect him to grow up and be a man?"

CJ had stopped crying to look at his furious grandmother's face. Now, her show of anger frightened him again, and his lip started to tremble.

Darla picked CJ up and whispered in his ear, "It's okay, sweetheart. Daddy is just tired and fussy, like you get sometimes." She handed him to Addie. "Go with Aunt Addie." She asked, "Would you please take him out of the room?"

Addie took him in her arms and instructed Macy and Garrett to join her.

When the kids were out of the room, she turned to her mother-in-law. "When I want your opinion on bringing up my child, I will ask you. Until then, don't you ever speak to me in front of my child like that again. I think it's time for you to leave."

Lottie instantly turned to Charles who was now shaking and staring at the floor. Without looking up, he went into his office and closed the door. Lottie grabbed her purse and stormed out of the house.

Darla reached for Connie's arm. "Do you mind finishing up in the kitchen? I need to see to Charles?"

Connie ached for both of them. "Of course, sweetie."

Dani took Sam's hand and looked like she was going to cry. Reassuringly, Sam squeezed her hand. Dani shook her head. "Now I know why you are so concerned about his mental state. My god, I've never seen him like that."

Darla had quietly entered the office and softly closed the door behind her. She wrapped her arms around her husband, letting him sob until he was able to stop. They remained in the, now quiet, office, while everyone busied themselves feeding the kids and themselves and acting like nothing had happened.

Darla came out of the office, alone, about an hour later. She could see that everyone was concerned. She smiled and reassured everyone that he was fine.

Dani made her a plate of food and sat down next to Darla. "Are you okay, too?" Everyone left them alone to talk.

"He has been under a lot of stress." Pleadingly, she looked at Dani. "You have to know he is not like that. He is so good with CJ. They adore each other. Charles is a good father. He just snapped under the pressure. I asked him to get some counseling, with or without me. He said he would think about it. It was not the time to push or threaten him."

Dani smiled. "I know why you are telling me this. I promise I won't add to his stress." Dani kissed her on the cheek. "That doesn't mean my mother isn't going to get a kick in the ass from me."

Darla leaned over and also kissed her cheek.

Dani found Sam in the backyard, playing with the kids. CJ was laughing, having already forgotten the angry moment. Sam immediately asked about Charles.

"Darla said he is okay. They talked, and she said he would consider counseling. Baby, I'm going to go over to my mother's for a little while. I know you have to pack tonight; I'll meet you at home later. I won't be too late."

Sam held Dani's face in her hands and with a concerned look, she asked, "Are you sure that is a good idea right now?" She didn't wait for a response. "I can cancel the book signing. It's not for another two days. I was just going to stay with Julia and Ed and visit, before I drive to up to Sacramento for the signing."

"No. Please don't. I'll feel terrible if you do. I just want to try and point out what she is doing to Charles. Maybe she will listen and back off of him and Darla if she knows how miserable he is."

Actually, Sam was more concerned about Charles needing to talk. They had gotten close since he and Darla had moved to Tucson, and they enjoyed their conversations and respected each other's opinions. As much as Sam reminded him that she was not his mother, he continued to confide in her, as if she was the mother he had always wanted. Maybe it was best that he sorted this out on his own and hopefully take her and Darla's suggestion to seek some counseling.

"Okay, but please try and not lose your temper. I don't want you driving home like a maniac. You speed, even when you're not angry."

Dani tilted her head. "No I don't..." She smirked and playfully wobbled her head for emphasis. "Okay, maybe sometimes I do. It's only when I can't get home to you fast enough."

Sam slapped her on the butt. "Really, you little kiss-up. So if I'm not in the car with you, how do I know you speed? So much for your logical mind. Maybe we should get rid of that sports car and get you a smart car."

Dani let out a hearty laugh and moved in for a deep, reassuring kiss.

Matt walked by, smiled and said, "Jesus, get a room."

Chapter 18

Dani knocked at her mother's door. Lottie opened it immediately, and her face looked disappointed. Dani knew she was hoping it was Charles, coming to console her. She let her daughter enter. Dani looked around the room. There were still boxes everywhere, yet to be opened. Her mother had been there two weeks, at least.

"This is a nice place."

Her mother just looked at her.

Dani waved her hand to indicate all the boxes. "You need help with these?"

"Charles said he would help me this week." Not wanting a lecture about taking up his time, she said, "Dani, why are you here?"

"Actually, it's Charles that I wanted to talk to you about." They were both still standing. "Can we sit down?"

Her mother, showing annoyance, waved her toward the couch. "I would think you came to ask me how I was doing after being attacked by his wife!" She took a seat across from Dani and crossed her arms in front of herself.

Dani remained calm. "Mother, have you not seen how Charles looks and has been acting lately? He is very stressed and under a lot of pressure."

Before Dani could continue, her mother's hands flew toward the ceiling. "Well, of course he is, look who he lives with! I'm not blind, Dani, I see how she treats him. Always making rules and demands of him. I was trying to point out to her that Charles was acting responsibly with his son, and she threw me out of his house."

"Mom, please, you don't truly believe that's what happened. Charles is exhausted from worrying about the very thing you did. She asked you to leave, only after you went bat shit on her." Her mother's eyes got enlarged, and Dani held her palm toward her. "Please, just listen to me for a minute. I won't yell if you don't, deal?"

Her mother just glared at her.

"I am really concerned about Charles. He has tried so hard to please you and Darla. He cannot take the strain, and that is why he acted the way he did with CJ. He has never done that with his son before, and he feels terrible. They are not raising that child the way you and Dad raised us."

Dripping in sarcasm, Lottie volleyed back with, "And... just how were you raised, Dani? It seems to me that you and Charles grew up and became successful adults. I obviously did something right."

"You might want to let Charles know he is considered, by you, to be successful. We grew up in a house where love was substituted with disapproval and guilt. I was able to handle it, but Charles cannot. To this day, he associates your disappoint with him with his fear of failing you, and he feels that he needs to try harder to please you, so that you will love him. That came out today in a very scary moment for Charles and CJ. Love is not control. We never felt affection or love growing up. We never felt like a family."

Sarcastically, Lottie sneered at her. "Really? I thought your degree was a medical one, not one in psychology. Who are you to tell me how I raised my children?"

Dani leaned forward and looked straight into her mother's face. "I'm the surviving one. Charles is still trying to earn your love. Love shouldn't have to be earned, Mom. Love does not have to be bargained for with approval. It is unconditional."

Lottie placed her hands on her thighs. With dismissal in her voice, she asked, "So, is the lecture over now?"

Dani closed her eyes in frustration. When she opened her eyes again, she asked, " Is winning Charles's devotion to you over Darla, worth the toll it is taking on him? This is not a game, Mother. He loves her, and this stress is killing him."

Lottie set her jaw and remained silent.

Dani clapped her hands together, in defeat. "Well, now the lecture is over. At least think about it." She rose and saw herself out.

Sam was still up, waiting for Dani. She was reading in bed, when Dani climbed in next to her and reported how it had gone. She looked so unhappy.

"Honey, I still can cancel the trip."

"No. There is nothing more we can do. You have an early flight, and I have a surgery in the morning. Let's try and sleep."

Sam's trip went well. She enjoyed her visit with Ed and Julia, before driving up to historical Old Sacramento for the book signing. It went well, and she returned the car to Sacramento International and caught her flight home. She preferred not to pay the garage fees and leave her car at the Tucson airport, if she didn't have to. Clancy had been available to pick her up.

"How are things on the home front? Dani sounded weird on the phone last night and got off the call quickly."

Clancy said, "Dani asked us not to call you, knowing you'd be home today, and there is nothing we can do but wait. Two nights ago, Charles left Darla a note saying he needed some time to himself. He hasn't contacted her or Dani since. Darla said this is not something he has ever done before; it's not like him. She had to wait twenty-four hours before she could file a missing person report. She filed it first thing this morning."

Sam ran her hands through her hair. "Shit. She must be a mess. Does his mother know?"

"Darla and Lottie have not spoken to each other since the BBQ. Dani didn't want to alarm her mother, yet. She contacted her and just asked if she and Charles have had time to discuss what they had spoken about at her townhouse. She said he had not responded to her texts and is guessing he just isn't ready to talk about the incident, because she is supposed to talk to that bitch and not him. She said she is not about to." Clancy glanced at Sam. Her voice lowered and she sounded afraid. "Mom, he left his cell phone at home."

Clancy dropped her off at the house. Sam left her suitcase in the kitchen where she found Dani's note saying she was with Darla.

When she arrived at the house, Connie was there, getting CJ his dinner. Dani's hug with Sam lingered in a desperate need of support.

Addie arrived to take CJ back to their house for the night. Connie had been with Darla since she had discovered the note. Dani finally convinced Darla that she had to eat a little something to keep up her strength. Sam and Dani joined her since it was now evening and they, too, hadn't eaten.

Darla's cell phone sat in front of her, continuously being charged. She would stare at it occasionally, willing it to ring or text her. It was getting late, and Sam insisted that Connie and Dani go home and get some sleep, since they both had to work in the morning. She would stay the night with Darla.

Exhausted, Darla finally fell asleep after two a.m. Sam followed suit soon after.

The morning went by with no call from Charles. Darla was now frantically cleaning house, except vacuuming, too afraid she might miss his message, muffled by the noise. Sam took a book off their shelf and tried to read. Dani and Connie both checked in with Sam at their lunch breaks, afraid to startle Darla by calling her cell phone.

It was almost four in the afternoon when the doorbell rang. Darla opened the door to two police officers on her doorstep. Before they even spoke, Darla let out a bloodcurdling scream. Sam dashed to the door, just in time to help one of the police officers catch her before she hit the ground. Dani had been right; the situation with his mother did not have a fairy-tale ending.

Charles and his mother were found by the hotel cleaning woman. He had shot himself in the head. His mother was identified by her license in her wallet. She was lying on the bed as if she had been placed in a coffin, her hands crossed across her chest, with flowers placed in her hands. The florist's box sat on the desk. Until further investigation and an autopsy, they believed she had been smothered with a pillow. Charles had left a note addressed to Darla, and it was being held as evidence. A photocopy was presented to Darla with the promise that the original would be given to her after their required investigation. It was being held to be dusted for fingerprints. They asked her if she could verify that the note was written in his handwriting, by looking at the photocopy.

Darla read his note as she sobbed. She handed it to Sam and looked up at the officers. She nodded her head and verified it was Charles's handwriting.

The officers asked Sam if she was able to stay with her, until she could notify her family. As Darla clung to her, Sam stated, "Thank you, we are family."

Before Sam read Charles's note, she texted Connie and Dani, asking Dani to bring medication she felt would be appropriate to help Darla through the night. She picked up Charles's note, took Darla to her bed and held her close until Darla's body stopped trembling.

Darla looked at Sam through a tear-streaked face. "He tried, Sam, he tried so hard." She glanced at the note and began to cry again.

Sam held and gently rocked her. "I know. I know." When Darla laid beside her, limp from exhaustion, Sam read his note to herself.

'Darla, please know that since you have come into my life, I have loved you with all my heart. You brought meaning and purpose to my world. I could no longer watch the pain in your eyes, when I disappointed you with my lack of strength and courage.

This is the only way I knew to allow you, and my incredible son, to move forward in peace. He has the most amazing mother who will raise him to be an amazing man. I am so grateful that you now have family that you always deserved. I know they are there for you. Please thank them all for me. Please tell Sam that, if she likes it or not, I still wish she had been my mom. Tell Dani I love her, because I'm not sure we ever said those words to each other, and I need her to know. As you know, I have never been a religious man, but I can always hope that, in my death, I can still watch over you and CJ. I love you and CJ with all my heart, Charles'

Tears streamed down Sam's face as she read his words. It was Sam's turn to sob, as Darla curled up against her, and they held each other tightly.

Chapter 19

It was four days after the suicide, when Sam found an envelope tucked under her laptop on her desk. It was sealed, and only her name was written on the outside. Charles had methodically planned his death. The day after he and Sam had had their discussion about allowing his mother and Darla to handle their conflicts without him, he began to, once again, doubt himself, and he knew that if this didn't work, he had no other choice but to remove his mother from the equation, and in doing so, he would have to pay the price. He would not put Darla through a murder trial. Inside the note was a list of all of his and Darla's finances and where to find them. It included personal life insurance, business bank accounts, as well as his investments and shares from his business. He had paid off the cars. He asked Sam to help Darla sort out what needed to be done, since Darla would be in no condition to see to it herself. He thanked her for opening her arms to his family. He was sorry that he hadn't the courage to create a family life for himself and Darla, like Sam and Dani did for themselves. He thanked her for the talks, friendship and the love she personally had showed to him.

The police investigation had filled in the gaps during the time he had gone missing. They tracked down the gun and ammunition purchase to the day before the suicide.

They guessed that he had left his cell phone at home, so that his whereabouts could not be tracked. He purchased a burner phone and checked into the hotel. His mother's cell showed that he had called her and asked her to come to his hotel room. The coroner's estimate of his time of death was approximately less than two hours after his call. Sam knew he must have struggled with the letter he needed to write to Darla, because the police had found ripped up versions in the waste basket.

She knew, in her heart, that he had cried as he put the pillow over his mother's face and watched her take her last breath. In her mind, she could see him place the flowers in her hands and apologize to her for being such a disappointment to her. Then he sat in the chair next to the hotel bed, put the gun barrel into his mouth and pulled the trigger.

At first, Dani blamed her mother for his death. She was hurting for his loss and needed to blame someone for what happened. Her rage and grief played out only in front of Sam. When she finally let it all out, they talked about it more. The discussion changed from blame into the only conclusion there really was; when it was all said and done, the ultimate decision had been his. The question they struggled with was his decision caused by his inability to cope, or had his final act been one of sacrifice for Darla and his son? Like so many other controversies, this one, as well, turned into judgments.

The family members all had their own feelings about what Charles had done. They ranged from sympathy for his torment, to outrage at what he had done to Darla and his son. The feelings fluctuated as Lottie's death was thrown into the mix. all of it really didn't matter. They had lost a family member, and Dani had lost a brother and mother. What was most important was Darla's opinion of her husband's actions, for it would eventually have to be expressed to CJ when he was old enough to ask questions about his father.

Darla's opinion was not open for discussion by family — that was an invisible boundary, not to be crossed.